MUHAMMAD BIN
TUGHLAQ

MUHAMMAD BIN TUGHLAQ

TALE OF A TYRANT

ANUJA CHANDRAMOULI

EBURY
PRESS

An imprint of Penguin Random House

EBURY PRESS

USA | Canada | UK | Ireland | Australia
New Zealand | India | South Africa | China

Ebury Press is part of the Penguin Random House group of companies
whose addresses can be found at global.penguinrandomhouse.com

Published by Penguin Random House India Pvt. Ltd
4th Floor, Capital Tower 1, MG Road,
Gurugram 122 002, Haryana, India

Penguin
Random House
India

First published in Ebury Press by Penguin Random House India 2019

10 9 8 7 6 5 4 3 2

Muhammad bin Tughlaq is a work of fiction. Several incidents and dialogues, and
a few characters, with the exception of some well-known historical figures, are
products of the author's imagination and are not to be construed as real. Where
real-life historical figures appear, the situations, incidents and dialogues concerning
those persons are fictional and are not intended to depict actual events or to change
the entirely fictional nature of the work. In all other respects, any resemblance to
actual persons, living or dead, events or locales is entirely coincidental.
The objective of the book *Muhammad bin Tughlaq* is not to hurt any religious
sentiments of any individual, community, sect, religion or organization or be biased in
favour of or against any particular person, society, gender, creed, nation or religion.

ISBN 9780143446644

Typeset in Adobe Garamond Pro by Manipal Digital Systems, Manipal
Printed at Repro India Limited

www.penguin.co.in

MIX
Paper from
responsible sources
FSC® C047271

For all those who take pride in the fact that India is a secular nation

'We strutted about this world a good deal;
we indulged in luxuries.
We had many joys; till at last, we sank and became
hump-backed like the new moon.'

Muhammad bin Tughlaq

Author's Note

Muhammad bin Tughlaq is one of history's 'bad boys' and has exerted a strange pull over me ever since I heard about him in Grade VI during Sister Fabiola's history class. Being fascinated about him is one thing but writing a book on his life and travails was altogether a different kettle of fish, for the Sultan has put the complex in complicated and the puzzling in paradoxical. What a character he was and still is (even if it is only in my own head)!

Modern historians concur that he has been terribly misunderstood, and so-called scholarly accounts from the likes of Ibn Battuta, Barani and Isami reek of bias. He was exceedingly unpopular among the followers of his own faith for daring to be tolerant to his subjects who belonged to other religions, failing to zealously guard the principles of Islam from idolatry and heresy, and raising non-believers to high posts instead of dealing with them using the savagery he was infamous for.

The Sultan had a rough time of it with the orthodoxy, who sought repeatedly to undermine his reign, and even tried to have him killed. But Muhammad bin Tughlaq refused to give in to their fanatical demands, choosing instead to provoke them further by killing key religious leaders in spectacularly barbaric fashion. Needless to say, he paid a heavy price for his belligerent attitude. This probably explains why he issued an extraordinary proclamation prohibiting public prayers in the empire for a period of five years, though by all accounts he himself was a devout practitioner of Islam.

In addition to this, the challenges of ruling an unwieldy empire where his subjects in the various provinces had their own language and customs, and all of whom were uniformly proud and prickly about their roots, proved too much for him. As a result of these differences, his subjects were given to endless bickering and ceaseless hostility, which often erupted in bouts of communal violence. The unrelenting pressures of governance and the lack of support from his officials and subjects made him bitter and cynical. Not that it stopped him from doing his utmost to implement his outré innovations and 'madcap' schemes, which were viewed with alarm and disbelief by his contemporaries. They only saw his trademark impulsiveness and recklessness, which effectively shrouded the sparks of genius that went into the making of his grandiloquent plans.

The man was an exceptional scholar, well-versed in theology, rhetoric, poetry, philosophy, economics and finance, with a keen mind imbued with the spirit of enquiry. Many of his ill-advised reforms—particularly the one where he sought to replace gold and silver coins with alternative currency—were sound, but the manner in which they were enforced left a lot to be desired. The failure to seek the counsel of his councillors and experts, anticipate problems in execution, the rampant corruption which derailed many of his projects before they could take off, and the careless cruelty with which he dealt with his subjects when they failed to fall in with his plans led to untold suffering.

The Sultan had neither the pragmatism nor the patience to see his revolutionary ideas pertaining to administration, agriculture and taxation through to a successful conclusion. When confronted with successive failures that led to a loss of face for the emperor, he became increasingly embittered and his mercurial temper led to savage reprisals. As a result, he was universally reviled.

Yet, even his harshest critics have conceded that Muhammad bin Tughlaq was also a kind, generous and benevolent ruler.

He seemed to have genuinely cared about the welfare of his subjects and worked tirelessly to end their suffering during the terrible famine that beset his reign and laid waste to the countryside for long years. If only the Sultan had not been opposed at every turn by his subjects, circumstances and his own temperament—not to mention the rash of rebellions that robbed his empire of stability— he may have met with a modicum of success. He may even have changed the history of this land and realized his vision to make it a better place. If only . . .

This book is an attempt to recreate the life and times of Muhammad bin Tughlaq and clamber into the chaotic headspace of one who was considered to be a mad monarch. Painstaking research has gone into the foundation, and I am particularly grateful to Agha Mahdi Husain for his invaluable assistance. But when it came to building upon the character of this towering persona, I have taken some creative liberties. When confronted with conflicting versions of certain events, I have gone with what makes sense to me personally, or I have cobbled together missing fragments with chunks from my own imagination.

All chroniclers of Muhammad bin Tughlaq have been annoyingly negligent when it comes to the women in his life. His mother, Makhduma Jahan (Mistress of the World), is referred to with the said honorific, but no one saw fit to mention her real name, though she is believed to have been hugely influential and is known to have received foreign dignitaries and taken an active interest in governance. His sister, Khudawandzada, also gets a passing mention because the Sultan's munificence was on display during her wedding, and she dared to make a bid for power on behalf of her son, Dawar Malik, during his successor Firoz Shah Tughlaq's reign. There is next to nothing about his wife (or wives) or progeny, which is truly puzzling since everybody in those times had an unhealthy obsession with the love lives of their sultans and the fecundity of their wives (not that things have changed drastically in these enlightened times!).

Be that as it may, I have sought to give the royal ladies a voice, even if it is mostly my own. With regard to Muhammad bin Tughlaq's love interest, Girish Karnad gave me the germ of an idea in his wonderful play on Tughlaq, and I ran with it, though in a different, much darker direction. Feel free to make of it what you will, dear reader.

Every time I make a date with history, I see the present in the past as well as the past in the present. This book is my attempt to make sense of both in order to get an inkling of the potential and perils held by the future. Does that make sense?

PART ONE

PRINCE JAUNA

'Muhammad, son of Tughlaq, is the prince of kings;
his helper is God.'

(from an inscription carved on a stone monument)

1

The two young men stood in silence on the terrace, oblivious to the splendour of the setting sun, which was discarding its golden rays like a gorgeous woman undressing at leisure as the sky blushed and shut its eyes, allowing the darkness to descend. Both were lost in their own thoughts—Abu, at least, was more than a little worried. This was certainly not the best of times. Blood flowed freely and the spectre of death loomed over them all.

Jauna seemed composed. Relaxed even, for someone who seemed determined to embark on a reckless mission that was certain to get them both killed, or worse. If caught, death was the best they could hope for. But that was a fool's notion. Their captors wouldn't dream of giving them such a merciful release. But Abu knew better than to try and dissuade his friend. Fakhiruddin Muhammad Jauna Khan was nothing if not mulishly obstinate.

'It has to be done.' Jauna's voice was steadfast. 'There is no other way. Besides, my blood is boiling. That upstart slave, Khusrau Khan, and his posse of perverts are a disgrace to God and man!'

'Careful, old friend! The former slave is Nasiruddin Shah now and has been known to treat those who point out his lowly antecedents most cruelly. Those *panwari* scum of his are everywhere, spoiling for a fight. I still think it would be best to wait,' Abu's voice was low, 'for your father's response. You should play it safe.'

Jauna smiled at him in that easy, effortless manner of his. 'There is no need to whisper! It will only make people strain their ears to hear what we are saying. Besides, we have been silent and held our peace for too long. In doing so, we have been complicit in his wrongdoing.'

Jauna's eyes darkened as he remembered the things he had allowed to happen. He refused to dwell on them now. Not today. He forced himself to go on, 'But now, the fool slave is so busy keeping a wary eye on the father, he hardly expects the son to strike. It's time for the seeds of rebellion to be planted and nourished, all in plain sight. Under the circumstances, my position couldn't be more secure.'

'Secure? I wouldn't go that far . . .' Abu had to stop himself from looking around nervously to check for spies.

'If he had wanted to, Khusrau Khan could have had me killed easily. But if he were to do that, my father would mourn the loss of his heir and console himself with the fact that he has a few spares, before giving orders to march immediately and massacre the lot of them. With a single stroke, he would have avenged himself for the slaying of his son and the annihilation of his ill-fated benefactor, the late Alauddin Khalji, and his descendants. My father is efficient that way.' Jauna's smile was bitter.

'I'll grant that Khusrau has low cunning,' Jauna continued, 'but that reprobate is no strategist and he is no match for Ghazi Malik!'

'Yes, of course. Everybody knows that! Your sainted father, Ghiasuddin Tughlaq, was the Warden of the Marches, appointed by Alauddin Khalji himself,' Abu said enthusiastically, 'and he repulsed the Mongols on twenty-nine separate occasions, a feat that will never be matched, and led to his being appointed as the governor of Punjab. Everybody knows that he is loyal to the Alai family, or what remains of them, but he dare not make a move with the Sultan keeping his firstborn so close to him.'

'Which is why it is imperative that I join him at the earliest,' Jauna was unperturbed, 'or risk being held hostage to keep my father in check. That impostor becomes surer of his usurped position with every passing minute. He has no qualms about spilling innocent blood and has been particularly generous with the contents of the treasury that he has appropriated for his own personal use. The scions of the Alai family have been treacherously murdered by that monster. Yet he has managed to secure the allegiance of spineless scoundrels who formerly served the royal family—all with indecent amounts of gold! All that stands between him and success is my father, whose hands are tied as long as I am held here.'

'But you are most certainly being watched,' Abu pointed out. 'The Shah is not going to allow you to just saunter out of here!'

'I was thinking more in terms of a canter if not an outright gallop!' Jauna smiled at his own joke. 'Last time I checked, it was I who was the superintendent of the royal stables.'

'One way or the other, we will be free and clear of this unholy mess within a matter of days!' Abu sounded resigned. 'And hopefully we will still have our lives and all body parts intact so that we may commit a few transgressions of our own.'

The two men were silent for a few moments, reliving the turbulence and violence that had become the norm ever since the demise of Alauddin Khalji. Too many princes of the Alai family had been imprisoned, blinded or killed outright, their tender years notwithstanding. It was a blot against all who had served the emperor faithfully that they had allowed such a travesty of justice to take place.

The scions of the Khalji dynasty weren't the only ones to die, though. All those who hadn't convinced Nasiruddin Khusrau Shah of their loyalty, those whose property he coveted, and the unfortunates who merely looked at him wrong, were crushed. It was madness. Anarchy prevailed and roared along a river of blood.

Jauna drew in a sharp breath, his eyes blazing with fierce intensity. 'The Tughlaqs have Alauddin Khalji to thank for their exalted position today and we are grateful. But truth be told, he is entirely responsible for the inglorious end of his line. In his prime, he was a canny ruler and a capable administrator, but in his old age, the Shah managed to undermine every one of his achievements. My father refuses to hear a word against his overlord but despite Alauddin's many admirable qualities, his reign became accursed the day he murdered his uncle, father-in-law and Shah, Jalaluddin Khalji, for an empire.'

Abu looked at his friend. What a contradictory creature he was! No one could question his loyalty to the Khaljis, and yet he had never been one to support his benefactors blindly. Unlike Ghazi Malik, Jauna could never forgive the dear departed for their depredations.

'Personally, I think he did the right thing by murdering Jalaluddin,' Abu said. 'If there is one thing that is truly unforgiveable in an emperor, it is weakness. Intemperate kindness is a close second.'

'Every emperor has his faults, and some deserve to be killed, but staining your hands with the blood of your relatives is insupportable,' Jauna said firmly.

Abu nodded. 'However, it was Alauddin Khalji's unholy dalliance with another upstart slave, the late and not quite lamented Malik Kafur, that was even more inexcusable. He could not trust his own sons, convinced they may murder him for the throne, and chose to give his love to the eunuch instead.'

'It wasn't love that corrupted Malik Kafur,' Jauna remarked. 'It was the dizzying ascent to power and authority. That dog repaid the Shah's blind trust by having him condemned to an excruciating death by slow-acting poison. If that were not bad enough, he imprisoned and blinded the heir apparent, Khizar Khan, as well as poor Shadi Khan, who had his eyeballs torn out with rusty razors. Mubarak would have met the same fate, but at least he had the wherewithal to talk the *paiks* sent to do the nasty deed into sparing him. Being his father's loyal foot soldiers, they were happy to spare him and murder Malik Kafur instead. Fortunately, Kafur's reign of terror lasted only thirty-five days. If only Mubarak had displayed the same resourcefulness as a ruler!'

'Do you remember the celebrations on the streets after Kafur's passing?' Abu had been tempted to join the revellers himself as they raced down the streets distributing sweets and drinks, burning effigies of the eunuch in raucous celebration. 'But everybody's happiness was short-lived. Nobody expected Alauddin Khalji's son to be such a disappointment. He won himself an empire, but did not hesitate to throw power away to drown himself in all things perverse and pleasurable.'

'Alauddin's foolish passion for that treacherous eunuch was bad enough, but it was worse that his son inherited this particular vice and none of his father's virtues.' Jauna's smile was sardonic. 'Mubarak's fondness for Khusrau Khan made him every bit as foolhardy as his father. His lover got him addicted to every available intoxicant and inebriant, leaving him with addled brains, a taste for sybaritic excess and little else. History will remember Alauddin's achievements and the strength he displayed as a ruler. Mubarak will be remembered for allowing the palace to be overrun with prostitutes of both sexes and disgracing his father's legacy by prancing around in the nude on the terrace while insisting his companions urinate on the heads of visiting dignitaries or perform oral sex on them.[1] For shame!' His voice was hard.

Abu shook his head at the memory. He would never forget the debauched orgies that had desecrated the hallowed premises of the audience chamber and the shocking sights his eyes had borne witness to, and truth be told, his loins had been stirred by. Jauna had been repulsed by the entire thing, which was probably why he took care to devote himself solely to study and the duties allotted to him.

'He must have been insane to hand over so much power and privilege to Khusrau on a silver platter. Mubarak Shah not only raised the slave to the position of grand vizier but also handed over total command of the imperial army to him.' Abu, like the other nobles, had been flabbergasted at this display of stupidity.

'Clearly Mubarak inherited another vice from Alauddin,' Jauna went on. 'While Malik Kafur had placed five-year-old Shihabuddin on the throne as a puppet king he could manipulate, after his death, the nobles respected the young ruler's birthright and named Mubarak as his deputy. But Mubarak had his younger brother blinded and imprisoned in Gwalior. Having narrowly escaped such an awful fate, how could he condemn one of his own blood to the same? And when he came to know of the plots being hatched to kill him, he had his remaining brothers, Khizar Khan, Shadi Khan and Shihabuddin, killed in cold blood, all because he was unable to identify the conspirators.'

'I have heard that it was Khusrau who incited him to commit those murders, getting him to issue the orders while under the influence. But I take your point. Mubarak Shah must bear the responsibility for his misdeeds.'

Jauna shook his head in disgust. 'I have always wondered if it's power that makes monsters out of men or if it's only the monsters who successfully capture and wield power. Alauddin and Mubarak stained their hands with the blood of family to get their paws on a throne. It is hardly surprising that Mubarak's brief reign was accursed like his father's and he himself came to a bad end.'

Abu shrugged. 'A bad end indeed! It is hard to feel sorry for a fool, though. Mubarak had it coming! When well-wishers like Malik Tamar and Malik Taligha, veteran warriors who had suppressed the rebellions in Devagiri and Ma'bar, tried to warn him about the treachery of Khusrau Khan, he became paranoid, irrational and murderous. Both men were publicly flogged and flayed alive, but not before seeing their *iqtas* and worldly possessions handed over to Khusrau. Like Alauddin, Mubarak raised the beast that would slay him with his own hands.'

Mubarak Shah was dead now. But it was hard to refrain from thinking badly of him for inflicting the likes of Nasiruddin Khusrau Shah on his subjects. Anxious to hold on to his ill-gotten gains, he was draining the treasury to curry favour with the powerful Maliks, and had made short work of the remaining princes who carried the blood of the Alai family in their veins. Farid Khan and Abu Baker, aged fifteen and fourteen, had been killed on the orders of the new Shah. The younger boys, Ali, Bahar Khan and Usman—who was only five—had been deprived of their eyes.

According to the palace wags, the foul deed was done while they were with their teachers, being taught to read the Quran. It may have been a rumour designed to incite passions but given Khusrau's execrable conduct it did not seem exaggerated.

As far as Abu was concerned, the only sensible thing Mubarak Shah had done in the course of his four-year reign was to raise the talented and capable Jauna to the rank of Akur Bak, the superintendent of the royal stable, and appoint him as the Barid-ul-Mulk, postal superintendent.

Jauna had been careful not to jeopardize his precarious position by revealing his loathing for Khusrau Khan. 'How do you manage to keep your true feelings hidden from the false Shah?' Abu had asked him once.

'I keep reminding myself of what happened to Malik Kafur and assure myself that if the father's paramour got the comeuppance he deserved, there is no reason why the son's lover should fare any different!' came the reply. Whatever his reasons, it had been most judicious of him. The new Shah had allowed him to keep his head on his shoulders and not stripped him of these offices. This in turn had allowed Jauna to keep his father informed about the usurper's movements and formulate the bold plan, which, if not executed to perfection, would lead to his own execution. Now, he had decided that it was time to act.

'We leave shortly after breaking our fast tomorrow,' Jauna told him with a slow smile, which had the faintest trace of the devil in it. 'But let us get something to eat first, followed by a good night's rest. Something tells me we'll need all our strength and wits if we are to get through this in one piece.'

Abu swallowed and followed his friend inside.

2

The sun was peeking at them from behind the clouds as the two horsemen rode like the very devil. They were spared its overpowering heat during what was certain to be an arduous and life-threatening journey from Dilli to Punjab. Fortunately, it did not rain either and the horses weren't forced to slog their way past slippery mud tracks in poor visibility and high winds.

Jauna's hair streamed past him and his cheeks had a robust colour that enhanced his natural good looks. He had so much to lose and yet his manner was carefree. Abu was convinced, then, that here was one who was born to rule. At the very least, he certainly wouldn't develop a hankering for the hired help and piss away his prospects.

It had been a clean getaway. Jauna was a meticulous planner, after all. He loved every single horse in his charge, and it was well-known that he cared for them like his own children. Despite the high status he had achieved at a young age on the strength of his many merits, he gave himself no airs and joked with the stable boys as he cheerfully performed duties well beneath his station.

Jauna was so gentle with the horses that there were a few who were inclined to comment about it. 'He caresses and talks to the mare as if it were a beautiful woman!' 'He seldom evinces the same interest in the fairer sex. Perhaps his tastes are peculiar, if you know what I mean!'

The whisperers made sure the calumny never reached his ears, for Jauna was also infamous for his mercurial temper. Calm and measured on most days, his sudden rages would erupt without warning. Once, he had whipped a groomsman to within an inch of his life for daring to use the same whip to ill-treat one of the more temperamental horses.

When not brushing the manes of his horses till they shone or feeding them the little treats he always carried on his person, Jauna could be seen astride one, putting the thoroughbreds through their paces with the style and precision of the born horseman. He was most assiduous about fulfilling his other duties as the postal superintendent, which was why it usually went unremarked when he disappeared with one of the horses for the entire day and returned well after sundown.

Jauna had very respectfully sought and obtained permission from Khusrau Khan to train the horses on a daily basis to make them battle-ready. The Shah had concurred, pleased to note that Ghazi Malik's son seemed amenable and pliable to his will.

'Everybody knows that Ghiasuddin Tughlaq has emerged to eminence from a humble background,' he told his advisers, who wanted to know what he intended to do about the threat posed by Ghazi Malik. 'Unlike some of the others, he knows the merits of a man who has worked his way to the top on the strength of his own talent and hard work. He will not respond to force and I will win him over by elevating him to the post of supreme commander of my forces, with gifts of land and riches for him as well as his son. It will be an offer no sane man can refuse.'

'But he is loyal to the Alai family and is known to have openly voiced his outrage over your ascent to the throne. Your enemies will most certainly offer him the throne in exchange for declaring war. He is too dangerous!'

Khusrau only smiled at this outburst, but it did not reach his snake-like eyes, and his men swallowed their protests. He saw no reason to explain himself to the fools who surrounded him. Of course, Ghazi Malik was too dangerous. But in order to get rid of him, he needed to be lured out of his stronghold in the Punjab and present himself in Dilli. Which is why he had stayed his hand and refrained from presenting the grizzled veteran with his son's head.

Jauna would persuade his father of the good intentions of their generous new ruler and convince him to pay homage and swear allegiance as soon as possible. Then he would take care of them both. In the meantime, he could sport with the horses to his heart's content. Khusrau Khan was nobody's fool. Instructions had been issued to keep a wary eye on Jauna, lest he were foolish enough to conspire against his new ruler.

Even so, his bold move took them all by surprise. The absconding duo had managed a decent start but Khusrau Khan's panwaris, with a full regiment of the cavalry, gave chase. Nasiruddin's orders had been explicit and barked out to the full array of war chariots and elite troops armed to the teeth: 'By this time tomorrow, I expect to find that traitor whelped by a whore and his companion dragged back here on the back of your chariots!'

Their quarry could hear the sound of pounding hooves as well as the exhortations and grunts of their pursuers in the distance, but Jauna ensured that the gap between them never closed. He knew every inch of the terrain and had taken the trouble to familiarize himself with the routes and the time it would take him to traverse the distance.

In his capacity as the Barid-ul-Mulk, he had made it his business to personally arrange for relays of horses to convey messages from Dilli to the various provinces with the utmost speed and efficiency. Fresh teams awaited them now in prearranged spots, along with food and drink. The men were loyal to the handsome young man who treated them as his equal and had always been generous and genuinely solicitous when it came to their needs.

Once Jauna and Abu were on their way, man and beast melted away into the distance, having been instructed to make themselves scarce and catch up with Jauna in Punjab, where they would be richly compensated. And so they rode on for three days and nights, danger dogging them every step of the way.

The sun and the winds were not always their friends. Sometimes, the sun was hostile, threatening to bake them whole with their horses, while the wind was biting cold or inclined to whip the dust and grit into their eyes. The poor horses were showing signs of distress, unable to withstand the punishing pace and gruelling distances they were expected to cover.

Jauna was indefatigable, seeming to need no rest or sustenance— at one with the horses he rode. He encouraged them to give him their very best, devouring the distance that separated them from safety. As Abu rode behind Jauna, he couldn't help thinking about how handsome and heroic his friend was. Almost Godlike. Calm, confident, blessed with clarity and vision, unflinching in the face of clear and present danger. For the umpteenth time, Abu thought what a fine ruler he would make, if God Almighty willed it. Abu himself would happily die to make it happen. How lucky this land would be to have Jauna lead its citizens to the greatness that had always been well within their reach.

There was a strange smile on Jauna's face that offset the curious light in his eyes. It was hard to decipher his expression. Perhaps he was exhilarated, feeling savagely alive as he rode headlong to meet the destiny he had been singled out for. But every once in a while he would glance back, almost as if he yearned to return to the darkness and death he was leaving behind, fully convinced that it was better than what awaited him ahead.

~

To his dying days, Jauna remembered those three days and nights when they had ridden like madmen, uncaring of the encroaching menace, laughing like maniacs to keep the fear and fatigue at bay. On that fateful journey from Dilli to Punjab, Jauna felt his senses come alive like never before, and he was fully attuned to his body and mind. The light had an ethereal quality to it, revealing the things that lay blurred behind the boundaries of time, space and distance.

As they rode past the fields, rivers and huts that dotted the countryside, he felt every bounce and jolt, the sweat oozing from his pores, the fine dust that he breathed in and the moody breeze that buffeted him alternately with sapping heat and reviving coolness with crystal clarity.

Jauna was aware of the great heart of the beast that bore him towards safety past the hostile countryside, mindful of the exhaustion it battled as sweat lathered its flanks and the laboured breaths it drew, chest heaving painfully. He could sense Abu's raw excitement rising when they pulled ahead of their pursuers, ebbing to be replaced with crushing fear as they determinedly sought to close the gap. He felt Abu's gaze on him and the tremendous weight of his admiration and expectations.

The arrows flew hard and fast around them and Jauna never did figure how he managed to escape that deadly hail without a single scratch. He spurred his horse on, and it responded to his touch, blindly trusting the resolve and nerve of his master who never once faltered.

Jauna glanced back. Abu had wheeled around, having drawn his sword in a suicidal bid to slow down the pursuers gaining on him. He saw the shafts of the arrows buried in his back. 'Go, Jauna!' Abu had screamed. He did go, without looking back. He couldn't. The wind dried his tears before they could be shed.

Many were the people who had gathered to cheer him on. The news had spread like wildfire. Ghazi Malik's son had defied the tyrant and escaped his clutches in an unparalleled act of heroism. In doing so, he had become the spark that set off the flames of rebellion.

He heard the cries of 'Fakir-ud-Dawal!' and 'Fakir-ul-Haq!' over the whoosh of the wind in his ears, honouring him as the great pride of the state and of truth. From a tremendous distance, he saw himself afloat on a sea of adulation, accepting the approbation with graceful ease as he waved, without pausing or breaking stride. Jauna felt himself gather their hopes and dreams in a fluid embrace and hold aloft the promise to take them to a safe haven, far from the excesses of their unworthy ruler.

In return, they blocked the passage of the mounted and armed warriors who pursued him, willingly laying down their lives to ensure the safety of the hero they had already taken to their hearts. Dozens were trod underfoot by flying hoofs or impaled by thrown spears. The mobs tore down the rest from their mounts before tearing man and beast alike to pieces.

Still, Jauna rode on, aware of the blood, bones and senseless sacrifice that ensured his safe passage to glory. Of Abu's faith in him and the fate it had condemned him to. He felt it all in his head, heart and deep in his bones. Yet he was detached, removed from the frenzied activity he was so furiously engaged in. He shed no tears for the fallen. But he could not exult either. From his heightened place of awareness, he saw too much. With blinding clarity, he realized the price to be paid for every step he had taken. It was more than he could take, but he could not turn away. He was filled with dizzying excitement and nameless dread.

The terrors of the past he was leaving behind lay revealed to him. He kept thinking back to the bloody events of the fell night when it had all begun for him. They had been summoned in the darkest reaches of the night to the palace. Jauna remembered the flickering light of the hastily lit lamps throwing long shadows over the momentous but grisly proceedings.

The headless corpse of the late Mubarak Shah remained where it had landed in the courtyard, limbs and sleeping robes akimbo, pooling in blood and the contents of emptied bowels. A tragic but fitting symbol of the rot that had set in.

Khusrau was seated in the throne room. He had changed his blood-soaked robes, but there was a touch of red in his dishevelled hair, which complemented his audacity in holding court not far from the scene of his heinous crime. His thugs had taken over the palace, led by the despicable Jahariya, who Jauna later learnt had struck the killing blow, their mood jovial. They reeked of alcohol, blood and sweat. It had made Jauna's gorge rise as he stood solemn and stone-faced, along with the other nobles. Abu was with him but they couldn't bring themselves to meet each other's eyes.

They heard the sounds of women screaming and struggling as Khusrau's men invaded the harem. Alauddin's aged widow was throttled, but not before she was forcibly disrobed and made to endure the jeering abuse of her tormentors. The younger ladies of the harem and even the children who hadn't succeeded in fleeing or hiding probably envied her fate. Jauna refused to look up, but in his silence, he knew himself to be an accomplice to the unspeakable horror. Their piteous cries for help and mercy tore at his heart, but still he moved not a muscle.

He averted his gaze and glanced at the courtyard. Two women made their way to the fallen body, uncaring of the danger. Jauna recognized them. One was Devala Devi, the wife of Khizar Khan, Alauddin's eldest son and designated heir apparent, who had been blinded by Kafur and killed by Mubarak. She spat on the corpse before collapsing to her knees, pounding her chest and bewailing the fate he had condemned them to.

Jauna could not take his eyes off the other one. She was Alauddin's youngest daughter, Saira. Gently, she tried to clean up the worst of Mubarak's injuries and covered her dead brother with a richly embroidered quilt, which seemed incongruous in the macabre setting. Kneeling by the side of the corpse, she began to pray.

Khusrau followed his glance and frowned at the surreal spectacle. She was a jarring presence. An oasis of beauty, grace and goodness in the midst of the savagery, bloodshed and hysteria that surrounded her. At his command, his men dragged the two women away. Devala Devi screamed imprecations at her captors, frothing, gibbering and struggling. Saira seemed uncaring of the rough hands that violated her, strangely calm in the midst of the madness and violence that loomed ahead of her.

Jauna had started forward then, but stopped. For a brief moment, their eyes locked. There was nothing in her eyes, not the faintest trace of anger or sorrow. They were devoid of every emotion, save the faintest trace of pity. There was no judgement in that beautiful countenance. Yet he would carry that look to his grave. For he had tried himself on that day and found himself wanting. Not a day would pass by without him feeling guilty. Or entirely unworthy.

Finding himself land in the present with jarring intensity, he heard thousands of voices cheering as the flying hooves of his mount clattered past them, hailing him as a hero, saviour and champion. His heart would have soared, but it was too heavy with the haunting memory of the lovely girl he hadn't saved. Jauna couldn't forgive himself for not even trying. At that juncture, he had made his choice to live as a sinner rather than die a hero.

Jauna looked ahead and away from the demons let loose by his past. At that moment, he knew with the utmost certainty that the throne would be his. As would the power, prestige and untold riches it offered. He should have been beside himself with pride and joy, but all he felt was an aching emptiness and a profound sorrow that urged him to turn around and embrace the death that he had eluded. But he couldn't do that. No more than he could turn back time to save the worthy souls who had been far more deserving than him.

All he could do was ride. Without stopping. For as long as he could. So he rode on and on.

3

Ghiasuddin Tughlaq was on the move with his sons, supporters and troops, not long after Jauna's ride of glory. Having risen in revolt, they marched against the false Shah. En route to Dilli, large crowds gathered to see Ghazi Malik, whom they knew by repute and who was the man most likely to be declared the Sultan, should he survive the clash with Nasiruddin Khusrau Shah. Ghiasuddin stopped to address the people whenever possible, appraising them about the godless practices of the new monarch and the measures he himself would take to redress the wrongs done to them.

Jauna was impressed. His father was known for his military acumen and prowess as a general, but clearly his political skills and capacity for adroit manoeuvring were nothing to be sneezed at either. The masses adored him and screamed their support, though Jauna doubted it would amount to much.

'The goodwill of the people always counts for something, son!' his father told him, seeming to read his thoughts. 'It is their future as much as ours.'

Jauna nodded politely. It was nice to ride by the side of his father. They had received intelligence that Nasiruddin Khusrau Shah had sent a considerable force headed by his brother, Khanan Khan, and Amir Sufi Khan to confront Ghazi Malik. The army had gathered on the outskirts of Sarsuti.

Ghazi Malik clearly commanded the respect and goodwill of nearly everyone, and yet it was no easy feat even for him to put together a confederacy of the leading nobles, governors and military commanders. Only Bahram Aiba of Uch had allied himself with them. Most of the others were unwilling to risk their positions by throwing in their lot with what could well turn out to be the losing side. After all, if history was any indication—and it was—deserving rulers seldom managed to secure and hold a throne, although they did succeed in lowering their life expectancy.

It did not help that Nasiruddin Shah was distributing gold by the bushel, making generous gifts of land and prestigious titles to bolster support for himself. The lack of open support for Ghazi Malik did not seem to deter him. He took it all in his stride and focused only on the job at hand, backed by his loyal supporters. Jauna himself was disgusted.

'Now is the time to act, and too many are concerned only with protecting or enriching themselves at the expense of others. Worst are the nobles who had served under Alauddin Shah as well as Mubarak Shah and are all too familiar with the inequities of the false Shah. They ought to have known better. This land and its people do not deserve someone like you. They are better off wallowing in the filth with the likes of Khusrau Khan lording it over them.'

'You are too hard on them, Jauna!' Ghiasuddin's tone was measured. 'Remember that we cannot achieve the things we seek by depending on others. All you will ever have is your own head, heart and hands to help you do the needful. Make sure these are in fine fettle and everything else will fall into place.

'But even if you choose not to depend on others, it does not mean that disobedience, defiance or disrespect ought to go unpunished.' He had smiled bleakly at that. Later, Jauna understood what he meant.

Amit Mughlatti, the governor of Multan, had responded most rudely to Ghazi Malik's overture for aid. As a former *muqta* of Multan, Ghiasuddin had built a large mosque there and fought off the Mongols who were terrorizing the inhabitants with sudden raids. Many remembered him with respect and were incited to rebel against their governor. Mughlatti was forced to flee but was hunted down and hanged by the neck to die. As the crows plucked out his eyes, he might have regretted the lack of judiciousness he had displayed.

As a further retaliatory measure, thanks to the faultless intelligence they had been supplied, two convoys from Multan and Sivistan, loaded with treasure, weapons and horses to aid the false Shah in Dilli during the war effort, were waylaid by Ghazi Malik's men, and the goods appropriated. The troops loyal to him were rewarded with two years' worth of salary in advance. Needless to say, his men, who already worshipped the ground he walked on, were willing to gladly lay down their lives for him, should the occasion call for it. They cheered him with cries of 'Ghazi Malik, the true saviour!' and 'Sultan Ghiasuddin Tughlaq!'

Jauna was filled with admiration for his father's statesmanship and sagacity. Even so, he hoped his father would take a harsher stand against those who had failed to respond to his call. If it were up to him, all who denied their overtures for help would be spitted and roasted over live coals.

Ghazi Malik felt differently about these things, though. His father had also disregarded Jauna's opposition to his preferred stratagem. Jauna had insisted that pandering to the religious sentiments of fellow Muslims and accusing Khusrau Khan—who was a convert—of restoring Hindu rule wouldn't work, since the vast majority were Hindus themselves. He had been right, of course, and the ploy had done little to garner sympathy for their cause.

His father sensed the shifting tides of his mood. 'While watching someone work, we are always convinced we can do better, aren't we? And while actually engaged in a task, we are confident that none can do it better.'

Jauna gave a start, and for once, he was at a loss for words. Ghiasuddin persisted. 'What exactly is bothering you, Jauna? I wonder if it is defeat and death at the hands of the tyrant? No true warrior can afford to fear either.'

Appalled at the suggestion, Jauna replied without thinking, 'Defeat does not scare me. Victory does. And it is all but guaranteed, for Khusrau Khan is no match for Ghazi Malik. His is the last gasp of a dying man.'

'I am flattered but must admit to being puzzled as well. Victory is coveted by all and granted to too few, and yet you are wary. Why is that?' he asked as he looked at his son, reminded of a young Jauna of ferocious intellect whose teachers simply couldn't figure out what to make of him. One had been bold enough to assert that his son's undeniable genius made it harder to forgive his abject foolishness. This assessment of his firstborn had always bothered him.

Jauna sensed his lack of approval, and it stung, but he did not hesitate to answer. 'Victory will lead you straight to the throne. There is none wiser or worthier, and yet I can't help but think you deserve better. Remember what happened to the Alai family? When they started out, they weren't the monsters they eventually became. But it was as if they were all infected with the same disease that doesn't really have a cure.'

'Power does corrupt. There is no arguing with that.' Ghiasuddin was thoughtful.

'I am not saying that you will become like the others who sat on the throne, for you are destined to be the greatest of them all. But I am worried that it will corrupt those around you who are supposed to serve, but instead seek to wrest for themselves the power they are unfit to wield . . .'

His voice trailed off as he remembered the things he had seen in the palace. While his father fought the Mongol hordes and carried out duties assigned by the emperor, he had been stationed at the palace and present during Alauddin's last days. With his own eyes, he had seen the Shah reduced from a mighty monarch to a drooling imbecile who was too weak to get up from his bed to use the privy and had to be cleaned like a child. Kafur had made sure visiting dignitaries saw him in this state, chipping away at his self-esteem even as his master clung to him with desperate trust.

Jauna was still haunted by the image of the headless trunk that was all that remained of Mubarak Shah, whose reign had started with so much promise, the beautiful girl who had prayed by his side, and the friend who had sacrificed himself for his sake. He had known Mubarak as a bright young man who had been cheerful and kind. Who knew he would turn out to be an addict and a killer of king, kith and kin?

Would the Tughlaqs, like the Khaljis, devolve into killers who murdered their own fathers and brothers with impunity? It did not bear thinking about.

'I have given the matter a lot of thought, Jauna,' Ghiasuddin said in his measured yet authoritative voice, 'and my mind is made up. Too many are content to complain about those in power while being too lazy or caught up in the minutiae of their mundane lives to do something about it. If given the chance, it behoves all of us to do what we can to benefit the great majority instead of shirking such an onerous responsibility. But that said, something tells me I haven't the time left to clean up this mess. I have decided not to accept the throne should it be offered to me. We will place a surviving member of the Alai family on the throne and serve him to the best of our ability.'

He lapsed into silence after that. Jauna wondered at the equal amounts of disappointment and relief he was experiencing. Of course his father meant every word, but would he really have the strength to walk away from a throne? Would they let him? Besides, to the best of his knowledge, the choice was not really his father's to make. From what he had heard, Khusrau had hunted and killed everyone who boasted a drop of Alai blood in their veins.

With prophetic vision, he knew his father was fooling himself if he thought he could just walk away. The time had come for a new order. Ghiasuddin Tughlaq would be their Sultan, and his firstborn son would inherit the throne in good time. For better or for worse. That was the way of it.

'Let us not get ahead of ourselves, son.' Ghiasuddin glanced at him with a strange smile. 'Not when there are battles to be fought and a tyrant to be relegated to the trash heap of history. As for the rest of it, we'll cross the bridge when we come to it.'

With that, father and son rode into the future with steady resolve, not entirely sure if they were ready to have greatness thrust upon them.

4

The battle at Sarsuti—if it could be called that—seemed to end before it even began. Jauna had been ordered to head the charge, with his father bringing up the reserves in the rear. The old warrior hadn't been entirely certain about the unconventional battle formation drawn up by his son, but Jauna had been validated when he crushed Khanan Khan and Sufi Khan in a matter of hours.

Seeing young Jauna lead a seemingly isolated division, with Ghazi Malik nowhere in the vicinity, his opponents had been drawn into the attack. Carried away by the headlong rush, they had allowed themselves to be trapped when Jauna pulled back and signalled for two fresh divisions, which materialized at the flanks of the enemy, cutting off their retreat, and soundly defeated them.

By the time Ghiasuddin arrived, Jauna had restored order. He had rounded up the fleeing fugitives and presented them to his father, along with the rich booty and priceless valuables left behind by the fallen. Ghazi Malik had been pleased. As for the cheering troops, they were beside themselves when their commander announced that they would be richly compensated for their own contribution.

Jauna looked at the rows of rambunctious troops celebrating their victory and good fortune, feeling deflated. His father had needed them to fulfil his plans for the future and make his vision a reality. These were mean soldiers who gave their compliance and support to the highest bidder. Yet, Ghazi Malik had found a way to convince them to give their loyalty and very lives so that they may be wedded to his personal purpose. It was a tricky business and it made Jauna uneasy, knowing that he lacked his father's natural gifts. He hated the thought that some day his life and legacy would be inextricably linked to the competence of his underlings.

After the battle, Ghiasuddin allowed them a few days to rest and attend to the injured before they resumed the march to Dilli. He used the time to gather all the intelligence he could about his enemy's movements. Their informers brought news that the false Shah was disheartened but determined to make a fight of it. It had been his plan to bribe the high-ranking officials into supporting him. They had pretended to acquiesce, milked him for all he was worth, and promptly abandoned him.

Even the common soldiers who had been paid with gold from the imperial treasury had taken his money before turning their backs on him. The morale in his camp was at an all-time low. Heartsick and weary (in the words of the more eloquent spies) Khusrau Khan nonetheless marched from Siri with the imperial army.

Victory seemed certain. But Ghiasuddin was not one to take anything for granted and formulated his plans with care. The two forces met on the plains of Indarpat. This time, Ghazi Malik himself led the charge with 300 of his veteran troops. They were heavily outnumbered, Jauna noted (though he had been given embellished figures), and were certain to have a rough time of it.

He was right. Initially, they suffered heavy losses, and a lesser man would have quailed. Jauna watched with admiration as his father did not flinch in the face of overwhelming odds. Instead, he gathered his veterans around him and led the charge. 'Remember what is at stake here!' his bull voice roared. 'The tyrant will show you no mercy. He will grind you into the dust before going after your women and children. You are all that stands between him and your loved ones! Fight for honour! Fight for justice! Fight for the motherland!'

Galvanized, his troops rallied behind Ghiasuddin Tughlaq and struck back with almighty vengeance. Jauna fought his way to his father's side. Khusrau Khan's forces broke under the weight of that fresh onslaught while their Shah fled for his life. Within the hour, their ranks were decimated, forcing them to flee pell-mell from the battlefield.

While the men celebrated their triumph, Ghazi Malik sent for him. It wasn't over. Jauna was assigned the task of pursuing the coward and bringing him to his knees.

They found him in the garden of an empty house. His guards had abandoned him and made a run for it. But not before tying him up and looting him of all his remaining worldly possessions, as well as his fine steed. Nobody felt anything was owed to a former monarch who had succeeded only in losing everything. It was a pathetic sight.

Jauna called out to a detachment of his troops, 'Find the louts who have betrayed their overlord! Chase them to the ends of the earth if you have to but be sure to relieve them of their ill-gotten gains before hanging the miscreants by their sorry necks till they die. Report to me once you have carried out my instructions!'

As the soldiers clattered away, their companions hauled Nasiruddin Khusrau Khan to his feet and presented him to Jauna. To his credit, the man did not deign to plead for his life.

Instead, the deposed Shah looked him in the eye with typical audacity. 'You have seen fit to betray me, though I have treated you with benevolence. But I don't blame you. Having grown up a slave in filth and poverty, I clawed my way to the top, and for a moment there, I was the richest and most powerful man in the land. Even now, I am uncertain that this is all nothing more than a mad dream. And do you know the strangest thing about all this?'

He tried to laugh but wound up hacking and coughing violently. Flecks of drool and blood bespattered his armour. Jauna stepped back in revulsion.

'I genuinely am not sure whether it is better to be a slave or a king . . .'

Wiping away the tears of his mirth, he continued, 'You and your father aren't as different from me as you think. When it is your turn to be seduced by power, you too will do whatever it takes to hold on for as long as you can, your so-called fine principles and scruples notwithstanding.'

Jauna's eyes were cold. 'Don't you dare talk about my father! And I will never stoop to your level. You betrayed your benefactor, fed his addiction and had him killed as he lay in your arms on the very bed where you seduced him.'

Khusrau Khan coughed again and spat out a bloody blob. 'You think he was my benefactor? Perhaps, but it was I who stayed my hand when ordered by Malik Kafur to blind him. Having rescued him from a fate worse than death and won him a throne, I stood by his side and single-handedly administered an empire, expanded as well as enriched it, managed successful conquests and suppressed every rebellion that flared up. I did all that while playing at being his woman because he wouldn't have it any other way.[2] Do you know what it is like to be the whore of a madman dominated by his drug habit? To pander to his perverse whims knowing full well that you are his better in every way but your birth robbed you of everything?'

He was breathing heavily. 'Like your father, my intentions were merely to save us all from the tyrant. The throne was offered to me by an assembly of the noblemen who had suffered under the mad monarch, and you know it to be the truth, though you choose not to see it. And contrary to what you have been feeding the masses, the majority were Muslims. There is a reason they supported the claim of a Hindu convert when your father marched against the throne! In my position, Ghiasuddin Tughlaq and Fakhiruddin Jauna Khan would have done exactly the same thing. If you were to stop making excuses for Mubarak, you would agree that my deed was necessary, even laudable.'

'And if you stopped making excuses for yourself, you would agree that your actions were execrable and death is too good for you!' Jauna's voice was hard as flint and entirely devoid of pity. How dare this vulgar creature compare himself to Ghazi Malik and justify his vile deeds? Jauna had seen him comporting himself as the Shah's woman with his own eyes and he had not seemed put out in the least while displaying his silken garments and precious ornaments. Fancy him playing the victim now!

'I seek neither your pity nor your understanding, emperor-to-be!' There was resignation and even a certain dignity to his mien. 'All I offer are my wishes to you and your father in the foolish hope that the Tughlaqs will have a better time of it than I did, even though you too turned on a benefactor and paved the way to the throne with my blood. For that and more, you have my forgiveness!'

Jauna had had enough by then and gave the order for the wretched man's head to be struck off at once. He stayed only long enough to make sure the deed was done before turning his back on the remains of the false Shah. Dirt belonged in the trash, after all.

Riders arrived bearing urgent summons from Ghazi Malik. The nobles had assembled before him to commemorate his victory and to present to him the keys to the palace, treasury and the city gates in recognition of his victory. Jauna was to join him immediately.

On the ride back, there was a sickness in his heart and an overpowering dread that refused to be quelled. Jauna watched the joyful revellers who were celebrating the triumph of the Tughlaqs and resisted their blandishments to join in. Deep in his heart, he supposed, the false Shah was right. They had all risen from the dirt and it was only a matter of time before they were ground into the dust. What was there to celebrate but the supreme folly of mankind?

5

The next day, a triumphant procession with Ghiasuddin Tughlaq at the head wound its way to Siri and the palace with due pomp and ceremony. The citizens thronged the streets and showered them with marigold petals. Ever humble and devout, he prostrated himself and thanked the Almighty before making his way into the palace.

The courtiers had assembled to greet the victor and swear allegiance to him. Ghiasuddin was overcome with sadness and lamented over the fates of his patron's blood relatives and the inglorious end to his line. With an almighty effort, he controlled himself. Refusing the pride of place that was the right of the victor, he gathered the *amirs* around him in comradely fashion to say his piece.

'With the death of the false Shah, my duties to my patron and emperor have been discharged.' His eyes shone with tears. Jauna, who was watching from a discreet distance, decided it was a nice touch. 'Alauddin Shah was a good man and a great ruler. This land and her people will always remain indebted to him. I urge the eminent personages present here to bring forward one of his blood to restore the glory of his reign. But if none have survived the calamity that befell them, it is my suggestion that the amirs name one who is worthy to rule. I will abide by the decision and serve the chosen one to the end of my days.'

It was a masterly stroke, Jauna mused to himself. Alauddin may have been great for a brief period, when his four capable Khans rode in all directions to subdue all who had failed to bow before the Shah's authority. They had captured vast tracts of land and brought back more treasures than could be imagined, but that had been before the lot of them had been overcome by stupidity.

For the four, it had been wine, women, gambling and hubris that had derailed their careers. For the Shah, it was his need to love and be loved in return that had got the better of him. Why his father sought to glorify him and reinstate his unimpressive progeny on the throne, he would never know. Surely it was a bluff? But Ghiasuddin seemed sincere.

The amirs reacted with shock to this surprise announcement and whispered to each other while Ghiasuddin moved back, steady and resolute as ever. Jauna studied the faces of the amirs and he saw the longing on their faces for a chance to sit on the throne, knowing that it mirrored his own. Again, he wondered at himself. How was it possible to want something so desperately and yet not want it at all?

They wavered for long moments until one among them spoke up, 'I speak here on behalf of my fellow luminaries! Not a single man here can deny that there is none more suited than our beloved and most heroic Ghazi Malik to assume the mantle of rule. We beg you to restore order and put to rights the evils that have been perpetrated ever since the last days of Alauddin Khalji.'

Another voice spoke up, rightly gauging the mood prevailing in this august assembly, 'We have not forgotten our debt to you for ridding us of the Mongol menace.'

'You have been chosen by the Almighty to lead us to a new era of peace, prosperity and plenty. Don't turn your back on us at this crucial juncture!'

Others in the gathering shouted out their assent and a sea of voices roared in support of Sultan Ghiasuddin Tughlaq. It was the prudent thing to do, after all. None of them had been particularly forthcoming when it came to showing support when he rose up in rebellion, and now, with his victorious army at the gates of Dilli, they couldn't have been more enthusiastic. Jauna nearly laughed out loud at the absurdity of it all.

When Ghiasuddin started to shake his head in refusal, they persisted. One of the amirs leaned in and whispered in his ear, 'There is no turning back for you. By defeating the false Shah, you have emerged as the strongest contender for the throne and even if we were to choose someone else, the new ruler would never rest easy till he has wiped you out along with your family.'

Bahram Aiba Kishlu Khan called out, 'If you persist in refusing, we will have no choice but to install your heroic son upon the throne. He has also acquitted himself very well on the battlefield. In fact, it was he who finally rid us of the tyrant by striking his unworthy head off!' Jauna tamped down hard on the heady rush of eagerness and keen anticipation those words induced. His father's features were inscrutable.

A babel of voices rang out, and Ghazi Malik rose to his feet, his arms raised as if in surrender. Taking it at as a sign of assent, the gathered nobles tripped over themselves in their eagerness to bow down before him. That was when the cheering began in earnest. Jauna looked at his father, who was graciously accepting the wishes of the nobles. He continued to watch as the snakes, leeches and a few good men gathered around the new Sultan.

'So it begins . . .' he murmured. His words were swallowed up by the hullaballoo, but his father turned in his direction then. Almost as if he had heard.

6

Jauna was in Devagiri and in a foul mood. He confided in Abu, the way he usually did when he was upset, 'Unlike father, I am surrounded by none but the colossally foolish and the insupportably stupid.'

He had been thrilled when his father had given him his first command and sent him to Warangal, the Telangana province, to quell the unrest there and retrieve the territories. These had been lost by those who had come to power after the death of Alauddin Khalji. But he had been forced to lift the siege and return with his tail tucked between his legs. The only silver lining was that Qutlugh Khan, his former tutor and the vazir of Devagiri, had been fiercely loyal and had followed Jauna's instructions to the letter.

'Of course my father is to blame for this misadventure,' he went on, 'but not entirely. Bloody Malik Kafur did his fair share, as did Nasiruddin Khusrau Khan.'

Abu wagged his finger at him. 'And you were wondering where the rumours of the Sultan's supposed death and your so-called hand in it had sprung up from.'

'I know exactly how the rumours started . . .' he barked, refusing to elaborate. Being all too familiar with that terrible glare, Abu decided to change the topic.

'I understand your ire at the way the southern provinces have been governed by those who came before Sultan Ghiasuddin Tughlaq. It is all well and good to raid, grab and withdraw, with treasure enough to last you till the next such outing, but far more difficult to absorb enemy territory into an empire and centralize power in a land where every few miles people speak a different language, belong to a different caste, eat different food, worship a different God and take inordinate pride in the differences that are unique to them. Don't be so hard on yourself; these things take time.'

Jauna was not entirely appeased, but he nodded. Even if they were given all the time in the world, he had a bad feeling that this land would be wrestling with the same problems of cultural identity and personal pride.

Kafur had overrun Telangana and been on the verge of sacking its capital, Warangal, but the wily Pratapa Rudra Deva had offered to surrender in addition to accepting Alauddin Khalji's sovereignty and offering to pay regular tribute. The slave had also pocketed exorbitant sums for his personal gain, if the rumours were to be believed.

Jauna shook his head. 'Was there no end to his avarice? Having pocketed as much of the treasure as he could, he neglected to take action when the tributes came in irregularly, if at all, because he was too busy conspiring to take the throne for himself.'

'Khusrau was no better, I suppose,' Abu mused. 'He marched against Pratapa Rudra of the Kakatiya line and was similarly gulled by the lure of filthy lucre. Of course this particular potentate managed to wriggle free from the yoke of Dilli during the power struggle between our Sultan and Khusrau, and here we are again! Still, it was overly optimistic of him to try the same stunt with the Sultan's son by hoping to fob you off with a few baubles and the offer of support should you decide to hasten your father to an early grave.'

Jauna glared at him. He was still brooding over being forced to withdraw to Devagiri, where he had been licking his wounds for the past four months. The failure of the siege had caused him to lose face and it was not a nice feeling. Worse, he couldn't shake the notion that this had merely been a preview of what he could expect for the rest of his life.

Sometimes he wished his father had not raised him to be abstemious like himself. It would have been nice to drown these troublesome thoughts in alcohol, drugs or between the legs of an accommodating woman. Unfortunately, he cared nothing at all for such distractions.

The entire thing had been frustrating, especially since the siege had gone so well in the beginning. By dint of forced marches and leading from the front, he had managed the three-month journey from Dilli to the Deccan in half the time. His use of 'newfangled' (according to his detractors) war machines like catapults, fire throwers and siege towers—all built to his design—had had the most satisfactory results.

However, far from receiving credit, he had to deal with stiff resistance to his methods from the 'experienced and loyal chieftains' his father had insisted he take along. They questioned his every move and sniggered behind his back. Bloody old farts and doddering fools! Despite them, his men had managed to breach and secure the outer wall of the formidable fortress of Warangal. Jauna had almost tasted victory then.

But that was precisely when things had started to go horribly wrong. He supposed he should have seen it coming. They *had* been chafing at the bit from the protracted siege, uncomfortable in the sweltering heat and shitting blood from the ridiculously spicy food. But how could he have known that his underlings wouldn't do the jobs they were supposed to?

They had been sleeping on their feet while the damn rebels had cut off communication lines to Dilli, isolating them from the Sultan who had hitherto been monitoring the situation and offering his opinion at least once every two weeks. When his missives dried up and the inner walls resisted the efforts of his siege machinery—much to the delight of his detractors—his captains took to questioning his every move. Perhaps he should have paid heed to his instincts and lopped off their tongues.

Sensing the dissent among their officers, the troops grew restive and even more derelict in their duties, which forced Jauna to enforce discipline using severe methods that did not endear him to them. To compound matters, they were running short of provisions.

With the uncanny instincts of a cornered animal, Pratapa Rudra sent his blasted messengers with an offer of conditional surrender. If they lifted the siege, he would show his gratitude by accepting the suzerainty of the Sultan and would send them laden back to Dilli with all the treasures of Warangal. The nerve of that man! Jauna wasn't willing to bite this time, but the fools who surrounded him were blinded by greed and couldn't wait to get their grasping paws on the promised treasure. They had argued vehemently and nearly came to blows over it.

'Buggers would have happily sold their mothers for a gold mohur or two!' he had complained bitterly to Abu. 'Short-sighted morons who would happily settle for a measly handout when we stand on the threshold of a complete victory that would throw open the doors not only to the treasures of Telangana but the rest of the south as well.'

Then came the offer to support Prince Jauna should he make a bid for the throne. Those carelessly uttered words had the desired effect, and all hell had broken loose in his camp, with everybody determined to believe he was in cahoots with the enemy and openly questioning his loyalty to his father, the Sultan. It would have been laughable if it hadn't cost him the damn siege and a world of trouble besides.

'The Sultan is dead and it is his own son, whom he generously named as the heir apparent, who is responsible!'

'The prince is guilty of the twin crimes of parricide and regicide.'

'He has joined hands with the enemy and betrayed his own flesh and blood.'

'There is no assuaging Jauna Khan's bloodlust! He plans to assassinate every one of the senior officials who have been loyal to his late father and have accompanied him on this foolhardy expedition.'

As if the situation had not been dire enough, a vicious outbreak of dysentery had roiled through their ranks, and they were all up to their eyeballs in shit and blood. The disgruntled soldiers had been irrationally inclined to blame him for the battle being fought in their bowels.

'Prince Jauna may be clever, but what is the point if he is cursed with the worst luck imaginable?'

'By following him, we are forced to partake of the misfortune that plagues him so sorely!'

'God Almighty doesn't favour him and frowns on his enterprises! It is an ill omen and a future with him in charge will be an inauspicious one.'

Jauna knew his father would have wanted him to address the rumours and reassure the idiots who would not recognize the truth if it bit them on their incompetent and still sore backsides, but he had never been one to suffer fools gladly. Now he was willing to concede that his intractability could have been the reason many among the chieftains had withdrawn their support and slunk away like rats in the dead of night with their troops.

Meanwhile, Pratapa Rudra remained safely ensconced in his inner fortress, drinking, feasting and making merry, no doubt laughing himself silly over the foolishness of his enemies. The humiliation could scarce be borne.

'If it makes you feel any better, I don't think you are capable of killing your father, even though you are not above wishing he would die of natural causes,' Abu interjected, ignoring the warning look his friend shot him. 'You still haven't explained why your father is to blame for this debacle. I thought you were fully on board with his policies. It is about time we eschewed the smash-and-grab policies of yore and brought the entire extent of this land under the direct control of the Sultan.'

By way of reply, Jauna pointed towards the entrance to the fortress. Abu didn't bother to look. He knew about the two impaled figures which had been prominently displayed for many days now.

The mutilated flesh, missing appendages, multitude of maggots as well as the rank odour were impossible to miss. They did little by way of aesthetic appeal but did serve as a grim reminder for those who conspired against the Prince or spread vicious rumours.

'What do the sorry remains of Ubaid, a composer of middling poetry, and Shaikhzadah of Damascus have to do with your father? Though the Sultan has a reputation for being stern, none can accuse him of such savagery.' As his oldest friend, Abu was allowed to speak his mind, even though it was always a risky enterprise with Jauna.

The Prince sighed. 'It all started when the Sultan chose to address the grievances of good men who had suffered when power changed hands after the death of Alauddin Khalji. In his eagerness to redress such wrongs, my saintly father got into a bit of a kerfuffle with a fellow saint, Shaikh Nizamuddin Auliya.'

'I remember . . .' Abu nodded, scratching his chin. 'The Sultan decreed that all those who had wrongly benefitted from the tyrant's reign of terror would have to return their ill-gotten gains or make adequate recompense to either the injured party or the state. The holy man declined to do as much, declaring that the generous contribution of Khusrau Khan had been used for charitable purposes, and he couldn't possibly ask the poor to regurgitate the food they had eaten or deprive them of the clothes on their back. Needless to say, the Sultan was less than happy.'

'And my father made it perfectly clear that he believed the saint was defrauding him and he would face dire punishment if he failed to obey his direct order.' Jauna looked thoughtful. 'In the meantime, Nizamuddin Auliya's rabid followers—including but not limited to Ubaid and Shaikhzadah—decided that the Sultan and his son must pay for the perceived slight upon the saint. They sought to foment trouble between my father and me with their accursed rumour-mongering, thereby undermining his rule.'[3]

Abu was flabbergasted. 'And here I was under the assumption that you were very close to Ubaid, given the evenings the two of you spent closeted in the royal tent discussing mind-numbing poetry from ancient Persia and the more obscure points of Sufi mysticism, among other things.'

Jauna grinned. 'The man did have an excellent gift for conversation. It is too bad he allowed his religious beliefs to cloud his mind. And he was most unrepentant even under torture. But he was taken aback when he realized I had known about his designs all along.'

'But if you had identified the root cause of the problem, why didn't you pluck it out immediately?' Jauna frowned in response.

'Never mind; leaving the dear departed aside, what are you planning to do next? The Sultan isn't going to be happy that Warangal is yet to fall.'

Jauna shrugged. 'I was able to make a full report to the Sultan. Ubaid and Shaikhzadah were the chief troublemakers. On my orders, the captains of the army who had rebelled against my authority have also been rounded up and captured. Their men were given no quarter and their remains accompany their masters, who are currently being dragged behind their horses on their way to an audience with the Sultan in Dilli.

'It is not the ideal way to travel,' Jauna continued, 'but a fitting punishment for deserters, wouldn't you say? They carry with them my request for fresh troops with more reliable leaders and fresh provisions. Once these have arrived, we will march again. And history will record that Prince Fakhiruddin Jauna Khan eventually emerged triumphant. As always.'

Abu did not reply. After all, there was no arguing with that.

7

Jauna was happy for his father. Ghiasuddin Tughlaq's ascent to the throne had been a great success and people were in raptures over his wisdom, generosity and benevolence. All who had stood by his side were amply rewarded. He had famously restored law and order within a week of coming to power and kept up the good work with exemplary governance.

Though he revered the memory of Alauddin Khalji, he did away with the late Shah's more stringent measures, which was a blessing for the administrators as well as the administrated. He reduced taxes but took steps to replenish a depleted treasury by implementing economic reforms that encouraged trade. He helped farmers enhance the yield per acre with agrarian reforms. The Sultan came down hard on petty thieves and local gangs, allowing his people to finally feel safe and free.

The Sultan was blessed with the love of his people, success and prosperity. They all sang the same tune as the poet Amir Khusrau composed in honour of Ghiasuddin Tughlaq, 'He never did anything that was not replete with sense and wisdom.' His subjects were touched with the genuine consideration he extended towards their needs and the many ways he made their lives better.

The rich and powerful had no cause to complain either. Despite his welfare schemes, the Sultan had ensured there was plenty left for those who sought to fill their own coffers without resorting to criminal activities or exploitation, both of which led to swift apprehension and harsh punishment. Miraculously, the Sultan even managed to care for his Hindu subjects without alienating his fellow Muslims.

After the fiasco with the postal lines in the Deccan, the Sultan ensured that the postal system was up and running with unmatched efficiency, and in his wisdom did not reinstate his heir apparent, Prince Jauna, in his old position as the Barid-ul-Mulk. It was a stinging rebuke.

Abu's words had been conciliatory. 'The Sultan is wise and it is not your place to question his judgement. In all likelihood, he has bigger and better things planned for you since you will take his place one day.' They had not made him feel better.

Clearly, the Sultan wasn't too happy with Jauna's handling of the Telangana expedition even after his eventual triumphant return, which he made abundantly clear in front of his gathered court.

'The treatment meted out to Tamar, Tigin, Mall and Kafur, the maliks ordered to accompany you to Telangana, is unacceptable.' The Sultan's tone was level but his disappointment palpable. 'They were handpicked for this expedition and had proved themselves to be good, loyal men. Did the fact that their family members have served and continue to serve the throne not give you pause? None of them deserved to be dragged to their deaths in this barbaric manner.'

'I respectfully disagree, your majesty!' Jauna couldn't believe his father would take the side of cowardly deserters.

'What exactly do you disagree with, Prince?' It was the Khwaja Jahan, the grand vizier, who spoke, unctuous and presumptuous enough to take umbrage on behalf of the Sultan. 'On being falsely informed by self-serving individuals that there was a plot to overthrow the Sultan, they arrived immediately to lend their support to one whom they have sworn to serve unto death. Surely you are not suggesting that loyalty to the Sultan is to be punished with death?'

'That is certainly not what the Prince was suggesting.' The Sultan did not shout, but the steel in his voice was unmistakable.

'The amirs deserved punishment for deserting their posts, but the Prince overplayed his hand. They ought to have been sent to Dilli to face the Sultan's justice.'

The Sultan paused, and there was silence in the court as the nobles watched the Prince expectantly, wondering if he would lose that infamous temper of his. To their disappointment, he held his peace while managing to look respectful and unapologetic at the same time.

Ghiasuddin Tughlaq thawed. 'The lapse in judgement notwithstanding, your triumphs in Telangana are noteworthy. You did well to take a major chunk of Bihar en route to your conquest of Warangal and Bidar. It was chivalrous of you to treat Pratapa Rudra Deva and his extended family with respect and send them to Dilli with an armed escort. Your actions in pursuing the allies of the fallen king and storming Jajnagar in Utkala, where they had taken refuge, are also noteworthy. Thanks to your efforts, Telangana has been fully absorbed into the empire.'

The sudden smile that lit up Jauna's handsome features was a sight to behold as he bowed in acceptance of the praise he clearly felt was his due. The assembled nobles rose to their feet to applaud him. Even the Khwaja Jahan settled for a nod and half-smile, noting to the flunkies who flanked him, 'He is every bit as spirited and temperamental as those fine steeds he loves so much. But it is to be hoped that his father will have the time to break him into the finer aspects of rule and governance. He has the potential but is a little rough around the edges.'

The Sultan noticed with satisfaction the effect his little speech had created before clearing his throat. When the assembly fell silent, he spoke again, 'It pleases me that you enforced discipline among the troops and prohibited looting or desecration of places of worship. You did well to consolidate your conquests, divide the territory into blocks for administration by centrally appointed officials and set up military garrisons. Your accomplishments will be suitably commemorated at one of the sites of your conquest.'

His father then presented him with a magnificent robe of honour and declared a week's holiday to celebrate his victory. The applause began again, and this time, it did not stop for a long time. Jauna supposed it was his father's way of making it up to him for the dressing-down.

He smiled outwardly. Did his father think he was trying to usurp the throne and had conspired to assassinate him? Was he having second thoughts about having named him the heir apparent? A blind man could see that the Sultan favoured Mahmud over his other sons and kept him close at all times. Was he grooming the younger son to take his place?

Jauna was conflicted. It would be a relief to give up the trappings of power and settle for a life of ease without the added burden of responsibility. Perhaps he could work on the stories he had always wanted to write. Tales of adventure and brave warriors, tomes on history, philosophy, religion. It would be nice to cross the seas and see the world. Jauna had always wanted to visit his hero Kubilai Khan's lands. The possibilities were endless. On most days, he was tempted to walk away from the intrigues of the palace and wander through the land with no destination in mind, without ever coming back.

However, another part of him refused to relinquish the things he had never sought but had been placed within his reach. He had no wish to murder his father or brother for it, though. He hoped it would never come to that.

~

Jauna wished he had not learnt what he did when he visited his mother, Haniya Begum. He had snuck past her guards the way he had as a boy, when challenged by his friends that he couldn't enter the harem unseen. Pleased that he could still do it, and ruing the inefficiency of the guards, he was walking towards her chambers when he heard the voices from within. It stopped him in his tracks. The Sultan had chosen to visit her too, for she was the great love of his life.

'The only thing worse than a fool is an intellectual who is too clever for his own good,' his father was saying. 'The entire crisis in Telangana could have been averted if only Jauna had applied himself. Surely he sensed that the army chiefs were upset with his refusal to accept the Raja's profligate bribes to lift the siege?'

'You know Jauna hates to explain himself to his inferiors,' his mother interjected. 'He usually thinks things through and is thorough. What more can you ask of him?'

'As a commander, he need not justify his actions, but a good one would have assessed the situation and dealt with it before it escalated out of control. Somebody of his intelligence ought to have known that the troops were disgruntled and worked hard to prevent the rebellion that was brewing.'

'Those cowards who withdrew their troops and fled at the first sign of trouble deserved to die,' she said stoutly. 'You wouldn't have let them get away with it either. It is not his fault Ubaid and Shaikhzadah stirred up so much trouble.'

'Somebody in his position cannot afford to make these mistakes and palm the blame on to somebody else.' His father sounded disgruntled. 'There is a cruel side to him that is most disturbing. His troops will hold it against him and so will the families of the victims. For a commander or Sultan to be successful, the love and goodwill of his subjects is paramount. But he doesn't seem to know the value of these things and is keen to fritter it all away.'

'Are you done grousing about your heir apparent? With time and proper guidance, Jauna will ease into the role he was born to play.' Haniya always took her son's side, especially when his father was on the warpath, but Jauna suspected it was overcompensation on her part to make up for the fact that she worshipped her husband and felt that no man would ever measure up to Ghiasuddin Tughlaq. She was probably right too.

The Sultan's response made the knife turn in his heart. 'There is no denying his cleverness, but mostly his education seems to be getting in the way of his common sense. The boy has good ideas but he seems inept at executing them. I am worried about him. When he becomes the Sultan, his subjects will find it in their hearts to forgive him for his cruelty but they will never forgive him for his failures.'

'What is the point of dwelling on his shortcomings?' Haniya pointed out. 'Your time could be more gainfully employed if you were to spend a portion of it training him to be a good leader. Your late benefactor made the mistake of failing to prepare his offspring for rule. Thanks to his negligence, they were not well-educated, driven or disciplined. They got used to doing as they pleased, which is why they came to such a lamentable end.

'Jauna is nothing like them,' she continued loyally. 'He has always been most fastidious. You are too hard on him. All you do is complain about his mistakes while ignoring his many excellent qualities. You pointed out his cruel treatment of those cowardly amirs but conveniently ignored the fact that he treated Pratapa Rudra and the women of his household with far more respect and clemency than they deserved.'

'It was good of him to follow my orders precisely.' There was an edge to the Sultan's tone. Pratapa Rudra had committed suicide en route to Dilli. That was the official version, though Jauna suspected that his father knew that sometimes a man could be persuaded to take his own life, especially when the alternative was pointed out to him.

Haniya persisted, 'My son did not tear down temples and allow his men to violate those women. It is customary to do as much and curry favour with the more fanatical of our God's followers. And he showed a lot of political acumen by raising a splendid mosque to appease the Ulama. In addition to all this, he is generous to a fault, a thoughtful and dutiful son. Vice holds no allure for him.'

'Neither does virtue,' his father pointed out drily. 'Now Bahram and Mahmud on the other hand . . .'

Jauna could hear no more. He turned away abruptly and found himself staring into an arresting pair of eyes. Their owner was not unfamiliar to him. He spent the nights and most of his waking hours consumed by thoughts of her. It had been that way since he first saw her. He had been haunted by the fanatical conviction that in failing to save her, he had failed to save himself.

Saira smiled her sad little smile and whispered, 'The Sultan is merely concerned about your future. All parents want their children to have the best life has to offer and be spared its difficulties.'

Jauna would have given her an earful about his father but her proximity had made him forget his irritation. 'He is the Sultan and it is his prerogative to do whatever he thinks is best. If he wants Mahmud to be the next in line, I will respect his decision and wish them both the joy of the throne.'

Her gaze was steady and wise. 'It is not in his hands. Nor yours. It never was. None of us control the things that happen to us.'

Was he supposed to feel comforted, Jauna wondered. What exactly was she trying to tell him? 'Is that why you married him?' he asked her. His tone sounded a lot more accusatory than he intended.

'You are making it sound like the decision was mine to make.' She shook her head. 'Which is not to say I am not grateful to the Sultan for the kindness he has shown me.'

He supposed she was right. The Sultan had encouraged his higher-ranking courtiers to marry the few Alai women who had survived. As always, he had led by example and chosen the youngest, most beautiful one for himself. And of course she was grateful. The Sultan's 'kindness' had allowed her to retain the privileges of her old life rather than be dismissed as damaged goods who had formerly been the plaything of rough soldiers.

'I am glad you are happy,' he told her, and to his surprise, he actually meant it.

'I am glad you have made the acquaintance of your father's new wife,' Haniya's voice cut in, 'though you seem to have forgotten all about your poor old mother in the process.'

Jauna went to embrace his mother, noting that Saira bowed low and disappeared as quietly as she had materialized.

8

The Sultan had sent for his three eldest sons. Apparently, he wanted a word with them on matters of grave import. They stood outside his private quarters and waited for his summons to enter. Jauna glanced at his brothers, wondering if they knew what this was all about. Bahram's face gave nothing away. He had always been taciturn and a bit of a slogger, which led to people mistakenly underestimating his competence. Mahmud, on the other hand, was a talker with charm to spare. It was hard to say if he was really brilliant or merely pretending to be brilliant.

The brothers weren't particularly close, but neither had they ever felt it necessary to draw daggers on each other. Under the circumstances, they got along as well as could be expected from brothers born to different mothers, and who were in line for the throne.

It was Mahmud who spoke first, 'There has been trouble in Gujarat and the news is not good.'

Of course Jauna knew that, and he suspected Bahram did too. In fact, nearly everybody knew but nobody was certain how the Sultan intended to handle it. If the past was any indication, they could all expect a torrential outpouring of blood and gore.

Following the death of Khusrau Khan and his panwari associates, their clansmen had had a rough time of it. They had made their bid for glory and failed spectacularly. It did not help that during the brief reign of Khusrau Khan they had got drunk on power. Many openly claimed that they would restore Hindu raj in 'Hindustan' and drive away the Mussulmen from their land. They had even gone as far as to demolish prominent mosques while the faithful were at prayer, claiming that they were built on sacred sites that had formerly been temples. Of course, they had justified this injustice by hearkening back to the times of Ghazni and Ghori, the slave kings and the Khaljis, who they insisted had made it their life's business to smash and loot temples while slaughtering thousands of Hindus.[4] So naturally a debt of blood and large-scale destruction had been incurred and must be paid back in kind. The argument sickened Jauna.

Most of the extremists had joined Khusrau Khan on the other side of the grave, which meant that the panwaris who remained were considered fair targets by those who had lost loved ones during the reign of terror and wanted vengeance. Of course, the Sultan had dealt with the communal clashes with an iron hand, but even he wasn't entirely up to the task of making people of different faiths live together peacefully. The casualties kept piling up and the bad blood between the faithful persisted.

The politicos of Gujarat taking advantage of the unrest were using fickle public sentiment to fan the flames of rebellion. The Sultan had sent Malik Shadi Dawar, his son-in-law, at the head of a mighty force to deal with it. Having distinguished himself in two successive battles against the Mongols fought around the time Jauna had been preoccupied with Telangana, Malik Shadi had earned himself the regard of the emperor.

'Do we know for certain that he is dead?' Jauna inquired. He knew the answer, but when it came to games played for power, he had found it was best to play things close to the chest. He was sorry to hear about the loss of his brother-in-law, though. Malik Shadi Dawar had been a good man who was loyal and capable. His sister, Khuda, was inconsolable. He had held her hand and commiserated with her, knowing that it was what his father would want him to do.

Mahmud rolled his eyes at that. 'Of course he is dead, as you very well know. There was treachery at play, but the precise details that led to his demise seem unclear. It usually happens when there is massacre on a large scale and there are no witnesses who have survived to tell tales. I daresay you have a better grasp on the situation than I do. In fact, my spies tell me that your spies are better than even the Sultan's. As for Bahram's spies, like him they will reveal nothing. Not even on pain of death.'

Jauna grinned but was noncommittal. Bahram might have allowed himself a tiny smile but it was more likely that it was a trick of the light.

'It was most unfortunate,' Mahmud continued, shrugging his shoulders in resignation. 'Fresh from his success against the Mongols at Samana, where he fought under the command of Gurshasp, our revered cousin, now governor of Samana, Malik Shadi acquitted himself well. His initial successes were laudable, I am told. He won every skirmish and prevailed in open battle, only to lose the war. After forcing the rebels to retreat, he failed to chase them down and make an end to it.

'They say that the rebels disguised themselves as musicians or bribed a travelling troupe of minstrels who were to perform for the Amir to kill them all. It was a bloodbath, and the Sultan is furious. I daresay his retribution will be fitting!'

Bahram caught his eye then. Jauna was not surprised to note that he knew. What about Mahmud, he wondered. Was he aware of his father's deadliest arsenal? For all his genial ways and affable manner, his younger brother might be a lot smarter than he let on.

Of course, Sultan Ghiasuddin Tughlaq would not allow the foul murder of his son-in-law to go unavenged. Mahmud was still prattling on about it. 'It is likely that we will be called upon to march towards Gujarat immediately and teach the insurgents a lesson they will not forget in a hurry. You will probably be asked to command the imperial forces, Jauna, especially now that you have redeemed yourself after the fiasco at Telangana.'

Jauna bristled ever so slightly, but he refused to rise to the bait. Mahmud was just a puppy yapping away to glory and pretending he was a blooded, battle-hardened veteran. However, his conquests were limited to the boudoir, and they could hardly be called that, since they had mostly been bought and paid for.

Bahram frowned. 'We will know father's wishes in this matter soon enough.' They lapsed into silence after that.

Jauna's thoughts turned to the *hashashin* who had recently offered themselves for hire to his father. Formerly an elite troop of assassins, they had been the scourge of the world during their glory days. They were on the run now that their ranks had been decimated and their impregnable fortress Alamuth had been razed to the ground by the Mongol Hulagu, in whom they had finally met their match. Despite his best efforts, though, Jauna had been unable to ascertain their exact numbers or pinpoint their leader, who made himself known only to the Sultan and would answer to no one else.

Jauna had been fascinated by their history as a student, much to the distress of his instructors, who felt their charge was hero-worshipping a bunch of sinful misfits and glorifying their heinous deeds of murder and mayhem. Their founder, he recalled, had been Hassan-al-Sabbah, who belonged to the Shia sect of the Ismailia and had started the order of the hashashin sometime in the tenth century. Erudite and charismatic, his extremist views nevertheless got him into trouble with the law, which prompted him to lock himself away within Alamuth. If legend was to be believed, Hassan ventured out only twice in his lifetime and devoted himself almost entirely to the upholding of Sharia law. Apparently, he was so fanatical about his chosen vocation that he even executed his two sons when they were found guilty of minor infractions.

Even after the passing of their founder, the hashashin had been actively involved in the great power struggles of the age and made themselves some powerful enemies among both Christians and Muslims, having offered their services to both sides during the Crusades for a price.

Their sphere of influence had radiated from Persia to Syria and the rest of the known world. The executions were carried out in public as well as in private, and the sheer audacity of their crimes struck fear in the hearts of all. Now that their reign of terror had ended and most were cast out into the world, some among them saw no reason not to set their religious scruples aside and offer their skills to the highest bidder. They were dangerous men but their especial skills were invaluable when wielded by the right hands.

Jauna knew that the Sultan had set them on the trail of the cowardly killers of his son-in-law, who had already melted away. The hashashin were known to be relentless. They would devote themselves to the task and execute them even if it took them the rest of their lives.

It was typically efficient of Ghiasuddin Tughlaq. He would have avenged his son-in-law without exacerbating the situation with the Hindus, which would be inevitable were he to order a series of public executions. Eventually, a force would be sent to subdue the mess in Gujarat, but any action now would only be counterproductive, with only the innocent dying, when his attention and resources could be more gainfully employed elsewhere. Some day, Jauna hoped to cultivate a touch that was half as deft as his father's.

Therefore, Jauna knew that they would not be ordered to march towards Gujarat. The Sultan clearly had something else on his mind. Jauna supposed he could hazard a guess, and excitement stirred at the prospect of war, conquest and riches. His expedition to Telangana had been a nightmare, and yet he had felt more alive then and less lonely.

They were finally asked to enter. Jauna thought he saw Saira's retreating figure and his heart skipped a beat. If the gossips were to be believed, his father was quite taken with his new wife, who had already rewarded him with a son. Jauna could hardly blame him for being so enamoured of her, but did anyway.

The Sultan nodded to them, beckoning for them to take their seats around him. He looked frail, Jauna thought. Age was catching up with him fast. It made him sad. He wished his father would live forever. But he also wished sometimes that he would succumb to natural causes and leave every one of his possessions to him. Initially, he had been horrified by his thoughts, but now they were around so much that they were starting to feel like co-conspirators.

Jauna saw no reason to flagellate himself for it. After all, thoughts seldom translated into action. He forced himself to concentrate as he felt his father's piercing gaze on him.

'I assume all the preparations have been made and the imperial army is ready to march within a few days.' The query was directed to Bahram. Jauna and Mahmud stared at him in surprise. This was the first they were hearing about this. The Sultan had clearly confided in their brother. Why did their father make it a point to favour them in turns? Did he want them to kill each other?

'It has, your majesty, and your troops need but a moment's notice to carry out your orders,' Bahram replied, and the Sultan nodded with satisfaction.

'Well done, Bahram!' He smiled at his son, and Jauna felt even more ill-disposed towards him. Judging from Mahmud's smile, which had suddenly become snake-like, he felt the same way. 'Now the time has come for me to reveal my plans.'

'Within a fortnight, I will lead the forces and we will set out to Lakhnauti.' He noticed the looks of surprise mirrored on the faces of his three sons with satisfaction. 'As you know, I have coveted the prosperous Bengal province and hoped to absorb it into the empire ever since fortune smiled on me and placed me on the throne. Recently, I received an overture from a prince of the realm and am determined to respond, since I am convinced that the entire province is ripe for the picking.'

Jauna's mind was whirring. 'It has been an independent kingdom since the time of Balban's son, Bughra Khan, who removed himself from the power corridors of Dilli and was content to rule from Lakhnauti. They said he refused to involve himself in the internecine struggle following Balban's passing, not even when the Khaljis took the throne for themselves after deposing the last of Balban's line, which included Bughra Khan's own son.'

'Thanks for the history lesson, brother, but why don't we focus on things as they stand today?' Mahmud was impatient.

'He was getting to it . . .' the Sultan admonished him.

'Shamsuddin was Bughra Khan's descendant, and he died recently,' Jauna continued. 'He is succeeded by four sons: Shihabuddin, Nasiruddin, Ghiasuddin Bahadur and Qutlugh Khan. The smart money is on either Nasiruddin or Bahadur to take the throne. Bahadur seems to have the advantage, which is probably why Nasiruddin or one of the others has invited our father, the Sultan of Dilli, to join forces with him.'

'Very good, Jauna, it is Nasiruddin who has approached me. I suppose you can predict the outcome of this clash as well.' The Sultan smiled.

He did not miss a beat. 'You will prevail, your majesty! Bahadur will be vanquished, and with Nasiruddin having sworn allegiance to you, the kingdom of Bengal will be yours. Not even your beloved mentor managed this feat. May you live forever!'

The Sultan cracked a smile in acknowledgement of the fulsome praise. 'Bahram and Mahmud will march with me. In my absence, you will be my regent, for I have decided to leave the empire in the capable hands of my heir apparent.'

Bahram merely bowed his head in acquiescence. Mahmud was slightly put out that his father had not singled him out for special duties, but consoled himself with the thought of being on the road again. He winked at Jauna before turning to address the Sultan. 'Wishing you every success, your majesty! But surely we still have to take care of the situation in Gujarat?' Mahmud persisted.

'One of the keys to success is knowing when to walk away,' the Sultan replied somewhat obliquely, 'and when to persist. The unholy mess there will be cleaned up in time. Malik Tajuddin Jafar will leave for Gujarat at the front of a substantial force. If all goes well, he will rule as the governor and answer to me.' He looked at Jauna as he said this.

'And there is one other thing,' he continued. 'I hope the three of you will remain united no matter the circumstances and be a source of strength and support for each other. We have come a long way from our humble origins, which is all the more reason not to take the blessings showered by the Almighty or each other for granted.'

He paused. It was a long speech for a man of action. Mahmud was the first to reply, 'Of course, your majesty. We are your sons after all, and despite what everyone thinks, some of your nobility and good judgement has rubbed off on us as well.'

The brothers smiled at each other, and for just a moment, they all believed they were one big happy family.

9

It was the latest triumph in a distinguished military career. Bengal had also fallen with minimal resistance. The Sultan had vanquished his namesake, Ghiasuddin Bahadur, and placed Nasiruddin, who had sworn allegiance to him, on the throne. Satgaon and Sonargaon had also fallen, as had Tirhut. It seemed as if the Sultan could not put a wrong foot forward if he tried. As ever, he was merciful towards the captured. The common folks of the fallen kingdoms were treated with the consideration and kindness he was famed for and they were grateful.

In light of everything that happened, Jauna was happy for his father, for the fact that he had lived long enough to rule over an empire that was larger than even Alauddin Khalji's had been. It was a proud moment for the Tughlaqs. However, he remained immeasurably saddened that at the very zenith of Sultan Ghiasuddin's glory, death came calling.

Jauna considered himself a strong man, but he still had difficulty accepting that the worst had come to pass. That Sultan Ghiasuddin, who had left his indelible footprint on the pages of history and been hailed as a behemoth among the greatest monarchs of all time, was no more. How had it come to pass? Even now it was all a blur in his head. And the debilitating guilt did not help.

When the royal messengers had brought in the glad tidings of the Sultan's triumphs, he was surprised that the predominant emotion he was feeling was envy. Success came so effortlessly to

Ghiasuddin Tughlaq, whereas it seemed that for him everything was a struggle. His father had handed over the reins of administration to him and he had wanted to make him proud. But his courtiers, led by the curmudgeonly Khwaja Jahan, had fought him at every turn, and the entire experience had left Jauna with a bad taste in the mouth. It had reached a point where he wanted to execute the lot of them.

The resentment he was feeling kept him up at night. Which was why he had sent for Ahmad bin Aiyaz, the inspector of buildings, first thing in the morning and asked him to raise a magnificent pavilion at Afghanpur, where they would receive the Sultan on the eve of his triumphant return to Dilli. As usual, there had been pushback when it came to the execution of his schemes.

The courtiers had groused about the expenses and impracticability of raising a structure on the scale and grandeur he had envisioned within a span of three days. Fortunately, he had chosen the right man for the job, and Ahmad carried out his instructions by cajoling the courtiers to fall in line with their regent, before cursing and harrying the workers till they got the job done.

All had been in readiness for the Sultan, and his father had been most pleased. His mood had been expansive as he mingled with all who had gathered to celebrate his triumph, and there had been a festive note to the proceedings. The Sultan had displayed the treasures that had come into his possession at Lakhnauti and distributed weighty quantities of gold, silver and precious stones among those who had rendered distinguished service to the throne.

He singled out the heroes of the war, from lowly foot soldiers to stalwarts of the imperial army, honouring them with gold, land and titles. All basked in the warm approbation of their emperor. Like the others present, Jauna marvelled at the ability of his father to take note of and reward the little things that made all the difference in the world.

Then the thrice damned, richly caparisoned elephants had been brought out for the parade on his orders. It had been a blisteringly hot day and the air had a heavy, oppressive quality to it. The creatures had become increasingly restless, having waited in the sun for long hours prior to the Sultan's arrival. One of the mahouts lost control of his beast and there had been instant pandemonium as the creature trumpeted and charged.

The sudden blast of sound deafened them, and when the mountainous beast thundered forth with surprising speed, people began screaming hysterically. The panic goaded the pachyderm into a state of fury and he attacked, grabbing an unfortunate soul and dashing him to the ground, killing him instantly. Others were less fortunate as the swinging trunk struck down on unprotected backs with the force of an axe blade, breaking spines and maiming its victims.

In the ensuing stampede, the guards struggled to hold back the panic-stricken crowd. Jauna had asked Mahmud to stay with his father while he himself rushed out to deal with the situation and restore order.

'With pleasure, brother!' Mahmud had joked, though his forehead was beaded with perspiration. 'You have a way with animals. I would rather stay here where it is safe.'

Jauna would have liked to inform him that nobody ever feted the deeds of cowards who cowered in the safety of the pavilion, but there simply hadn't been enough time as he dashed out, taken aback at the extent of the carnage that had been wrought in those few minutes. Fortunately, most of the other elephants had been led away. Only the one remained, its back bristling with arrow shafts that seemed to have done little to improve his temper.

The mahouts and a dozen soldiers were trying to haul him back, using their spears to force him to submit, but succeeding only in making the poor creature furious, which in turn gave fresh impetus to his capacity for destruction. Before Jauna's horrified eyes, he trod on two more men beneath those massive padded feet and speared another with his tusk before raising him heavenward and pounding him into the dust. He heard every bone in the wretched man's body break before he took his last agonized breath.

Jauna cursed them all. What a disaster! And he was certain he would be blamed for this entire fiasco. As if it was his fault that the elephant had run amok. He wondered if his father was watching and with an effort stopped himself from waving his arms frantically while shouting instructions that were being completely ignored.

Finally, one of the swordsmen struck, driving the entire length of his sword into the space between the ribs and deep into the great beast's heart. Blood gushed out from the end of the trunk, spraying everyone in the vicinity. Even so, it was long moments before he died, fighting off the soldiers who swarmed over him, hacking and thrusting like butchers. Finally, the grey warrior succumbed to his injuries as his feet gave out beneath him, and he crashed to the earth.

The Prince was still trying to make himself heard over the hullaballoo when the crash and boom of thunder drowned out everything else. Rain pelted down on them without warning. Clearly, even the elements were determined to compound an already miserable situation. A wild premonition of disaster gripped his heart as he turned to gaze at the pavilion. Forked lightning tore across the heavens as the wind shrieked in his ears like a wailing woman bemoaning the loss of the most precious thing in her world. Lightning flashed again, and it seemed to strike with malignant intent.

Through a sheet of water, he saw the pavilion break apart and collapse to the ground with excruciating slowness. Jauna ran. As he struggled to speed across the slippery terrain, he heard the infernal screams of terror, torn from throats in mortal pain. He would never forget that sound. Struggling to get a grip on his emotions, Jauna spotted Ahmad and shouted for pickaxes and shovels. Over and over again, he tried to make himself heard even as the accursed storm swallowed up his words. 'Dig in the name of all that is holy!' he bellowed. 'Dig with your own damned hands if that is what it takes! Find the Sultan! Bring the hakim!'

He had tried frantically to get to his father, using his bare hands to work his way through the wreckage till they were shredded and bleeding. They needed to be bandaged for days afterwards. But his frantic effort was futile. It was far too late to do anything for his father and brother.

He held the Sultan's broken body in his arms, drenched in the driving sheets of rain, screaming again for the hakim, praying for a miracle. His father had thrown himself over Mahmud, and the back of his skull had caved in under the weight of a fallen beam. Bahram knelt by his side, head bowed, hands clasped as he prayed. Of all the things, that made Jauna weep. He had no idea how long they remained that way while the work detail, summoned by the ever-reliable Ahmad, worked their way through the wreckage to pull out the bodies of the deceased and the injured.

The storm raged on through the night, and for the life of him, Jauna had no idea what he did during those long hours. Later, his detractors would insist that he had paid off all those who had been a part of the conspiracy to kill the Sultan and used the time to cover his tracks so that the dastardly deed would not be traced back to him.

The next day, the funerary procession wound its way towards the mausoleum at Tughlaqabad, and the simple sepulchre the Sultan had designed for himself. Throngs of people gathered to say their farewells to the emperor they had loved so well, whom they had prepared to greet with petals and cheers to celebrate his greatest triumph.

Hysterical mobs converged on them every step of the way. Women tore at their hair, beat their chests and ululated wildly, lamenting the loss of one they had revered as a God and protector. Grown men were on their knees weeping like children and pounding on their heads, demented with grief. Prayers were conducted in the temples and mosques as for once the Sultan's warring subjects set aside their differences, united by their shared grief over the passing of a beloved monarch.

Jauna observed it all across the great gulf of his own profound grief, a lone figure in the middle of the multitudes of humanity, unable to stop the tears that streamed down his cheeks. Later, he won laurels for his so-called histrionic talents on the strength of those heart-rending tears. 'Can you believe the nerve of him?' they whispered behind his back. 'He commits parricide and then sheds copious fake tears to divert suspicion from his despicable deed.'

'Stop blaming yourself!' Abu whispered urgently. 'Even if the Sultan had died peacefully in his sleep at a ripe old age, fingers would still be pointed at you. If you carry on nursing this senseless guilt, your old friends the rumour-mongers will have a gay old time carrying on.'

But Jauna did feel responsible. For the resentment he had harboured in his breast over the success of his father, the happiness his new wife had found in his arms and the paternal love enjoyed by his brother, Mahmud. It had been a malignant infection of the spirit that had spilled out of him and struck down his loved ones, hadn't it?

Worst of all was the tiny part of him that was inexplicably happy because the path ahead had been cleared. Even though it could lead nowhere but to damnation. He was sure of it.

10

In the days leading up to his coronation, Jauna wished he could be fully rid of old friends. Like rumours. And Abu. They were everywhere, circling around him. Ephemeral spirits that taunted and teased armed with their barbs. Always out of his reach when he lashed out.

Parricide. That was what they were accusing him of. It was felt that the freak accident that had claimed the life of Ghiasuddin Tughlaq had been too much of a coincidence. And worked out a little too conveniently for his son, who would ascend the throne as Muhammad bin Tughlaq. Abu, bless his soul, felt otherwise.

'They don't know you like I do,' he said staunchly. 'You are too much of a good planner to leave so much to chance. Even if you built a flimsy structure designed to collapse, the forked lightning is beyond the powers of even an aspiring monarch.'

'Some are saying there was no storm to speak of,' Jauna replied moodily. 'Apparently, on my instructions, Ahmad built the pavilion using poor quality wood with a hollow foundation, triggered to cave in on command.'

'It does not help your case now that everybody knows you intend to promote him to the post of Khwaja Jahan once you ascend the throne,' Abu mused. 'That is quite the leap for the former inspector of buildings. These late converts to Islam seldom ascend the ladder of power so quickly.'

'He is the best man for the job and it goes without saying that he has proved his worth. As the son of the former ruler of Devagiri, he has been well-trained as a warrior and administrator. More importantly, he was converted to the true faith by Nizamuddin Auliya himself. Besides, his predecessor also lost his life when that accursed pavilion fell. It was considerate of him to exit life when he did, otherwise I might have been tempted to have him executed.'

'Speaking of Auliya, you must be aware of his "prophetic" words uttered during a trance, which many believe led to the death of the Sultan. It is all his faithful followers can talk about. Apparently, the royal messenger carried a missive saying that if the saint did not pay back what was owed the state by the time the Sultan returned, Dilli would not be big enough for the Sultan and the saint, and it would be best if he left the city. To which he is said to have replied that Dilli is still pretty far . . .'

'*Hunuz Dilli dur ast*,' Muhammad finished for him. 'Everybody is saying that we colluded to make this tragedy happen. But saying such things about a saint or Sultan is not really good for one's general health, is it? You would think that would stop people from spreading filthy lies, but no!'

'We have the venerable Shaikh Rukhnuddin to blame for that. He claims to have been an eyewitness to your conduct on that day. As a rabid follower of the true faith, he has always been voluble about the fact that your father was a traitor because of the benevolence he has shown the Hindus,' Abu whispered. 'Convinced that you will follow the same policy of tolerance, he has seized this opportunity to begin a smear campaign against you.'

'I know. He claims that I pretended to summon the work detail with their pickaxes and shovels while giving them orders to wait till sundown to commence digging, and it was the delay that killed my father.' His eyes filled with tears as he remembered that awful day.

'That is not all!' Abu continued in a hushed voice. 'He also claims that the Sultan was still alive and your men finished the job with spades. Perhaps you should make an example of that lying

Shaikh and all the slanderers out there. Have his toxic tongue ripped out to caution others.'

'That would merely give credence to the rumours.' Jauna sighed.

Abu sighed in tow. 'It didn't help that before the prescribed period of mourning was completed, you met petitioners who came on behalf of Nizamuddin Auliya and agreed to change the name of Ghiyaspur in his honour, and sanctioned a request to build a fabulous dargah for him. It gave your detractors a chance to insist you were in cahoots with the saint and his followers.'

'First of all, he is ailing and doesn't have much longer to live. It was verified by my informers. Secondly, I cannot begrudge him these things given that he has devoted his life to the propagation of truth, wisdom and purity,' Jauna insisted. 'Not to mention the many welfare schemes he implemented to help the poor and needy. Granted, he had his differences with the late Sultan, but I know my father respected him. I did it to maintain goodwill and preserve peace. And he had no more to do with the Sultan's death than I did. Denying him his due to still insolent tongues would be an exercise in futility.'

'All I can say is that Sultans are easier targets than saints.' Abu was thoughtful. 'Ahmad has been wise too. He busies himself with his job and ignores calumny, which is the only way to deal with it. You care too much about what people say. It makes you susceptible to their attacks.'

'You would be bothered too, had it been you who stands accused of murdering your father and brother.'

'Don't be childish, Jauna, and stop brooding about the past when the future awaits,' Abu lectured. 'Your father's legacy is a shining one and he would have wanted you to outshine him. You have inherited a vast empire from him that extends from the Himalayas in the north-east, the Indus in the north-west, all the provinces up to the sea in the east and west, and up to Madurai and Malabar in the south. You also have a treasury filled to overflowing. With all this, you have the chance to make a truly remarkable career for yourself.

'As for the rumours, those with an iota of sense would realize that unlike Alauddin Khalji and his ilk, you were directly in line to the throne and your father was an old man. Therefore, you had no reason to kill him. Besides even if you had conspired to do so you would have done a neater job of it. A pillow over his head while he was sleeping would have been far more elegant and effective as opposed to rampaging elephants, bolts of lightning and collapsed pavilions.'

Ignoring Jauna's reproving glare, Abu ploughed on, 'So what if your mother looks at you with doubt in her eyes because you allowed love to cloud your judgement and had your stepmother Saira and your half-brother Masud Khan moved to new quarters at Jahanpanah with indecent alacrity? So what if the accusation of parricide hangs over your head for the remainder of your life? So what if petty historians refuse to give you the benefit of doubt and taint your good name for all of time? You know the truth and so do I! That is all that matters.'

Sensing his desolation, Abu tried again. 'Remember that you have a thankless task ahead of you. Don't get distracted; focus on what needs to be done. People will forgive murder, but they will not forgive either stupidity or failure. Be careful and make certain that you are guilty of neither. If you can do that, there is every reason to believe that your reign will be remembered as the greatest in the history of this land.'

Jauna grunted. Sometimes he wished Abu would just shut up and leave him to his misery. But he was right. There was a lot to look forward to. Tomorrow was the day of his coronation. It would be a glittering occasion in the Red Palace built by Balban, which had been renovated and suitably spruced up on his orders. And he had a beautiful speech prepared, even if he did say so himself. All wasn't well. But he supposed it could have been worse. He could have been sitting in that pavilion with his father and brother when it collapsed and his life would have been over before it could even begin.

PART TWO

SULTAN MUHAMMAD BIN TUGHLAQ

'Muhammad Shah is the ambitious and
magnanimous king of the whole world.
In comparison to the waves of his heart,
the river found itself reduced to a drop.'

(inscription found carved into stone monuments from
Muhammad bin Tughlaq's time)

1

Sultan Muhammad bin Tughlaq was a thinker. Sometimes, when his thoughts started running amok in his head, he wished he wasn't one. Surely his head would feel lighter when emptied of thoughts?

Given the circumstances of his father's death, everything had gone smoothly. He had just inherited a mighty empire without having to kill for it, as well as the woman of his dreams and an enviable treasury. His mind and body were sound. It appeared to him that he had all the advantages he could have asked for. Yet he could not shake off the foreboding that hounded him relentlessly.

As a child, every time he spotted a rainbow or a cloud, he would do his utmost to touch it. He had even started to build a ladder that would help him achieve his aim. Having seen the amount of time and effort he was lavishing on his ambition, to the detriment of his lessons, his tutor had made him tear down the edifice. Furious, he had launched himself at the man and would have torn off a chunk from his arm if a blow to the face had not stopped him in his tracks.

Prepared for a whipping, he had been surprised when his tutor addressed him quietly instead, 'If you spend your life with your gaze turned towards heaven, you will certainly miss the treacherous openings in the world of the living and fall headlong into the fires of hell. Be prudent with the expenditure of your resources, Jauna!'

That damnable incident was on his mind these days. Some nights, he dreamed of it. Every step on the ladder of his design would take him closer to the rainbows and clouds. Closer and closer. He was a heartbeat away from touching it and so intent was he that he did not notice the gaping, fiery maw that had opened up beneath him. It had consumed his creation, and the moment he realized that, he fell. Then he would wake up with a hollow feeling in the pit of his stomach, convinced that now he had climbed as high as he could, all that remained was the fall.

~

The coronation had gone without a hitch. After all, he had planned it to perfection. It was a new beginning for them all, and he wanted to commence his reign in a blaze of glory, not a cloud of mourning. Besides, it would set the tone for what would be a magnificent reign.

For the first time in living memory, the transition to power had been a smooth one, free of insurrection and bloodshed. It pleased him that the bureaucrats as well as common citizens, irrespective of their faith, had accepted his ascension wholeheartedly.

His father's body had been interred in the mausoleum at Tughlaqabad, the famous gilded citadel that Ghiasuddin had built for himself, preferring not to live with the ghosts of the Alai family at Siri or the preferred bastion of the slave kings, the Qutub complex at Dilli. Tughlaqabad boasted of fine palaces, the grand assembly and one of the marvels of the known world: a treasury made of bricks coated in gold. This housed all the valuables he had accumulated and boasted a deep cistern filled to overflowing with molten gold. Muhammad would have happily traded it all for his father's life.

Forty days had been spent in mourning, and he had sat at his mother's side throughout, holding her hand and nursing her past the worst stages of her grief. She had aged considerably, barely able to bear her terrible loss. Her eyesight had always been weak and he worried about her frailty. Muhammad insisted she partake of her meals and take the potions prescribed for her by the royal physician, Wasim.

'I always thought it was a barbaric practice to burn those poor Hindu women along with their husbands, but now I truly understand why they do it . . .' Haniya had confided in him during an unheard of moment of weakness.

'Don't you say that, mother!' Muhammad had taken her hand in his. 'This land needs you. We all do. Without your wisdom and strength, we are lost. As for that abominable practice of burning good lives away, I will abolish it if it is the last thing I do!'

Haniya extricated her hand and used it to nurse her head. Muhammad wished he could make her feel better. And for some reason, she had difficulty looking him in the eye and seemed ill at ease with his presence by her side. It saddened him. If only she knew that she was providing fodder for the gossip mills.

Saira, understandably, had been less distraught, but then, sometimes, she reminded him of a statue sculpted from the purest alabaster—breathtakingly beautiful but also cold and unyielding. It was frustrating because he could sense the warmth at her core. It was what had drawn him to her.

When Muhammad inquired about her well-being after the tragedy, Saira had said, 'My husband was a great Sultan and his premature passing is an insurmountable loss. But more importantly, he was a good man and kind. There will never be another like him and I will always be grateful for the benevolence and consideration he showed me.'

Her words irritated him. He concealed his feelings under a practiced veneer of courtesy and graciousness but she must have sensed it for she never mentioned Ghiasuddin Tughlaq's name in his presence ever again. As to her opinion on how he measured up to his father, she never shared it with him. But then she didn't have to. He could always sense her thoughts, and they hardened into certainty soon enough.

The consensus was that he was but a poor imitation of the great man. At best. Originally, it had made him sad. Then it drove him mad.

Grief had done nothing to make Bahram less reticent, and his brother kept his thoughts to himself. 'Do you think I had something to do with father's death? And Mahmud's?' Muhammad couldn't help but ask.

He had shrugged. 'It would be most unlike you. Besides, if I thought you did it, I wouldn't be standing here before you, taking the risk of getting murdered myself, now, would I?'

It had been Muhammad's turn to shrug. Bahram looked at him for a long moment. He seemed to be choosing his words carefully. 'For what it is worth and to the extent you will allow yourself to believe me, you have my support.' His brother's gaze was steady and unwavering. It was Muhammad who had trouble looking him in the eye.

Their cousin Firoz, the son of Ghiasuddin's brother, Rajab, had approached him too with the utmost politeness and correctness that was typical of him. 'The Sultan, your father and my uncle, was a legend, and his legacy remains in good hands with you, his worthy son. You can count on my loyalty and unwavering support, your majesty!'

It was most considerate of him. But later, Muhammad could not help but wonder if Bahram or Firoz had an eye on the throne and murderous designs towards him. After all, that was the way of it, wasn't it?

He remembered when his younger brothers Nusrat and Zafar had died. Neither had survived the notorious ailments of childhood. Their funerals had been solemn affairs and Muhammad had been immeasurably saddened then. He had also received the whipping of his lifetime for wondering out loud, 'Why should God take children? Why did he make them suffer so much? They were so little . . . if he were as merciful as everyone says he is, he wouldn't have done this to them!'

But now he was glad they were gone. There was also a palpable sense of relief that they or their children weren't around to kill or be killed by him or his own sons.

It was with relief that he had marched out of Tughlaqabad in a stately procession towards his new life. His instructions had been precise, and he was pleased to note that the decorations had been done with elegance and taste. The dusty roads and avenues leading to the city had been cleaned and paved. Foot soldiers posted at regular intervals stood at attention, their armour and helmets polished to a bright sheen.

The streets and turrets had been festooned with streamers and brightly coloured banners of silk, trimmed with gold, with painstakingly embroidered images of his handsome mien, which he had inherited almost entirely from his mother. Musicians played their instruments and pounded on drums. The citizenry were exuberant as they came out in droves to welcome the new emperor and call out their blessings.

Seeing his smiling countenance, some felt confident enough to call out ribald suggestions, referring to his royal sceptre and the desirable creatures who would warm his bed. One was bold enough to cry out, 'May you have brave sons who won't have you killed with stampeding elephants and collapsible buildings!'

Muhammad did not respond, but the smile disappeared from his face. The crowd fell silent as the guards used the butts of their spears a little more freely to dissuade the loose-tongued and insolent.

Sultan Muhammad bin Tughlaq then proceeded stiffly and in state beneath the royal parasol, accompanied by his courtiers who would take office on that day. His officials, mounted on elephants, worked the catapults and showered the assembled with armfuls of gold and silver, which he was no longer sure they deserved. The crowd went berserk with joy and scrambled around scooping up coins, pushing and shoving, while the guards continued to use their weapons to keep them in line.

He had planned another surprise for his subjects at the instigation of the ambassador from China, who had enjoyed his hospitality during the period of Muhammad's regency. Initially, the citizenry had reacted with alarm at the sudden explosion of light and sound high above their heads, but then the shock and amazement had made them forget about the coins. Those who were craning their necks instead of closing their eyes in terror spotted the source of the explosion behind the turrets arcing towards the heavens. Ear-splitting booms accompanied the brightly coloured streaks radiating outward in spirals leaving behind a trail of dense smoke.

Once they got used to it, they laughed and cheered at the marvel, excited as the children jumping up and down trying to catch those splintered pieces of gold, silver, ruby red and emerald green. A propitious way to mark the beginning of a new era, Muhammad patted himself on the back, trying to distract himself from the bitter taste that flooded his mouth.

Before proceeding to the palace where his coronation would take place, Muhammad had addressed his subjects, 'My father believed in justice for all, and I do too. It will be my life's mission to ensure that none of you will ever have to suffer from unjust acts and unfair deeds. The old and infirm in my realm will be treated the way I would my own parents. The youngsters are akin to my siblings. And your children are my own. It is my wish that every single one of my subjects enjoys a life that is blessed with peace, prosperity and plenty, irrespective of their status at this moment. With your blessing, it will be my duty to dispense justice and uphold it till your emperor's name becomes synonymous with justice!'

The Mullah had recited the litany of prayers and outlined his duties in a sonorous tone. Muhammad barely registered what the man was droning on about before placing his father's glittering crown on his brow. As the petals rained down on his head, he felt the sheer weight of every single one of them, and the crushing burden of the great Sultan Ghiasuddin Tughlaq's formidable legacy.

At that moment, he realized that he wouldn't achieve in fifty years what his father had in five. It was a sobering thought.

I may never measure up to you, father, but I swear to do my utmost to make you proud. I swear it with every fibre of my being!

The new Sultan had kept his emotions in check and held himself erect with the steadfast resolve and fortitude that had characterized his father in life.

Once the formalities had been dispensed with, and after enduring one flowery speech too many, the Sultan got down to business.

In keeping with tradition, Muhammad had conferred titles on the deserving, confirmed appointments and released prisoners, all of which he had worked out beforehand. Of course, there were many who would have preferred to be consulted, but Muhammad believed that when you wanted a job done, it was best to do it yourself.

Ahmad, of course, was given the title of Khwaja Jahan. Muhammad's cousin Firoz was named the head chamberlain. Firoz had managed to cultivate a manner that was friendly yet reserved. He enjoyed a decent rapport with his cousins, though they weren't particularly close. His neutrality and dutiful air, however, seemed to endear him to one and all. As for Muhammad's youngest brother, Mubarak, he had decided it was best for him to be given a post in the judiciary department, where Ahmad could keep an eye on him.

Bahram was told to take command in Lakhnauti, where their father had enjoyed one of the greatest triumphs of his military career. The ill-fated Nasiruddin, who had solicited his help against his brother Ghiasuddin Bahadur, had succumbed to injuries sustained in the war and had not lived long enough to savour his success.

As usual, it was impossible to ascertain whether Bahram was pleased with the post or not. However, he did look less than thrilled when informed that Muhammad would be releasing Ghiasuddin

Bahadur, who had been imprisoned by their father. Bahadur and Bahram would be joint governors of Lakhnauti.

Everything had gone as well as could be expected, and it was the near-perfect start to his reign. He had honoured his mother with a title too: Makhduma Jahan (Mistress of the World). His sister, Khuda, however had felt left out and waylaid him when he went to visit their mother. 'How come I did not get a glorious title? Personally I think I wouldn't mind being called the brightest light of the world. Noor Jahan! Or something.'

'Or something it is then,' he teased, and she wagged a finger at him in warning. 'I am going to find a nice husband for you instead and you shall have a splendid wedding,' he added. Khuda winked at him and he could tell she was pleased. He was sure his father would have been pleased too.

He knew the title would make his mother happy and proud, but you wouldn't know it from the tirade she launched into on seeing him. There was no sign of the disconsolate, broken woman from earlier who had been contemplating ending her life, and he wondered if he had imagined it all.

'I didn't raise you to be so sinfully extravagant,' Haniya began with a flash of the same iron spirit he knew so well. 'Your father left you an abundant treasury, and if you carry on like this it will be empty in a matter of days. Allow me to remind you that Sultan Ghiasuddin Tughlaq did not feel the need to buy the love and respect of his people, preferring instead to earn it. Alauddin Khalji, on the other hand, felt compelled to resort to such cheap tactics on his coronation day because he hoped the glitter of gold would blind his subjects to the inescapable fact that he had murdered his king, who had also been a father to him.'

Muhammad had seen it coming, but her pointed barb made him wince anyway. He could have explained that he had merely wanted to infuse some joy after the dolorous period of mourning, but what was the point? His mother had already made up her mind, and she was only getting started.

'And what is this I hear about the latest addition to Dilli?' Haniya went on. 'Am I to be forced to leave Tughlaqabad and made to take up residence in Jahanpanah, as they call it? Your father built Tughlaqabad and it is good enough for me, even if it isn't for you. Thanks to your abandonment, its splendour will be lost to the encroaching decay, and it will be land fit only for grazing cows, just as that odious Nizamuddin Auliya predicted. How can you dishonour your father's memory in this manner?'

She paused, waiting for her son to explain. When nothing but imperial silence greeted her words, Haniya tried to work herself up into a proper fit of rage. But he was massaging her feet gently and she sighed. Her Jauna was a good boy even if he frustrated her and could never hope to be the ruler his father had been.

'Promise me that you will be very careful about all the things that have come into your possession recently. Especially the things that have wormed their way into your heart.' Muhammad was pleased to note that the anger had left her to be replaced with concern.

Haniya's heart ached with worry. If only God had paid heed to her prayers and allowed her husband to live long enough to prepare and guide their son. How was a mother supposed to warn her firstborn about that vixen he was obsessed with? That same creature who had entrapped her own husband and sidled her way into his bed and heart? Why couldn't the men in her life see the obvious? That seeing her family slaughtered and being made to endure great evil had wounded and hardened the woman they were obsessed with? That she neither liked nor trusted men?

Her Jauna needed a girl who was loving and dutiful, just like his mother. Instead, he went chasing after that which was already lost to him. It all seemed so hopeless to her.

He smiled sadly, almost as if he could read her mind. 'Don't you worry, mother. A Sultan can't afford to have a heart.'

2

'What is needed are sweeping reforms,' Sultan Muhammad bin Tughlaq was saying to Ahmad, his grand vizier, his chief executioner, Najib, and the historian, Barani. 'Serious changes that will usher in a new age of peace and prosperity for people from all walks of life. If done right, this land will achieve its full potential for glory and I will be at the head of the greatest empire in history.'

He paused, giving the impression he was lost in thought but was actually studying their reflections in mirrored surfaces placed around the room. He was fond of setting them up in strategic positions to fully observe the reactions of his ministers, and the better to separate the truth in their thoughts from the falsehoods uttered by their tongues.

They all held their tongues, which made it easier for him to read their expressions. *I wonder which scroll he read it from*, Ahmad was thinking tiredly. *Grandiose schemes can easily derail everything we are working so hard to keep together.* The man was loyal but he clearly thought his Sultan was most impractical. It was typical of him to feel that the emperor was someone who should be handled with extreme caution. A prudent man, which made him ideal for the job, but Muhammad couldn't help but wish the Khwaja Jahan would exercise his imagination once in a while.

Barani, on the other hand, had a harsher viewpoint which was entirely at odds with his pacific expression, *It is bad enough he has such a cavalier attitude towards the scions of our oldest noble families who carry the blood of the mighty Chagatai Turks in their veins, and consorts with those who have converted to the true faith simply to advance their careers, but he has also gone so far as to appoint these pretend Muslims to important offices. All manner of baseborn creatures and even the infidels now hold the same rank as the eminent nobles or higher. It is disgraceful!*

Muhammad stroked his beard and tried not to laugh. Of course Barani dared not give voice to his thoughts. Especially since the Khwaja Jahan was one of those converts he loathed. Ahmad also carried the blood of kings in his veins and could not be lumped together with the baseborn, though Barani would never deign to acknowledge that. As for Najib, it was true his antecedents were not what one would call illustrious, and he too was a recent convert.

The grand vizier kept up appearances, but he had also been known to look out for the Hindus, especially since his Sultan had never discouraged him, and regularly made contributions for the renovations of their temples and financed charitable schemes for adherents of his former faith who had been ground into the dust by fervent Islamists. Which was as it should be. It was pragmatic men like Ahmad as well as the tolerant and large-hearted from all classes of society who had been responsible for building the fragile bridges between the various faiths.

Najib, on the other hand, seemed not to care a whit for Hindu or Muslim or Buddhist or Jain and treated them just the same when they wound up on his executioner's block. Which was also as it should be. In Muhammad's opinion, there were good, bad and ugly people in every religion, caste and community, and there were no exceptions to that particular rule.

As for Barani, like a lot of scribes Muhammad knew, his boldness was limited to his words. In real life, he was frightened of those who had the power to crush him for sedition in thought or word. Of his Sultan who could ensure that he would lose his cushy job with its generous stipend and order his execution.

The historian had adopted a diffident air to mask his dislike for the grand vizier—not that he had succeeded in fooling anybody. As for Najib, whom he considered a butcher's son, he didn't bother to even pretend and was suspected of having coined the term Sag-al-Sultan—the Sultan's dog—which, luckily for him, Najib took as a compliment since he preferred the company of his bloodhounds to humans.

Muhammad expected Barani to say something obsequious to overcompensate for his overwhelming opposition to most things his emperor did. His family had fallen on hard times and had little left but pride. The historian was dependent on the emperor's patronage and largesse, which did not improve his feelings one bit towards his mercurial Sultan. But Muhammad liked him well enough. He could turn a phrase and he did not lack an imagination. Even his lies were beautiful things which he had no doubt would cure and preserve the stories he would some day chronicle for future generations.

'Your visions for a grand future are bold, sire! I call down Allah's blessings upon you and urge you to begin this or any other enterprise with the name of the Almighty on your lips. For it will be blessed and the kingdom of Islam will be realized in this world as envisioned by the Prophet . . .'

Ahmad was impassive but Najib groaned out loud. 'In politics there is no place for any sentiment, religious or otherwise.' He sneered, 'Even the shaikhs and mashaikhs you revere so much can't expect to succeed in their war against the so-called infidels if they are going to stick to the true spirit of Islam. They are all consummate politicians, perfectly capable of manipulating their followers to part with hard-earned money for the ostensible purpose of propaganda or building places of worship. All they do is incite their followers to hate those who do not belong to the same sheep-brained flock, riot against authority and kill to undermine the authority of the Sultan. Moreover, they have no scruples when it comes to relieving Hindus of their ancestral land, tearing down temples or violating their women. It is the very height of hypocrisy.'

Barani replied hotly, 'Don't listen to this blasphemer, sire. His Hindu past has warped his understanding of faith, virtue and truth. The holy men only seek to reform those who revere false gods and engage in idolatry, so that they might rise from the muck and embrace a better path that will prove to be uplifting . . .'

'Don't listen to this fanatic, sire,' Najib shot back. 'Things like faith, virtue and truth have little role to play when the conqueror imposes his will on the conquered. The holy men are a plague upon this land and need to be weeded out with an iron hand. Especially those who spread calumny about their betters from their pulpits.'

Muhammad had to give it to him. Some of the sheikhs were calling for his abdication, accusing him of committing *haraam* by lying in sin with his stepmother, which was also being bandied about as the reason he supposedly killed his father.

Since the Sultan himself was famous for encouraging total freedom of thought, word and deed, his detractors had brazenly discussed allegations of parricide from a pulpit and gossiped about his incestuous relationship, pointing out that the penalty for such a grave offence was execution. Trusted and high-ranking members of his court had been persuaded to rebel on the strength of this particular argument. Muhammad sighed.

'Was this the sort of petty infighting you were hoping to avoid when you conceived your scheme for a better future, your majesty? It would certainly stabilize the government,' Ahmad remarked politely. Barani lowered his eyes in chagrin. Najib merely looked amused.

Muhammad nodded. 'I am tired of this constant bickering, Ahmad. It is the reason the empire has been vulnerable to the attacks of the Mongols and other foreign invaders. The Hindu rajas were so caught up in their petty rivalries that they practically invited Mahmud of Ghazna and Shihabuddin of Ghor to fight their enemies.'

He frowned. 'The Muslim invaders are hardly better. We may have united to destroy our enemies, but now the disunity in our midst threatens to destroy us too. I know that nobody will be happy to hear this, but it is necessary to unify the people by force if necessary.' Muhammad paused, but none of them seemed willing to volunteer an opinion so he continued, 'It is not merely a question of religion. On the one hand, we have the privileged wallowing in the lap of luxury, while the poverty-stricken live in squalor, unable to scrape together enough for a single meal. It won't ever do for the rich to keep on growing richer at the expense of the poor.'

He closed his eyes for a moment. It was his dream to make Dilli the most beautiful city in the entire world, which was why he had commissioned the building of Jahanpanah. The imperial town planners and architects were doing a remarkable job. But he had realized that it would be impossible to realize his vision while the great unwashed roamed the streets.

Through the gaps in their threadbare clothing, one could see that their begrimed bodies had not made the acquaintance of water or soap in ages, and their ripe smell was like a blow to the nostrils. They spat and pissed on public monuments, defaced imperial property and defecated in the open. Even the luxurious hammams he had built for the use of the public based on the Turkish model had been so badly desecrated and looted that they had to be shut down. The ruffians had made off with the splendid objets d'art, towels, sponges, robes, oils, spittoons, soaps and scrapers. He supposed it was a miracle they hadn't carried away every brick and slab of marble that had gone into its making as well. Savages!

Muhammad had appointed guards to prevent the more wretched of his subjects from behaving in such an unseemly fashion and appointed sweepers to clean the streets regularly, but it was an uphill task.

Then there was the question of the vastness of his domains. Thanks to the military genius of his father, his empire on the day of his ascension included twenty-three provinces: Dilli, Devagiri, Multan, Kahram, Samana, Sivistan, Uch, Hansi, Sarsuti, Madurai,

Telangana, Dwarasamudra, Gujarat, Badaun, Oudh, Kanauj, Lakhnauti, Bihar, Kara, Malwa, Lahore, Kalanor and Jajnagar. He was determined to consolidate as well as expand his empire and do his father proud.

Muhammad was an able administrator even if he thought so himself. He had done a good job of establishing an efficient system headed by capable officers handpicked solely on the basis of merit, much to the chagrin of Barani. Wealth poured in from all directions and straight into his coffers.

The damnable thing, though, was that in each province his subjects spoke a different language, worshipped a different God and jealously guarded their own customs, culture and traditions handed down over the ages, which were all at odds with their neighbours'. If that weren't enough, there was further division on the basis of caste, sub-caste and class. Needless to say, all of them were at loggerheads over conflicting ideologies, identity and questions of religious dogma which grew so bitter, they were forever fighting or plotting to kill each other. He wouldn't have cared if the sticky mess had not interfered with governance.

'You were talking about unification, your majesty . . .' Ahmad prompted him courteously, breaking into his thoughts, and Muhammad bestirred himself.

'Yes, of course,' he said. 'I have a few schemes in mind that if implemented would put an end to the communal tensions that are tearing my empire apart. We are going to toss people from all the provinces into the pot of governance and force them to coexist or risk their emperor's wrath. It is about time they all learn to put aside their differences and work for the betterment of this land. Can you see the possibilities if this happens?

'If I can count on peace and am free of petty regional overlords struggling to achieve independence and spiritual authorities interfering in temporal matters and fomenting trouble, then it is my intention to march onward and outward towards fresh conquests. I want to march to the ends of the world and see all the marvels it has to offer. To die at the head an empire that is at least three times the size of this one.'

Muhammad ignored the sceptical looks the three of them shot him, suddenly united in their unwillingness to follow him down this bold path. The Sultan cleared his throat and glanced meaningfully at Barani. 'For those who feel that I am not practising and enforcing the tenets of Islam to the best of my ability, my new edict will put an end to all doubts, and in emphatic fashion.'

Ahmad was definitely looking nervous. Barani merely looked hopeful and Najib seemed anticipatory, no doubt convinced it would all be very entertaining.

'Henceforth, I am going to be very strict where religious matters are concerned, particularly the observance of prayers, attendance at which will be mandatory. Those of the faith will be expected to know the prescribed prayers by heart, as well as ritual observances, obligations and articles of the Islamic code. Court-appointed officials will question the congregation arbitrarily and also monitor them minutely during the hours of prayer. Anybody caught wrong-footed or derelict in the performance of their religious duties will be caught and put to death immediately. I trust my chief executioner will be up to the task?'[5]

'Of course, sire! I will be certain to strictly enforce the edict with all the resources at my disposal,' Najib replied with alacrity.

Barani blanched but made an effort to look approving. Ahmad was made of sterner stuff. 'With all due respect, sire, don't you think you are being a little too harsh? Even if your heart is in the right place, Muslims will feel they are being persecuted since it would have to be Hindus who take up patrolling duties during prayer time. It can prove to be counterproductive and exacerbate tension between the warring factions.'

'Rest assured, Ahmad, good Muslims like you and Barani have nothing to fear. Am I not right? As for me, I know the Quran and every prayer, rite and rule outlined in the religious texts by heart, and it has been so since I was five.' He glanced at Barani, who swallowed twice before managing a nod of assent. 'And to ease your fears, I will make it clear that false or fabricated charges are a grave offence that merit execution. That settles it. Make certain that the new rule is enforced immediately.'

All three men bowed their heads in submission and kept their eyes on their feet, refusing to look at each other. He knew they hoped to be dismissed, but he wasn't done with them yet.

'The south has been ignored for too long, and my subjects there feel cut off from the warmth and sunshine of their Sultan's benevolence. I am told the prevailing sentiment is I care little for their pressing problems and am content to let my underlings rule over them and force them to pay tribute. But all that is going to change.'

Three pairs of eyes filled with a mixture of unease and anticipation looked at him. 'My mind is made up and I would prefer it if you didn't try to dissuade me. For strategic reasons, I intend to move with my court for a limited duration from Dilli to Devagiri, which will be renamed Daulatabad. It is equidistant to all the key provinces in the realm and will serve as the second capital of the empire. As for Dilli, it will not be abandoned, since my beloved Jahanpanah will be built here. I have also commissioned the building of a new fortress which will be called Adilabad. The move will be made once all the arrangements have been made, so that those moving will not suffer any undue inconveniences. I trust I have your cooperation and support during this period of transition, after which we will stride forward to build the mightiest empire this world has seen.'

Without waiting for a reply, the Sultan dismissed them and turned to gaze out of the window. Even so, it took a few minutes before the three men could pick their jaws off the floor, pay obeisance and retreat. Muhammad smiled in satisfaction. They were sceptical now, but would see the merit of his actions soon.

3

They brought Bahauddin Gurshasp to him in chains. Muhammad had not been surprised at his rebellion. He had been conspicuous by his absence on the day of his coronation. Muhammad should not have let the slight go unpunished. But Baha was his cousin and had been a great favourite of Sultan Ghiasuddin Tughlaq's. However, he bitterly regretted his lapse in judgement, for things had become unspeakably ugly between them.

When Baha raised the standard of rebellion from his bastion at Sagar, backed by local Hindu chieftains, Muhammad had deployed his troops with Ahmad at the helm and Malik Majir by his side. Never one to leave things to chance, he had travelled to Devagiri to oversee things with reinforcements in tow. Muhammad had no doubt that his father could have subdued him with a few well-chosen words and half the number of casualties, but as always, he had a difficult time of it.

'The truth is, I overestimated him!' he had lamented to Abu.

'Whatever do you mean?' Abu wanted to know. 'Ahmad and Majir decimated his entire army and you have him on the run. The rank traitor and coward!'

'Exactly! The man is a coward and far more dangerous to others unlike the courageous at heart. I offered generous terms for his surrender: his family and troops would be spared and he himself would be unharmed but placed under house arrest. Even his land and monies would not be seized and left for his offspring. Yet, that ingrate threw it back in my face, and abandoned his family as well as his men.'

'Well, you do have a reputation for being capricious and cruel.' Abu was blunt as only he could be. 'There is no doubt that Bahauddin did not believe a word of the terms offered, convinced that he would be put to death, but only after being tortured by the Sultan's hound, one Najib who is already infamous for his preferred sadistic measures.'

Muhammad swore. 'The word of the Sultan is gold and don't you dare say otherwise.'

'I didn't.' Abu was unapologetic. 'But we were discussing your increasing penchant for brutality, which was already formidable to start with. Let us not forget that you ordered the execution of many of the Ulama's enforcers for neglecting to say their prayers with the rest of the congregation and for failing to pass the gruelling exam on some of the more obfuscating passages from the Quran. It hardly enhanced your reputation in the eyes of the faithful.'

The Sultan grunted by way of reply but Abu was relentless. 'And with a stunning capacity for foolhardiness, you made enemies out of the hardliners among the Hindus even while championing the spirit of tolerance by handing out the death penalty to all who came forward with false claims about their Muslim brothers. Sometimes, I am convinced that you are more fool than genius.'

'That will be enough!' Muhammad bit out but Abu ignored him with his usual blithe indifference.

'You know very well that Sheikh Imamuddin has been openly accusing you of parricide and rallying his followers against you. They are convinced that your dalliance with your stepmother is further proof of your guilt. Of course, you could set the rumours to rest by taking a wife and trotting out sons by the dozen! But you refuse to do the sensible thing and insist on carrying on with blatant disregard for a volatile situation.'

Muhammad did not bother with a response, and his oldest friend sighed. 'It is the reason Bahauddin rose up in rebellion.

He is outraged that you could do this to his beloved uncle, and who can blame him? At the very least, you could surround yourself with nautch girls and conduct orgies all through the long nights. It would be considered more respectable than this strange obsession with your father's wife.'

'You of all people know better than to suggest that.' His eyes grew stormy as he harkened back to Mubarak Shah's reign of terror. There had been hundreds of nautch girls as well as boys, and so much food, liquor and intoxicants it had made the senses swim. Forced into a state of inebriation, they were ordered to sport with these men and women, all for the viewing pleasure of the sadistic, debauched reprobate who had the power of life and death over them. Ever since, Muhammad had not touched a drop of alcohol, disliked rich food and had next to no interest in pleasures of the flesh. He saw no reason to take a string of wives either. After all, what was the point of being the Sultan if he was going to allow himself to be reduced to a prize stallion put to stud?

Besides, there were other things to deal with. Like rebellion and betrayal. Finally, after a lengthy song and dance, Baha had been brought to his knees. Najib had been busy and the fallen rebel had been relieved of every one of his fingernails, and that wasn't even the half of it. But his cousin was still defiant.

'You are a murderer!' Baha had spat out. 'And you will get your comeuppance for your foul deed. When I first heard the news, I couldn't believe it. What possible motive could you have had, especially since you were already the heir apparent? But you did it all to indulge a taboo passion. I will not answer to the likes of you!'

Muhammad nodded, and Najib plucked out Baha's tongue with a pair of heated tongs. It was all very messy and unpleasant, and the Sultan looked away. Barani was right. Najib was definitely more of a butcher than an artist.

'You know, cousin, I was prepared to issue a royal pardon on account of the fact that my father held you in high regard.

Mistakenly, as it turns out. Even now, it is not your infamous words that will be the death of you but your despicable cowardice.'

Baha glared at him as he choked on the blood spilling from his mouth. 'You should have accepted the terms of surrender, but you chose to run and sacrificed the lives of thousands. You didn't even spare the Raja of Kampila and his family, who died to save a traitor like you. Were you not aware that little girls, pregnant wives and frail, elderly women were made to commit jauhar while their men sacrificed themselves on our swords? What madness possessed you to become the instrument of such evil?'

His chest heaved as the rage coursed through his being again. The almighty conflagration had been a terrible sight that would be seared into his brain till the day he died. The Rai was beyond all reason, and Muhammad had been convinced that he was in the grip of madness. He hadn't been far wrong. Later, they told him that the Rajputs dosed themselves as well as their women with kushumba, a drink laced with opiates, before they rode or burnt to death. Never had he seen such a senseless and utterly useless sacrifice.

Even now, those flames and the screams of the dying women tormented him night after night. And his damnable cousin had nearly brought about a similar finale for Rai Bilal Deo, the Hoysala king of Dwarasamudra. However, this Rai was a sensible man who actually cared about his subjects and his family. He had refused to subject them to such a fate over the wretched creature who sought refuge. Baha had been trussed up and handed over to the Sultan. Bilal Deo had also sworn fealty to Muhammad, and, having made and accepted rich presents, he had returned to his people. Now the traitor awaited judgement.

The Sultan did not keep him waiting. He turned to Najib. 'You can carve up Bahauddin Gurshasp while he still lives and cook his flesh with fragrant spices and rice. Then serve it to the male members of his family as their last meal, before they too are executed. Stuff the remains with straw and parade them across the length and breadth of my empire! As for the female members of his family, they will not be made to suffer for the stupidity of their men, and will be placed under the care of the Makhduma Jahan. Take him away from my sight!'6

Ignoring the gasps of shock and horror that greeted his sentence, Sultan Muhammad bin Tughlaq leaned back on his throne, reeling from the heat of his own implacable rage.

4

Muhammad was with Saira when his mother thundered into his private chambers. She was almost completely blind now but none suspected as much because of how sure-footed she was and the strenuous activities she packed into a given day. In the eyes of the public, the fault lay with the Sultan, who had seen fit to have those fiery marvels displayed on the day of his coronation. Their harsh brightness had blinded the poor queen, it was said.

It didn't seem to slow Haniya down in the least. She had a number of projects that demanded almost all her attention. The veterans of Ghazi Malik's armies and wars who had been crippled or incapacitated had been reduced to wandering the streets with begging bowls. She had ordered the guards to round up these poor souls and house them at establishments she had personally erected, where they were fed from the royal kitchen and treated by imperial physicians who would have protested had it not been Makhduma Jahan herself who had issued the orders.

Besides, who could complain when the Sultan's own mother worked by their side, feeding bowls of nourishing soup with her own fair hands to wretched creatures who had lost the will to live, talking to them endlessly of God and hope, unwilling to give up on them.

'Any man who doesn't bother to save himself is usually not worth saving,' Muhammad pointed out to his mother, worried that she would catch some terrible infection. 'The world will be a better place if people dealt with their problems manfully instead of giving up and becoming a burden to themselves and others.'

'The Sultan knows best,' she had retorted sarcastically, 'but while he bestows favours upon the already privileged and the *ferenghi*, some of us seek to make sure that all of Allah's children get a fair share of his merciful bounty.'

Muhammad refrained from pointing out that she was being philanthropic with *his* money, which had been bestowed on her as a *favour*. But he couldn't stop himself from arguing further, 'Whenever people are struck down by misfortune, be it disease, loss of limbs, property or loved ones, war and its attendant horrors, it is only the fittest and worthwhile among us who survive. It is nature's way of rooting out the disposable on whom the limited resources of the land are wasted.'

She rounded on him, her eyes flashing in sudden fury. 'How dare you say that? Sultan or not, I will slap you senseless if you talk like that again. Nature is an arbitrary mistress who acts on her whims and destroys without discrimination. Never forget that Sultan Ghiasuddin Tughlaq was the best, fittest and most worthwhile among us. He certainly wasn't dispensable, and I still weep that while his inferiors have lived and prospered, he is gone, never to come back.'

That was the last time he had argued with her about her charities, and, to make up for his lack of delicacy, personally allocated abundant sums from the treasury to finance her large-hearted schemes.

Makhduma Jahan extended her kindness and compassion to orphans and ragamuffins as well. These were plucked from the streets on the her orders, where they had been roaming like feral dogs, fighting for scraps and stealing from honest shopkeepers and citizens. His mother had conscripted those among the clergy whom she favoured or who owed her favours and tasked them with making civilized human beings out of the ruffians and making them learn the Quran.

To nobody's surprise, the majority disappeared back into the uncivilized wastelands from which they had emerged and grew up to be petty thieves, rapists or bar-room brawlers who wound up in prison or the executioner's block. But a few did grow up to be halfway-decent citizens of a great empire. On his mother's recommendation, some were given high posts in administrative offices. Muhammad never denied his mother. In fact, the rise of these creatures pleased him almost as much as her.

The Sultan's mother was also the champion of whores, widows, abandoned women or those of ill-repute. She even set her religious scruples aside to argue the case of Hindu women who were being made to commit sati and had forced the Khwaja Jahan's hand in preventing the death of child widows, quickly taking these cast-offs into her fold.

Being a practical woman, she refused to allow them to wallow in their misery but put them to work. They were taught to cook, clean, embroider or stitch clothes and uniforms for the troops as well as the inhabitants of her homes for the wretched. She also allotted funds for the families of soldiers who had been killed while fighting for their Sultan, in addition to bearing the funeral costs. His subjects loved her dearly.

Now that she was getting on in years, she found an unlikely ally in Saira, who had quietly taken over the running of her mother-in-law's projects while giving her the impression that she was still in charge.

The two women went about their business amicably enough, even though Haniya felt morally obliged to point out that women who were guilty of incest deserved to be stoned to death. 'You are probably right, your highness!' Saira agreed quietly as she handed her a bag of coins to be given to a young girl's family. The victim had been killed by her husband. Later, Saira knew she would have a word with Najib, who in exchange for a sum would cheerfully have the perpetrator executed on a trumped-up charge.

Saira also knew that it pleased her mother-in-law when rank beggars refused the bowl of food she held out to them. 'It is better to die of starvation than to accept help from a sinful wretch guilty of incest.' They would hawk and spit in her direction but it would take more than that to break her. Haniya never defended her but would usually step in with a malicious cackle.

Later, though, Haniya would invite her for a meal which they would both consume in silence. Then Saira would receive an item of jewellery or some costly work of art from her mother-in-law. *And people wonder why the Sultan is such a study in contradiction!* she would muse to herself.

Makhduma Jahan faced her son in his chambers, more furious than he had ever seen her. 'Are you out of your mind?' she launched into her tirade. She became angrier still when he failed to respond and she registered Saira's presence. 'Did you put him up to this?' she asked her unnecessarily.

'If you are asking whether I am the reason he ordered the cruel execution of his rebellious cousin, then I think you already know the answer to that,' Saira informed his mother coolly. 'In fact, if I believed it would make a difference, I would have told the Sultan that it is barbaric to make the surviving members of his cousin's family, and by extension his own, pay the price for Bahauddin Gurshasp's perfidy.'

Her unapologetic demeanour took the wind right out of Haniya's sails. But she recovered swiftly when her son rolled his eyes in exasperation over the delicate sensibilities of the women in his life.

'You must learn to control your temper,' Haniya told him firmly. 'You have lost the goodwill of so many thanks to your rashness and intemperate mood swings. Besides, this level of brutality does not make much strategic sense either.'

'Why don't you leave him alone, mother?' Khuda had also barged in, and Muhammad decided that he must do something about the lax security. 'My dear brother usually knows what he is doing even when it looks like he hasn't a clue. Cousin Baha should have known better than to pick up arms against the family, and he refused to listen to reason even when the Sultan offered him terms of clemency he certainly did not deserve.'

Only Khuda would have dared talk to their mother that way. But then again, she was his fiercest and most loyal supporter. 'And what do you mean, his actions don't make strategic sense?' she demanded. 'Every time people gorge on biriyani with succulent pieces of meat, they are reminded of the fate of traitors and the importance of good behaviour approved by the Sultan.

'Why, there is not one single person in the land who would dare disobey their sovereign. Taxes and tributes are paid promptly. Every single high and mighty Khan, Malik, Amir, Isfahla, Raja, soldier and slave knows better than to harbour treacherous thoughts. It seems to me that he did the right thing, and if you didn't insist on comparing him with Father, you would agree.'

Muhammad sighed. As always, Khuda had come out charging, lost control and gone too far. His mother turned her blind gaze unerringly towards her garrulous daughter, who quailed under the matriarch's withering scorn.

'It is thanks to sycophants like you that even good Sultans nurse delusions of infallibility and come to a bad end.' Haniya was well and truly furious now. 'If my counsel was good enough for my husband then it ought to be good enough for my son, and I'll thank you not to contradict older and wiser heads than you. If you wish to remain, I suggest you hold your tongue.'

Khuda seemed suitably chastened as she retreated and sat next to Saira, who offered her a plate of sweetmeats, but she winked conspiratorially at her brother. It may have been to spite their mother, but Khuda and Saira got along reasonably well.

'Indiscriminate cruelty may get you short-term gains, but if things aren't going well and your people are convinced that you are a mad tyrant who would have them unjustly killed without rhyme or reason, they might just decide it will be worth the effort to kill you first,' Makhduma Jahan said.

As always, Muhammad listened dutifully to her words but refused to respond or explain his actions. What was the point? She wouldn't understand anyway. His spies had told him that Bahauddin had saddened her with his actions and she had spent the long nights on her knees beseeching Allah to show him the right path. Her heartbreak had been complete when she heard about the fate of the Raja of Kampila's entire family, and yet she expected him to treat his cousin with compassion. But of course, that was not what was bothering her.

Haniya, as always, lacked confidence in her son's ability to rule and seemed convinced that he would lose everything his father had won before coming to a gory end himself. And she wasn't finished with him. Haniya may have been beside herself over Baha's fate, but she was even angrier about the fact that he had humiliated himself, thanks to his recent actions which had seen a Kazi rule against him in two separate cases. He had been accused of wrongfully appropriating someone else's land and physically assaulting a noble's son. That hadn't been all. He had even submitted to a beating after the Kazi gave his sentence.

The way Muhammad saw it, he had handled an embarrassing situation with grace, giving the impression that justice was not an inaccessible commodity in his land and proving that the Sultan's word was gold. How would it have looked if the plaintiffs who had filed cases against him had been arrested on his orders and beheaded in public? A little finesse often went a long way.

'Forget nipping a problem in the bud, you would do well not to plant seeds that will yield nothing but bitter humiliation.' Mother spent the next hour berating him in a similar vein. But Muhammad was in no mood to listen. He had other things on his mind, such as his plans for the future. They would all be risky, but surely at least one would be an unqualified success?

5

Makhduma Jahan was entertaining a distinguished guest at her son's request. Muhammad knew she had been inclined to turn him down, especially after what happened during their last meeting, but he had known she wouldn't be able to resist.

Who would have thought she would be talking to a Mongol prince and serving him delicacies from her own kitchen? She who had accompanied Ghazi Malik when he fought the Mongol hordes swarming over the land and prayed to Allah to destroy them?

Tarmashirin had come as a friend to the court of Muhammad bin Tughlaq. As a recent convert to Islam, he was a fervent believer. In fact, it was his fanaticism and commitment to promoting his own Sunni beliefs over other faiths that had landed him in hot water with his brother Kabek Khan and his people, who were famously tolerant or infamously indifferent when it came to religion in the Mongol tradition—exemplified by the great Kubilai Khan.

Unfortunately, more than willing though his spirit was, his flesh was weak. On his becoming the king of Transoxiana (a bastion of the Chagatai Khans), after Kabek Khan's death he had moved against Abu Said, the Ilkhan of Persia, who had accepted the Shia faith. The sectarian rivalry surged back and forth, with Kabul, Ghazna and Qandhar coming into the hands of the Chagatais, with Tarmashirin determined to invade Khorasan. Eventually, though, a force led by Hasan, a general of Abu Said, took Tarmashirin unawares near Ghazna, forcing him to flee and seek the aid of Sultan Muhammad bin Tughlaq.

Tarmashirin and Muhammad had discussed many matters and come to an understanding. The former's son-in-law was now Amir Nauroz and a member of the Sultan's court. The visit had created quite a ripple and initially the assumption had been that they were facing another Mongol invasion.

Since Muhammad was involved, it didn't just stop there. His people were already angered by the impending move to Daulatabad, arrangements for which were going on in full swing, and wild rumours that Dilli was to be handed over to the Mongols began to circulate. They took to the streets, rioting and protesting against the non-existent threat of Dilli being razed to the ground and reduced to rubble, forcing the Sultan to have the insurgents arrested and executed.

The warm reception given to 'the invader' and the loss of lives on account of his visit infuriated the malcontents further. Suddenly, everybody was an expert on the ancient past as sordid stories of atrocities perpetuated by the Mongols were dredged up to deliberately inflame the public and denigrate their emperor's foreign policy.

'His father, the great Sultan Ghiasuddin Tughlaq, answered the Mongol threat with blood and steel!'

'Which is the only way to deal with scoundrels who have devoted their lives to smashing our temples, making off with our livestock and enslaving able-bodied men and women. They have been doing this for hundreds of years!'

'They used to kill our brave soldiers, and then consume their flesh and drink their blood! Filthy fiends!'

'It is said that the Mongols are conceived by the flesh-eating mares that carry them to battle!'

'And how does our Sultan receive them? With open arms!'

'Do you think that is the reason the Sultan is yet to produce an heir? Because he likes to . . . you know!'

'If his father hadn't been murdered, he would have wept at his son's shameful conduct.'

'Did you know that the Sultan has emptied the treasury to buy peace because he is too much of a coward to give a fitting reply to the Mongol rogues on the battlefield?'

'It may be he prefers to be the one who gets buggered as opposed to one who is doing the buggering . . .'

Of course, his spies reported it all to him and Muhammad listened stone-faced as they sputtered their way through all the profanity at his insistence. It was all hearsay and utter nonsense. But Muhammad knew that many including his mother and vizier blamed him for the constant outpouring of vile bile, and he supposed they weren't entirely wrong.

In one of his public speeches where he had addressed his people directly, Muhammad had declared: 'It is my desire that the citizens of my empire shall enjoy the fruit of liberty, embrace their individuality and shape their own destiny, caste and class be damned. Cast aside the fetters that shackle you to a wretched existence and seek to improve your status in life by dint of hard work and stalwart enterprise. Have the courage to climb out of the morass of poverty and aspire towards a life of ease. You can count on your emperor's support in your endeavour to rise above your limitations.

'Discover your voice and speak freely, knowing that your Sultan is your benefactor and friend. Don't be afraid to criticize unjust or immoral acts even if they have been committed by your sovereign lord. Let us all strive for justice, equality, peace and prosperity. Together we shall strive for greatness!'

Muhammad's brilliant speech had been received with thunderous applause and he had basked in the adulation of his subjects. However, all too soon, he had cause to regret his words. His subjects were only too happy to talk however they saw fit, with scant regard for decorum or decency.

They raised their voices against him at every single opportunity, irrespective of whether it was warranted or not. In fact, complaining or making fun of him had become their favourite pastime. They painted vulgar caricatures on the palace walls of him engaged in incest, sodomy or bestiality, composed disrespectful songs in his honour and disrupted his assembly with strident complaints and poison-pen notes that were tossed amidst the gathering.[7]

Worthless, witless fools who spent their days whining and whingeing. Something drastic needed to be done. Perhaps Ahmad had been right all along.

His Khwaja Jahan did not believe in giving anyone too much rope. 'Why should mindless morons be allowed to spout their gobbledygook?' Ahmad had wanted to know.

'My dear Ahmad! Sometimes I am convinced you are a relic from a bygone era. Do you not see that the days of absolute rule are numbered?'

Ahmad was so shocked at his response, he actually hissed and would have shushed his Sultan but thought better of it. 'I wouldn't risk saying such things, sire! It would never do for people to get it into their heads that they too deserve to have a say in governance. It is best for all concerned if they kept their useless thoughts to themselves and simply did as they are ordered to.'

'Is that so?' Muhammad sighed. Why were people deliberately blind to the things that were so clear to him? Didn't they know that there were lands not so far away where government and administration were patterned on the republic system of ancient Greece? That officials were elected to power by the people and their tenure of rule was limited by law?

'Whether you wish to acknowledge it or not, in future, freedom will not be a luxury enjoyed by too few but a basic human right. People wish to shape their lives as they see fit and will not be denied. The chains holding them in thrall are fragile, and it is only a matter of time before they snap.'

Ahmad hesitated for a moment, and Muhammad watched, amused, as his vizier ironically debated the merits of speaking his own mind. 'It has to be asked, your majesty! Do you really think that if people are given equal rights, they will use them wisely and to better themselves?

Now it was Muhammad's turn to hesitate. 'In theory, it is possible.'

Ahmad shook his head vehemently for emphasis. 'A lot of things are possible in the realm of theory, sire. It is easy enough to theorize since it costs nothing. But in truth, a truly worthy man or woman would make something of their lives with what is given, irrespective of whether they are offered the freedom and opportunity to do so or not. On the other hand, someone who starts with all the advantages life has to offer may still amount to nothing.

'Take Mubarak Shah, for instance. His life was miraculously saved when the eunuch conspired to uproot Alauddin's entire family, and he was handed a throne and an empire. But that hardly stopped him from frittering it all away on drink, drugs and debauchery. I repeat, those who are intended to rise up the food chain will find a way to do so. For it takes grit, guts and gumption to do that, and too few possess these qualities. That is unlikely to ever change.'

Muhammad stroked his beard contemplatively as the man carried on with his tirade. 'Tomorrow, if you were to inform your citizens that they are to be freed, do you think they will be better for it? Of course not! Chaos will prevail until the next tyrant takes charge, stamping and sealing his absolute authority with the blood of his predecessor as well as his extended family and just about anybody else who gets in the way.'

Ahmad took a few deep breaths to calm himself. Muhammad couldn't help thinking that though the Khwaja Jahan was right about a lot of things, he was wrong about the future. A republic may have its flaws, but it was still superior to an absolute ruler who was almost always unequal to the demands and pressures of the job. Power was addictive and utterly ruinous. Muhammad knew it to be true, especially since it was he who had been cast in the role of an absolute monarch, and not a day went by without him being made painfully aware of his limitations. His people had tied their hopes and aspirations to his destiny, confident he would soar heavenward and take them with him, but he himself knew that they were doomed to disappointment. He could never be the saviour they needed him to be.

He cleared his throat and tried again. 'In an ideal world, people would do the right thing simply because it is the right thing to do. However, since that is not the case, I am left with little choice but to put the fear of God and the Sultan in their hearts!'

Najib had come in just then. 'It is done, your highness! We can rejoice, for justice has truly been served.'

Muhammad nodded in acknowledgement but didn't smile. Ahmad looked at the two of them for a brief moment before understanding dawned on his features.

'I am relieved, your highness,' he began. 'We simply cannot condone a state of affairs where a citizen files a suit with the Kazi against his majesty, accusing him of seizing his land illegally and demanding compensation. And another, even if he is a noble's son, accusing his majesty of physical assault.' *And paying him back in kind.*

Muhammad frowned at the memory. He had tried to conduct himself with as much dignity as could be mustered while he was being beaten black and blue by a mere stripling, but Abu had laughed himself silly over the entire fiasco. 'Why do you do this to yourself? You should have had the rapscallion's impertinent hide flayed off his back!'

'I gave my word. And the Sultan's word is gold.'

Abu snorted. 'And you wonder why your citizens insist you like to get buggered.'

Muhammad gave himself a mental shake. 'He will not be doing anything of the sort in the foreseeable future,' Najib was saying. 'Nor will the callow youth who struck the emperor twenty-one times, simply because the emperor had exercised his royal right to hit him. It is most unfortunate that the kazis who ruled against the Sultan are no longer in a position to sit in judgement of others.

Even the anonymous sons of anonymous fathers who composed poisonous notes filled with vile invectives and hurled them into the assembly while the emperor was holding court won't be able to show such blatant disrespect now that they are good only for the worms and maggots to burrow into.'

'Don't let Barani find out about any of this,' Ahmad cautioned him. 'The man is a typical writer, waiting to use such sensitive information in his own misguided narratives.'

Najib shrugged. 'My duties are conducted in the utmost secrecy as decreed by the Sultan, and barring the public executions, few will be able to ascertain the fates of those who have been summoned or taken captive by the emperor's executioner. But nothing I could possibly conceive would match the gore and horror supplied by Barani's imagination.'

Muhammad ignored their banter. His thoughts were with those who had discreetly disappeared. But Ahmad was right—he couldn't let those who took advantage of the judicial system to file false suits or those who blatantly disrespected his authority get away with it.

Muhammad turned his thoughts back to Tarmashirin, who had given Muhammad a lot to think about, which he decided to share with Ahmad after Najib had taken his leave.

'Our Mongol friend is having a spot of trouble . . .' he began, 'which I am sure you are aware of.'

Ahmad nodded. 'We are familiar with the situation in Transoxiana, sire.' His voice was curt. The Khwaja Jahan did not like the Mongols. But Muhammad suspected that his hostility arose from the fact that Tarmashirin had made a few requests, gambling heavily on the Sultan's not-ill-deserved reputation for generosity and largesse.

'Tarmashirin has requested my assistance against Abu Said, the Ilkhan of Persia,' he began. 'He requires arms as well as money. We discussed mounting an expedition to take Persia, Khorasan and Iraq.' Muhammad's eyes were aglow with keen anticipation.

If successful, he would be on his way to surpassing even the achievements of Alexander the Great.

Ahmad, however, could not mask his doubt. Muhammad continued regardless. 'As of this moment, we will establish direct communication with Ghazna. I would like a postal relay in place, with our best teams of horsemen. It will be a new diplomatic centre in my empire, and we will send money, men and other materials, as requested by the government of Ghazna. Send word out to all the old regiments who fought the Mongols under my father. Their depleted ranks will be reinforced, and I want no expense spared as we begin preparations for the Khorasan expedition.'

'What about the move to Daulatabad, your highness? Are we to put it on hold?'

He shook his head. 'We will move as planned. It should go smoothly. It will take time to get the imperial army ready for the Khorasan expedition. In the meantime, Amir Naroz will gather intelligence from his fellow Mongols who have rebelled against the Il-Khanate. Arrangements must be made to receive them. It is also important to reach out to the religious leaders there so that I can be assured of their support. Such an overture may even placate the Ulama, though I doubt it. Preparations for both ventures must be carried out with painstaking attention to detail. I will brook no dissent or disobedience in this matter.'

Ahmad bowed his head. 'It will be as you desire, your highness! May Allah bless your enterprises with victory.'

Muhammad hoped so too.

6

They were finally on the move and Muhammad was pleased. He had hoped he could bring about a smooth transfer, and had devoted months to intensive preparation and planning. Inns had been constructed at various points along the 700 mile journey to Daulatabad, and arrangements for amenities like food, baths, medicine and clothes were to be provided for the travellers on his orders.

Advance riding parties had cleared and readied the route. Every governor of the minor provinces along the way and even the leaders of villages had been notified about the Sultan's eminent arrival. They had spent months making arrangements for him and all who passed through with the royal family.

There were comfortable beds, hot meals, fresh horses and the best accommodation waiting. New wells had been dug to ensure there was adequate water for man and beast. The Sultan, his family members and his nobles would be moving along with their households and entourage. Mostly, they found the journey to be a comfortable one and Muhammad was pleased.

Leading builders, traders, artists and city planners with their helpers and teams of slaves had been sent ahead to expand and beautify the city of Daulatabad and make sure that everything was in readiness for their arrival. All who had shifted would be provided free board and lodging. Those involved in trading would be allotted land free of cost to build their houses and set up business establishments.

Despite everything, there were malcontents who complained endlessly and blamed him for minor discomforts ranging from plain country fare to aching backsides. There were also a lot of ruffled feathers over the lack of intoxicants and the unavailability of women for the enjoyment of the nobles. His famous disdain for such vices did not endear himself to the pampered courtiers.

Key members of the Ulama had also been conscripted for the move. As expected, they had resisted him might and main, convinced that he was forcing them to leave their beloved Dilli so that they may be killed on the dangerous journey to the 'land of the infidel', as they insisted on calling it.

As always, their recalcitrance and frustration was unnecessary. Here he was, giving them an opportunity to spread the tenets of Islam among the Hindu-dominated regions in the south, and they were fighting him tooth and nail.

'I have a good mind to have them catapulted to the second capital with *manjanik*s. Or better yet, I could give the order to tie their feet to my warhorses so they can be dragged to Daulatabad.' Barani was present while he contemplated thus and looked so scandalized that he burst out laughing.

'Perhaps you could try reasoning with them, your majesty . . .' he ventured timorously.

Muhammad *had* tried to reason with them and address their concerns personally.

'The Deccan has been a hotbed of conflict primarily because the Hindu majority seems convinced that its religion is under threat. I daresay other minorities feel the same way.

'I feel it would be best if the mashaikh follow in the footsteps of Nizamuddin Auliya, Muhammad Bhaktiyar and Fariduddin, who used their warmth, wisdom and compassion to spread the teachings of Islam. Needless to say, they were beloved and their teachings widely disseminated because they preferred to adopt pacifist methods that were sensible and had the added merit of not leading to large-scale communal strife and violence.'

'With all due respect to the Sultan, it is thanks to your patronage of the kafirs that those of the true faith have been subject to endless persecution,' they complained. 'You spoke about the sentiments of Hindus, Jains and Buddhists, but you don't have the same regard for those belonging to the true faith! Your faith!'

'Seduced by their dark arts and disreputable yogis, you would have us leave our homes and send us to the land of the infidel, where we will be killed like dogs. The graves of the Mussulmen will stretch from here to Daulatabad and you will have our blood on your hands!'

Muhammad had had enough, and sent everyone away with orders to prepare for the departure to Daulatabad. The idiots responded by declaring a jihad against the infidels. Even the most reasonable among them caused him trouble. He had sent for Shaikh Shamsuddin, one of Nizamuddin Auliya's disciples, but the man had refused, insisting that he was getting on in years and could not involve himself in politics. When Muhammad insisted, the man pleaded a medical condition.

The Sultan instructed the saint be brought to court so that Wasim, the royal physician, could take a look at him. As it turned out, his condition was critical and the saint was dead the next day. Naturally, he was blamed for the death and accused of unnecessary brutality. The Ulama had risen up in arms against him.

Support had come from unexpected quarters, though. The disciples of Shamsuddin, led by Shaikh Burhanuddin, sought an audience with him.

'Shaikh Shamsuddin knew he was not long for this world. Our master, Nizamuddin Auliya, appeared in his dreams to summon him to a better place. It had been his wish that we spread the teachings of his master far and wide. Shaikh Shamsuddin believed the Sultan's heart was in the right place and we must assist in his endeavours.'

'Was that all he said?'

They hesitated, then surrendered. 'He said your heart is in the right place even if your brains aren't.' Muhammad had laughed at that.

Barani had also made himself useful, despite his extreme repugnance for the move. He had convinced himself that sooner or later the Sultan would succumb to the allure of Dilli. 'I remember your stories from the campaign in Warangal. You didn't like it all that much. Dilli is the beating heart of your empire and sooner or later you will be back.'

'Of course I am going to be back!' Muhammad said in exasperation. 'For certain strategic reasons, which I have explained thousands of times, this is merely a temporary move. I don't know why everyone is behaving as though I forcibly pulled a babe off its mother's teat and hurled it southward!'

Barani was unconvinced and had decided he was better off having like-minded company in Daulatabad. At his instigation, the poet Amir Hasan, a student of Amir Khusrau, decided to make the journey south. Every other eminent poet, scholar, historian, painter, artist and musician immediately felt it would be entirely worthwhile to make the move so that they could find themselves patrons with large purses and taste enough to recognize their genius. Those who depended on the largesse of the Sultan and his mother also felt it would be best to make a fresh start in Daulatabad.

However, many were still dead set against what they thought of as the shifting of the capital from Dilli to Daulatabad. Among the mashaikhs, Shaikh Siraj and Mubarak were less than accommodating. The former decided to escape to Lakhnauti but met with a tragic end, while the latter decided that the time was ripe to perform the Haj, but had an unfortunate accident on the high seas. Muhammad then had to order Najib to use his especial powers of persuasion to convince others among the clergy and noblemen not to take similarly foolish decisions. Why did people have to vex him so?

Matters became complicated when an old man by the name of Aziz Isami, who was nearly ninety, hobbled along the path to Daulatabad, then proceeded to douse himself in oil and publicly immolate himself, proclaiming that he was protesting the Sultan's barbaric insistence on killing holy men. 'Down with the *zalim* Sultan!' had been his last words.[8]

His grandson had wept over his charred remains. 'The Sultan must answer for the death of my grandfather! His hands are tainted with the blood of the innocent and he must pay! I swear on all I hold dear to bring the Sultan's sins to light. Future generations will curse him and spit upon his name.'

Najib wanted to have the eloquent little chap strung up by the neck but Muhammad felt otherwise. 'He is just a child now. And a clever one with a gift for words. Contrary to popular belief, I am not a murderer of children and women. But keep an eye on him. If he grows up into a seditious young man, let him feel the wrath of his Sultan.'

After all the unwarranted agitations, upheavals and uproars, the great exodus had begun. The Sultan, his household, nobles and other distinguished heads had departed in a glittering procession. The Sultan sometimes rode on his elegant, wondrously ornamented chariot pulled by four pairs of the finest, milk-white Arabian steeds, or in his plush howdah, atop his own elephant. His menagerie of falcons, cheetahs and tigers accompanied him, tame as dogs.

The rest of the company followed, behind the emperor. The lords and ladies of his court were only slightly less magnificently arrayed. Whenever they passed one or more of the villages, his subjects would be waiting to greet their emperor. Muhammad made it a point to stop briefly to address them and present them with bags of coins. Makhduma Jahan would send her attendants into their midst to distribute sweets among the children, while the elders would receive cloth and utensils. Their joyful cheers would resound to the very heavens, and Muhammad was always surprised at how gratified he was to hear them.

The ladies of his household had been excited about the prospect of travelling and seeing new places. They were all in high spirits. Even Saira seemed to have brightened and her eyes were unusually animated even though she had been against the move initially. His mother told him that she was feeling like a young girl again.

'Then perhaps you should find a husband for her as well . . .' Khuda had whispered in his ear. 'People keep forgetting that old people have needs too. What is the point of having so much power if you won't address these pressing issues?'

'Thank you for the suggestion, Khuda! From now on, I shall prioritize the sexual needs of my subjects.'

'Power has gone to your head!' she sighed. 'You didn't even consult me about making Daulatabad your temporary new capital. I could have advised you on how best to convince your stupid subjects. As for me, I have conflicting feelings. We ladies spend so much time in the harem, it is exciting to travel on horseback, see the countryside and make our home in a new place. I am partly relieved you have deferred my second wedding, but unfortunately my bed will remain cold a little longer.'

Muhammad rolled his eyes. 'Don't let Mother hear you!' he whispered.

'Hear what?' Haniya glared at them both.

'He has promised that once I am married again and blessed with a son, my boy will be named his heir apparent since he has been so lax about propagating the Tughlaq bloodline. I keep telling him I will be the better choice but the grand Sultan is not particularly enthused,' Khuda lied through her teeth with her customary cheek.

'By that logic, *I* am the best choice,' Haniya had huffed. 'There is little a mother can do when her son won't heed her counsel to produce heirs immediately and prefers to make a fool of himself.'

Muhammad did not respond but wished his mother would actually give up on him instead of merely saying so. And she wasn't even the worst of his detractors.

Saira had been dutiful and obedient as ever, though he knew that Dilli was the great love of her life. She had been born and brought up there, which explained the haughty arrogance that she, like the other denizens of the place, had clearly inherited, which convinced them that they were truly superior to all else in the empire. The prevalent belief was that Sultans would come and go, empires would crumble, but Dilli itself would remain at the very epicentre of power.

That was just like Saira. She wore even her natural hauteur with elegance and the quiet confidence that nothing could outshine or mar her radiant beauty. There was not much left of the girl she had once been, but the lines on her face and the haunted look in her eyes gave her a quiet strength and dignity. There was a stillness in her being that merely hinted at the hidden depths of the sorrow she had survived.

It was Saira who had convinced him to commence building the Begumpuri mosque. 'A sanctuary of prayer and peace,' she told him in a rare moment of eloquence, 'for those who need it to bolster their spirit and find the will to go on. This mosque is needed now more than ever when blood and pain are the price exacted for survival and the scant prospect of pleasure.'

He had gladly acceded to her request and she had thanked him most prettily. But even now, after all this time and all the kindness he had showered upon her, she still had the same haunted expression in her eyes, from that fell night when her brother, the Shah, had been murdered. As if she was certain it was only a matter of time before bad things would happen not just to her but to them all.

He wished he could tell her that she need never fear being hurt by him. Surely she knew that he just wanted her to be happy? With him? Perhaps their time in Daulatabad would bring them closer together. The Sultan was hopeful that the move would do him and his subjects a world of good.

Muhammad had provided free accommodation for all who had been chosen to move to Daulatabad. They had also received generous stipends to make a fresh start. Although it was to be wondered if they had received the fair share that was allotted to them. It was the job of the enforcers of the law to quell corruption, but no matter how much he cracked down, double-dealing, deceit and unscrupulous conduct refused to be weeded out. In fact, they had seeped into every aspect of their lives. It wasn't the smooth transition he had hoped for but Muhammad felt his spirits lift when they all managed to settle down to a semblance of routine in Daulatabad. He was sure everyone would eventually benefit from the move. Even the idiots who were pining away for their beloved Dilli. 'Dearest Dilli!' they wept over and over again. 'We would have been content to live and die within your warm embrace, and if it hadn't been for the Sultan, no force on earth could have induced us to abandon you!'

Muhammad was incensed. One would think he had ravaged the city, set fire to it, sowed salt into its fields, and driven its denizens away. It was ridiculous! Idiots! He took a deep breath. 'They will get used to the change. Besides, it is not as if I have sworn never to set foot in Dilli ever again.'

'I'll have to disagree with you, your most royal highness,' Abu piped up. 'Have you not seen the many graves that have sprung up along the entire length of the passage from Dilli to Daulatabad? Your people aren't going to forget this in a hurry.'

'So there were a few deaths. It has been hard on the old, sickly and the very young. But the great majority have made it here safe and sound. And I did not force anybody to move.'

'Tell that to those mourning the loss of their loved ones. And those who tried to stay behind but were not allowed to because you insisted that their services were needed.' Abu could be relentless when he so chose. 'Your careful arrangements served the purpose for you and your royal household. The poor had a rougher time of it. Many died from heat, fatigue and hunger. Of course, you gave orders for relief camps to be set up where travellers would be provided with free food, water and medicine. But there have been stories of hundreds being turned away.

'The corrupt elements in your court have wrongfully evicted landowners just so they can snatch their property. They even paid off guards to force people to leave their homes with little more than the clothes on their back. Even here in Daulatabad, greedy officials have pocketed most of the funds allotted for free housing and stipends. So your optimism is ill-founded. Your people are not going to forgive you for your sorry implementation of a hastily conceived scheme.'

Muhammad frowned. 'Why are you so determined to focus on the things that went wrong, as opposed to the things that did go right? Dilli does not deserve the monopoly of the Sultan's fortune it feels so entitled to. The rest of the empire needs to have access to the same amenities that Dilli takes for granted. The other towns and cities also deserve to have canals, bridges, inns, gardens, orchards, and magnificently constructed citadels, mosques, temples, libraries, bathhouses and centres for learning.

'By shifting the locus of urban activity, I wish to welcome more into the welcome shade of civilization. The great divide between the south and the north, Hindus, Muslims and the other faiths will be bridged. Daulatabad will be a place where people from diverse backgrounds will live together in peace, and it will be a model state for the rest of the empire.

'It is my intention to irrigate and cultivate vast tracts of arable land so that the problem of starvation may be entirely eradicated. I am going to build dams, dykes and canals so that the flow of the big rivers is controlled, and water scarcity becomes a thing of the past.

'I want more cities to become centres of learning and culture, so that in the next generation those with the aptitude can go on to become poets, mathematicians, astrologers, physicians, chemists, musicians and physicists. How long are we going to allow those whose birth and circumstances deprive them of opportunities for self-improvement? We need more thinkers, planners and artists. And none of this will be possible if I were to hole myself up in Dilli with its smug self-satisfaction, superiority complex and unwillingness to throw open its coffers for the betterment of outsiders.'

'That is quite the moving speech.' Abu sounded bored. 'But you are a brilliant thinker and an ambitious dreamer whose skills frankly aren't up to scratch when it comes to execution. Your sincerity is touching, which makes it all the more painful when you set yourself up for failure repeatedly. Perhaps it won't be the worst thing in the world if you pared down the sheer scale and grandeur of your visions.'

Muhammad shook his head stubbornly. 'It is only when we reach for the stars that we can touch the sky.'

Abu nodded sagely. 'You have the soul of a poet. It probably explains why you are such a lousy Sultan. I am not surprised. In this land, it is the least qualified who end up with positions of great power. But you know that, don't you? Just look at those politicians you have to hobnob with on a daily basis! Not a brain or an original idea between the lot of them, though they are all natural-born thieves and killers. I don't envy you one bit. Only a fool thinks the Sultan has it all.'

Muhammad wished he could send Abu off to Najib. If only it was possible to silence a dead man. But he was starting to agree with everything his outspoken friend said. Being a Sultan took the combined skills of a cutthroat, thief, saint, scholar and fiend. He still couldn't make up his mind as to whether he was all or none of those things. It made him shudder and wonder morosely about how much worse things were going to get.

7

Bahram Aiba Kishlu Khan was a thrice-damned fool. Didn't he know that Sultan Muhammad had neither the time nor the inclination to deal with a rebellion? Especially not now, since he had declared a period of official mourning to mark the death of his poor brother, Bahram Khan? He had returned to Dilli with his mother, Khuda, Saira and a contingent of nobles to bury him.

Khuda was irrepressible as ever. 'Now that Bahram is gone and I am yet to marry again and bear a son, who are you going to name as your heir apparent? Mubarak or Firoz? You better not be considering Masud, though he does carry the blood of the Khaljis and Tughlaqs in his veins.'

'Not now, Khuda. Show some respect for Bahram,' he bit out.

'You know, I liked him, but he is gone now, like my husband and father. Mourning does not agree with me, and it is pointless because none of them are going to come back. You will have to name an heir sooner rather than later!' she grumbled and flounced away, not bothering to hide her delight that they were back in Dilli.

Muhammad shook his head to clear it. This time, even he wasn't convinced that he was exempt from blame. After all, it had been his decision to release Bahadur, formerly the king of Lakhnauti, who had been defeated by Ghiasuddin Tughlaq and taken captive. On the day of his coronation, he had appointed him as the joint governor of Bengal with his brother, Bahram. At the time, people had questioned his decision, but he had reasoned that Bahram and

Bahadur would have their hands full with each other and be less likely to give him a headache.

Of course, Bahram had taken with him a detachment of the imperial troops to help maintain order. But it was always going to be a challenge, given that Bahadur was on his home turf and Bahram had been the interloper, surrounded by hostile locals who had forgotten the kindness with which they had been treated by Sultan Ghiasuddin Tughlaq.

Muhammad had stipulated that Ghiasuddin Bahadur send his son to Dilli to be the emperor's ward, but he had failed to comply. He should have acted then, but he had been preoccupied and assumed that Bahram had everything under control.

According to the reports, simmering tensions between Bahadur and Bahram soon escalated into open conflict. Muhammad had sent an army headed by Tatar Malik. In the ensuing clash, Bahadur's forces had been defeated. The rebels had all been rounded up and made to watch while Bahadur was force-fed ordure till he choked on the stuff and breathed his last. His body was then stuffed with straw and paraded around the provinces. All surviving male members of his family were also executed.[9]

Unfortunately for Bahram, it had been too late and he had been treacherously slain by the time Tatar Malik arrived with reinforcements. Muhammad found himself apologizing profusely, even though he felt his brother had carelessly allowed himself to be killed. But death had clearly made a philosopher out of Bahram.

'Why are you apologizing?' Bahram asked him, sounding mildly querulous. 'You don't mean it, and it wasn't your hand that killed me. It was Ghiasuddin Bahadur who did it.'

'That is true,' Abu pitched in helpfully, 'but your father, the great Ghiasuddin Tughlaq, knew a treacherous snake when he saw one and decreed that he be imprisoned for life. He should have executed him and been done with it. Unfortunately, when one is a ruler, acts of kindness are regretted more often than cruelty.

'Our Sultan Muhammad, however, compounded his father's mistake and saw fit to not only release him on the day of his coronation but also send him straight back to his former kingdom with you in tow so that he could make all kinds of trouble before assassinating the Sultan's brother.'

Bahram thought it was funny. Muhammad didn't. 'There is no need to look so gloomy!' his brother patted him on the shoulder. 'To tell the truth, it is good to get away from the strife and madness of rule and politics. Power is a cruel taskmaster and certainly not worth the trouble or effort.'

'I wish I could get away too.' Muhammad meant it. At that moment, he would have gladly traded places with his brother. Or Abu.

Muhammad shook his head in frustration. Kishlu Khan had also raised the standard of rebellion. The man had been his Warden of the Marches and the governor of Multan, Uch and Sind. Like Gurshasp, he had fought by his father's side and was one of the most respected figures in the realm. What cause could the man possibly have to rebel? He wasn't even particularly ambitious.

With a start, Muhammad realized that Ahmad was staring at him with a look of acute worry on his face. As usual, the Khwaja Jahan seemed convinced that the Sultan was dangerously close to full-blown madness.

'Why exactly has Kishlu Khan chosen this time to rebel?' he snapped at him.

'His son-in-law was killed during an altercation with a fellow noble during the move to Daulatabad. It was a property issue. The noble in question may have bribed a few officers of the law and managed to get away with his crime as well as the property.'

'But in the interest of upholding the law, I hope someone was punished, Ahmad.'

'Of course, your highness! As per your command, the Kazi must find and punish the guilty party, or he will himself be subject to the punishment prescribed by law for the crime. So, naturally, somebody was found and punished. It just wasn't the noble who actually committed the crime. Kishlu Khan is convinced justice wasn't upheld.'

'How very unreasonable of him! As I recall, the grieving widow was cared for by my mother. And she made sure that satisfactory arrangements were made for her children's future because Kishlu Khan was a loyal ally of my father's, though clearly he does not feel the same way about his son.'

'Well, sire, Kishlu Khan is furious and blames you for his son-in-law's death. He proclaimed that you made a promise to uphold justice but have become a tyrant instead. The unfortunate demise of Gurshasp is also being cited as an example of the zalim Sultan's excesses.'

'The nerve of that man!' Muhammad growled. 'This is the last thing I need, especially after the trouble in Lakhnauti. And my plans for the Khorasan expedition have suffered one setback after the other, now that Tarmashirin has gotten himself killed. If that weren't bad enough, Abu Said has allied himself with the Caliphate at Egypt and is virtually untouchable. Which means I have to extend the hand of friendship to him and forget all about my plans for conquest. After all the expenses incurred for the training and upkeep of a massive force! I suppose from this point, their only purpose will be to deal with rebels and fools. It is like sending a pride of lions to swat a few flies. In the middle of all this, must I deal with Kishlu Khan as well?'

'You don't have to deal with him personally, sire,' Ahmad said crisply.

'Whatever do you mean? Of course I could send you but I prefer to handle him on my own.'

'That is not what I meant, your majesty. If you recall, a few days ago we discussed Shaikh Imamuddin's vile insinuations against you and his repeated calls for your abdication. The people are stunned not only by his words but by his striking resemblance to you.'

Muhammad smiled slowly. 'Why, you have quite the devious mind, Ahmad! They say that even my mother might have trouble telling us apart. Imamuddin would be the perfect ambassador to represent the throne in the negotiations for peace with Kishlu Khan. After all, he wouldn't want Mussulmen killing each other senselessly now, would he?'

'Of course, "ambassador for peace" does have a better ring to it than "decoy who will lead our forces with the royal parasol placed over his head".' Ahmad allowed himself a rare chuckle.

Barani was admitted into their presence just then, and Muhammad nodded to Ahmad.

'We were just talking about Shaikh Imamuddin and his extraordinary resemblance to me, Barani,' Muhammad told him.

Barani looked a little nervous. 'Your highness must not judge him too harshly. He seeks only to disseminate the teachings of the holy book and convince people of the importance of the Sharia code. If he occasionally uses a strident tone, it is because he is so passionately committed to his chosen vocation. Ultimately, he is a good man and we need more like him, who are committed to protecting Islam against the encroachment of the infidel.'

The Sultan sighed. 'But that is precisely the problem. If all the holy men would choose to give up their proselytizing ways and actually take up gainful employment, this land would be a much better place.'

Ahmad nodded in agreement.

'Well, sire, we all serve the purpose that God in his infinite wisdom intended us to. But that is not the reason I sought an audience with you.' Barani paused to collect his thoughts and was heartened when the Sultan nodded encouragingly at him.

'If I may, sire, I did wish to beg a favour from you,' Barani began, 'on behalf of Shaikh Imamuddin's brother, the saintly Rukhnuddin, who desperately needs funds for his *khanqah*. Unlike the others, he has no wish to question the authority of the Sultan. Shaikh Rukhnuddin cares only to spread the message of peace and love. If you would be kind enough to oblige him with your famed generosity, I am sure the Shaikh and his brother would be grateful and proud to name themselves as your majesty's most loyal servants.'

'I wasn't aware that the loyal service the Sultan is entitled to from his subjects had terms and conditions,' Muhammad said. Barani blanched. 'But you know I cannot refuse you, Barani,' the Sultan continued warmly. 'Of course Shaikh Rukhnuddin shall have his funds and his khanqah need never worry about any lack in the future. I am an admirer of his. As for his brother, Imamuddin, I have nothing but respect for his honesty and eloquence.'

Barani looked relieved but the Sultan wasn't finished. 'It gives me pleasure to do this for the Shaikhsahib. In these dark times, it is always comforting to know there is still some goodness left in this evil world. Kishlu Khan was like a brother to me but he has forgotten my kindness and generosity. He has declared the independence of Multan, Uch and Sind from my empire. How aggrieved my father would have been! Now I have no choice but to march with the imperial army. It is going to be a bloodbath. Muslim brothers will slaughter each other and the sin will darken the days ahead. Just thinking about it makes my heart break.'

There were real tears in the Sultan's eyes and Barani was moved. 'Perhaps we could work towards a peaceful resolution of this conflict, your highness. I am sure this is all just a dreadful misunderstanding.'

'Don't think I haven't tried, Barani.' Muhammad was mournful. 'People think of me as a bloodthirsty tyrant. But the last thing I want is a war that could prove disastrous for us, Muslims who are brothers of the same faith. But Kishlu Khan will not see reason, and he refuses to meet with any of my envoys. Apparently, I have lost his trust. If only there was somebody eloquent who enjoys the love and respect of all the Muslims in this land . . . someone who is as committed to preserving the peace as I am.'

Barani's eyes lit up at once. 'I know just the person for the job, your majesty. Shaikh Imamuddin could reason with Kishlu Khan and persuade him to set aside his arms in the interests of upholding the tenets of Islam. This state of disunity among us simply cannot be allowed to prevail. The ungodly infidels will laugh themselves silly while we massacre each other. Sheikh Imamuddin has always stressed the importance of joining hands and forgetting our differences. I know he will be happy to help.'

Ahmad sighed. 'That is all well and good, but Shaikh Imamuddin has made his disdain for the Sultan painfully obvious and has been trying to incite your subjects against you. How can he be trusted with such a delicate mission?'

Barani frowned. 'The Shaikh Imamuddin's character is beyond reproach. I can assure you of that. He is merely a little overzealous on occasion. He can be counted on to do the right thing. You will see! Your majesty, with your permission, I will go to Shaikh Rukhnuddin and tell him about your generosity towards him and the khanqah. He shall also be apprised of the present crisis, and the saint will prevail upon his brother to act as your ambassador for peace.'

'What would I do without you, Barani?' Muhammad said effusively. 'You must go this instant to Shaikh Rukhnuddin and tell him that the Sultan humbly solicits his help to avert a grave crisis. Take with you a robe of honour to be presented to Shaikh Rukhnuddin as a token of my goodwill. If Shaikh Imamuddin consents to act as my peace envoy, he shall be presented with one too. He must do his utmost to convince Kishlu Khan that I merely wish to clear this misunderstanding and seek to reunite on cordial terms. Everything depends on you, Barani!'

'I will not let you down, your majesty!'

Barani bowed and departed at once, eager to do the Sultan's bidding. Muhammad glanced at Ahmad and was amused to note that for once his Khwaja Jahan approved wholeheartedly of his actions.

8

Shaikh Imamuddin was nobody's fool. He wasn't as trusting as his brother and was convinced the Sultan was up to no good. His unease mounted as they marched towards Abrogha, where Kishlu Khan waited with his own troops. The hot, muggy air was thick with tension and he couldn't shake the feeling that something was wrong. It didn't help that the emperor had taken considerable pains to set his mind at ease.

'I really appreciate that you have agreed to be my peace envoy,' the Sultan said warmly during the course of the forced march, acting for all the world as though they were comfortably seated from across each other doing little more than sipping on sherbet. 'It is kind of you, especially since I know you disapprove of some of my policies and personal conduct. You will find me most grateful once we conclude this business.'

'Your majesty is kind and magnanimous! However, I am sure he is aware that I am not one to mince words and will forgive me for voicing aloud my suspicions, especially since he has been known to put men of faith behind bars when he is not having them tortured or killed by his dog.'

'Men of faith, if wise, would limit themselves to the kingdom of God and work towards spreading it on Earth without the use of force, which alone would be in keeping with the tenets of Islam. Instead, they dabble in politics, spread hatred and manipulate their followers into committing atrocities against those who belong to other faiths.'

'There is only one true faith, and we have sworn to uphold it. It always saddens me when a scholar of your eminence chooses to misinterpret the Quran in keeping with his personal biases or petty political conveniences. Encouraging and supporting infidels is an act of treason against God and a far worse crime than even parricide or incest.'

He wondered if he had gone too far but the Sultan seemed amused. 'If I truly were the tyrant everyone claims I am, I would have ripped out your tongue and fed it to the crows for uttering such spurious claims. But I have always appreciated honesty. Know then that I wouldn't ever betray the essential principles of Islam. You believe I should use the power of the throne to impose my faith on my subjects, who feel every bit as strongly about their gods as we do about ours.

'Would you have me destroy them if they won't embrace my religion? Would you have me enforce the fanatical views of the Ulama and preach religious dogma at them when there are too many who cannot make ends meet? Will prayer fill the bellies of the poverty-stricken? Will God rescue the diseased and infirm when the hakim turns them away because they cannot afford to pay? They look to their Sultan for solutions to their problems, and I cannot in good conscience respond by forcing religion down their throats the way you would have me do.'

'What can *you* do to alleviate the problems of your people, your highness?' the shaikh ventured boldly. 'Have you provided your subjects with a surcease to their suffering or have you contributed to them? By forcing your careless whims and reckless impulses on them you have made their lives utterly miserable, well-intentioned though you may be. Can you really believe that a solution to all their troubles lies with you? Are you presumptuous enough to think that their salvation is in your hands, not God's?' His chest was heaving and he felt the fingers of the angel of death cold upon his spine.

'There may not be much I can do to lift people out of the morass of suffering, Shaikh Imamuddin,' the Sultan said courteously, clearly enjoying their little debate, 'but I owe it to them to at least try, instead of giving up and leaving their welfare to the care of the Almighty.'

Imamuddin found himself thawing slightly. The Sultan was the most misguided man he had met, in addition to being a murderer and tyrant, but who could deny his generosity or sincerity? And it was commendable that he would cheerfully work with his biggest detractor towards ensuring peace. Perhaps there was hope for their monarch after all.

They had been riding like the very devil on the Sultan's insistence. He told the Shaikh, 'We must make haste before fraying tempers on either side lead to irreparable damages. Once our mission is successful, we can carry on our discussion.'

As they neared Abrogha, the Sultan ordered his men to make camp. 'If Kishlu Khan is to see me at the head of a large force, he will be convinced that I am here to crush the insurrection, although I have merely brought them as a safety measure. It would be best if I remained behind while you begin negotiating for peace, accompanied by a select contingent of my personal guard.'

The Sultan's attendants helped him get ready for the meeting. They dressed him in a magnificent robe of honour and adorned him with the emperor's own jewels. His headdress was adjusted by the Sultan himself. The shaikh had never looked so resplendent. Muhammad enveloped him in a warm embrace. 'Go with God and may the Almighty grant you every success!'

'Those who place their faith in God will never have cause to regret it,' he assured the Emperor. 'I urge you to surrender to the Almighty and devote the rest of your life towards using your position to contribute to his glory.'

At Muhammad's insistence, he was helped atop the Sultan's own royal elephant, and they held the parasol over his head.

The emperor watched him leave with a heavy heart. For once, his plan was being executed to perfection, but he could derive little satisfaction from it. He watched dully as the Shaikh drew within shooting range of the enemy ranks. His men sounded the charge and the snare closed around the saint.

Kishlu Khan's front ranks watched in disbelief as the Sultan lumbered into their midst. Without waiting for a command, they loosed volley after volley in a desperate bid to destroy the tyrant. Muhammad flinched as arrow after arrow thudded into Shaikh Imamuddin and he was toppled from the howdah, his mouth gaping open comically in utter disbelief.

While the fools dropped their weapons and celebrated the Sultan's demise, the rest of the imperial army entered the fray on the command of the real emperor. The battle didn't last long in the ensuing confusion.

Muhammad had been in many wars, and he hated the messiness of it all. He couldn't get used to the stink of sweat, blood and excrement, and it would assault his nostrils for days afterwards.

He couldn't help but wish that his overture for peace hadn't been false. But it had been a risk he couldn't afford to take. Mercifully, this time it was over soon. The victorious troops put the surviving men to the sword and brought the whole thing to its inevitable bloody conclusion.

But Muhammad would not allow them to go on rampage—harm the civilians, raze Multan to the ground and engage in rape or looting. He was determined that such savagery would not be allowed to happen on his watch. Sultan Muhammad bin Tughlaq was his father's son, after all.

Those troops who would not be denied their share of looting, burning and raping were relieved of their limbs and male organs, and left impaled on stakes sharpened for the purpose so that they could inspire their comrades towards decent, God-fearing behaviour.

As for the citizens of Multan, Sind and Uch, the mood was sullen, though they were fortunate to be the recipients of the Sultan's mercy. But it was understandable. They had endured a crushing defeat and Muhammad had declared that they would be bearing the costs of the war effort. Muhammad was less compassionate when it came to the leading mullahs, sayyids and Sufis, who his informants told him had been responsible for the large-scale disaffection that had culminated in rebellion. These he rounded up mercilessly and had their beards ripped off, scourged till their flesh hung in tatters and fed them the contents of their stinking bowels. He hoped it would serve as a deterrent to those who sought to spread dissent.[10]

The stupendous victory ought to have enhanced his prestige considerably, but as always, he somehow managed to incur the enmity of his own troops as well as the vanquished, on account of what they viewed as his heavy-handed actions.

As for Kishlu Khan, who had single-handedly been responsible for such large-scale destruction, Muhammad had wondered if he should listen to his mother for once and spare him, but the decision was taken out of his hands. The rebel governor had fallen on his sword and ordered his guards to burn the remains so they wouldn't be desecrated and paraded across the realm. Muhammad supposed it was better this way.

The Sultan named Kannu Brahmin as Kishlu Khan's successor. He had been sold into slavery, but he was a resourceful man who had risen up the ranks. His ascent became even more rapid when he converted to Islam, started calling himself Maqbul, and proved he was a dab hand at administration and taxes. Naturally, the Sultan's decision infuriated the nobles. They considered Maqbul a lowborn who couldn't even speak Persian, which was the language of the aristocrats, and despite his conversion, he wouldn't touch meat. But the way Muhammad saw it, if Kannu did not get himself killed in office, he would be more than adept at handling the demands of the job.

On the Sultan's instructions, Shaikh Imamuddin's remains were attended to by the physicians who had to stitch him together before embalming and preparing for his burial in a beautiful mausoleum of marble the Sultan had commissioned in honour of the great man. He commiserated with Rukhnuddin, who seemed a broken man and blamed himself for his brother's demise.

Barani was devastated, too, and wracked with guilt over his own role in the affair. However, he was a prudent man who was a little too attached to his own skin. He buried his anger and resentment over the Sultan's conduct, along with his own culpability, deep in the innermost recesses of his memory. All that remained was a lingering trace of resentment that would explode out of him one day and poison the words he would some day put down.

Muhammad supposed he would be long gone by then, and in a place where words and memories couldn't harm him. Even so, he was sorry and remained particularly solicitous towards Barani, though he knew the historian would hold on to the hurt and hate for dear life.

'Congratulations on your magnificent triumph, your highness!' Ahmad had beamed at him. 'How would you like to celebrate this glorious occasion?'

'Declare a thirty-day mourning period for Shaikh Imamuddin and have a memorial built to honour him,' Muhammad replied.

'As you wish, sire!' As the Khwaja Jahan departed, Muhammad could practically hear the words he left unsaid: *Not that it is going to make any of this better . . .*

9

Khuda's wedding was a happy occasion. There were so few of these that Muhammad was grateful for it. For someone who had been singled out to wield limitless power, he couldn't help thinking that his life had whittled down to a succession of gloomy episodes. Which was why he had a fresh appreciation for the little things that pleased him: a ripe mango, a glass of cool sherbet, a job well done, an act of simple goodness, anything at all that made him smile, and yes, his sister's wedding.

Naturally, the great majority felt that his choice of an Arab groom was simply insupportable, yet entirely typical. The Sultan's love for the ferenghis was universally known and deplored. Did he not address them as *aziz*, his dear friends, and shower riches on them while his own poor subjects toiled to pay the exorbitant taxes he demanded?

It amused Muhammad when it didn't depress him. His father would have wanted him to do his God-given duty by his subjects without expecting anything in return. However, he couldn't help feeling a little ill-used with the endless torrent of scorn and contempt for his painstaking efforts. As for the never-ending and cruelly creative expressions of dissent directed at him, they made him a contrarian, and Muhammad became even more profligate when it came to making presents to all the ferenghis who thronged his court.

The fact that it was Makhduma Jahan who had chosen the groom did not matter to any of his subjects. The Queen Mother loved receiving the envoys and dignitaries sent by foreigner rulers. 'They have a less prejudicial eye,' she had told him once by way of explanation. She would never admit it, but she loved how much they fell over themselves to please the grand old lady whose reputation for generosity rivalled her son's.

Haniya arranged lavish and exotic entertainment for them, featuring the best musicians, acrobats, and circus menageries, including wild beasts, snake charmers, knife- and fire-eaters, as well as dancing girls from across the realm. She loved receiving and giving lavish presents, and had even appointed an accountant to note down these transactions.

'I suppose it is so posterity can remember your great and noble deeds?' Muhammad had teased her. 'Perhaps I should build you a statue that would touch the very heavens!'

'As if they could ever forget the legendary Makhduma Jahan, the great love of Sultan Ghiasuddin Tughlaq, who forbade the squandering of valuable resources on useless things like statues!' she retorted haughtily.

His mother had taken a shine to Amir Saifuddin Ghada, who had visited them from Arabia, and it was she who felt that he would be an ideal match for Khuda. Muhammad had been less sure. From what he could tell, the Arabs preferred their thoroughbreds to be fiery and spirited, while their women were expected to cower modestly behind their purdahs. But on his mother's insistence, he had given his blessing to the union.

He himself had thought Malik Firoz, their dependable cousin, would be a better choice for a groom because he was besotted with Khuda and had always been. But he had been overruled by his mother and sister both.

Khuda preferred the Arab and informed her brother that in addition to being bold, dashing and masculine, unlike the toadies in his court, he was extremely easy on the eyes, which, in Muhammad's opinion, were all terrible reasons to get married, but who was he to rule on matters of the heart?

His sister had a caveat, though. 'I don't mind marrying Amir Ghada,' she informed her brother, 'as long as he doesn't expect me to sail away to faraway lands where I have heard that savage sultans take a new bride every day only to behead her on the morrow. Why, I am told the Arabs whip their women for showing their ankles, remove the external genitalia of girl children and grab every opportunity to stone their women to death. I would rather remain right where I am. Besides, you would be completely lost without your lone supporter.'

'Don't worry about it. I have no intention of sending you anywhere, though if mother is to be believed, a good whipping will do you a world of good. Amir Ghada may be persuaded to stay here for the duration of his life. As for your other fears, between mother and I, we will keep an eye on you to make certain your groom doesn't whip you or stone you to death.'

'Who is getting stoned to death? What a terrible way to go . . .' It was Saira who had spoken. Muhammad looked up in surprise. Usually she seemed content to give him a wide berth.

'Thankfully nobody is,' Khuda assured her. 'It was just my wonderful brother making light of my fears. He is every bit the cruel tyrant people are forever accusing him of being. But he is going to give me a grand wedding and I am going to get busy making a son and a slew of daughters. Then he will have to name one of them as his heir apparent! Aren't you excited?' She grabbed Saira by the arm and twirled her around the room.

'You are going to be a beautiful bride,' Saira told her, eyes sparkling with warmth. 'I wish you a lifetime of happiness, and may every one of your wishes come true.'

Khuda whispered something in her ear and they giggled together like children. Muhammad watched them both with amusement. He wished he could make Saira laugh like that.

The royal wedding was celebrated lavishly with due pomp and ceremony. Muhammad was determined to spare no expense and make it a memorable affair. The festivities went on for seven days.

Grand pavilions were erected, and this time, they were sturdy structures that wouldn't collapse even if an army of elephants went on the rampage or even if they were struck repeatedly with bolts of lightning.

No royal celebration was complete without aspiring demagogues mounting pulpits to call out the emperor for his wasteful expenditure in the face of the rampant starvation and poverty that wracked his poor subjects. But even they couldn't dampen the proceedings as the masses swarmed towards the palace gates, hoping to catch a glimpse of the handsome couple and become beneficiaries of the Sultan and his mother's munificence.

Even the mullahs seized the opportunity to point out that the emperor was marrying off his widowed sister, which was what civilized people did, as opposed to barbarians who burned their widowed women on funeral pyres. The Hindus muttered that it was just like the invaders to create such a hue and cry over an obscure ritual which was practised only by those who didn't know better, or among the royalty for reasons of political expediency. Thankfully, everybody was having too much of a good time to get into a fight over it.

The halls were adorned with gilded, richly embroidered tapestries, the finest carpets and a profusion of flowers. Painters worked on pictures depicting their Sultan, Makhduma Jahan, his sister and the groom in their nuptial finery. Jugglers, dancers and acrobats kept the visitors amused with their colourful displays and exquisite, perfectly coordinated performances, which included ropes, trapezes, burning hoops and flaming torches.

There were singers and bands of musicians who kept the audience entranced with drums, cymbals, pipes and vocal performances that stirred the soul and made the heart sing.

There were elaborate fireworks displays as well, courtesy of the Chinese ambassador, and this time they lit up the night skies much to the joy of the crowds watching from below. Muhammad had tried a few experiments of his own with the burning powder that went into their making. He was convinced that the magical substance was meant to be more than a toy and could change the way wars were fought.

Unfortunately, the men who had been put to the task had only succeeded in blowing themselves apart, and provided more fodder for the gossip mills about his so-called idiosyncrasies. The Sultan wouldn't give up, though, and those in his court with a more logical turn of mind were packed off to China so that they could learn about the powders. None of them would ever make it back, though. But the Sultan didn't know his ill-advised experiments would come to nought during Khuda's wedding, and his mood was expansive.

Muhammad insisted that on this happy occasion even his lowliest should eat like Sultans. The royal kitchen churned out platters and platters of mouth-watering delicacies, as chickens, ducks, goats and game birds were slaughtered in the thousands to make savoury dishes to go with the mounds of flavoured rice, richly spiced gravies, rotis and vegetarian preparations. The Chinese ambassador had also presented the Sultan with sets of intricately carved ivory tongs fashioned from the bones of an ape, which he said would turn black if they came in touch with poisoned food. They delighted the Sultan and he had mastered the art of using them with ease.

Out of respect to his Hindu subjects, no beef was served. And of course there was no pork. But there were flaky pastries, sugared confections and sweetmeats aplenty as well as fresh fruit, tender coconut and iced sherbet. Enormous tents were erected for the commoners so that they too could partake of the Sultan's largesse and be a part of the royal celebrations.

Though the feasting and entertainment were known to go on until the wee hours of dawn, the Sultan was most particular that the celebrations be conducted in a manner that was sober and sedate in the Islamic manner so that the occasion wouldn't be marred by unseemly drunkenness and debauched licentiousness. This did not go down well with those who felt no celebration was complete until they had had their fill of intoxicating beverages, but the Sultan compensated by being even more generous.

Robes of honour, richly embroidered with gold and encrusted with precious stones, were presented to the guests with matching turbans, jewellery and bushel loads of gold and silver. The groom's party, which consisted mostly of the Sultan's own relatives, was dressed magnificently as the Arab had travelled alone. They made a big show of fighting their way past the bride's party and making away with her, much to the Sultan's amusement, and his laughter bounced off the walls.

The bride wore robes of the finest brocade and was adorned head to toe with exquisitely wrought jewellery. Her mother distributed heaps of gold and silver among the poor and needy. At the conclusion of the wedding ceremonies, the Sultan presented the happy couple with vast tracts of land in Malwa, Gujarat, Khanbaya and Naharwala. Khuda was radiant with happiness, and the sight gladdened the Sultan's heart.

The Sultan wished the celebrations would go on forever. Even his detractors were too stuffed with good food and in too high spirits to spout their bilge at him. The entire realm was at peace and there was not a calamity in sight. As always, though, once the celebrations wound down, there was a lot to deal with.

Khuda's husband, Saifuddin, turned out to be every bit as wild and uncouth as his Bedouin ancestors, and did not wait long to make a nuisance of himself and embarrass the royal family that had taken him in.

'This is all your fault,' Muhammad's mother informed him. 'I have spent my life giving you sage counsel which you have ignored or dismissed, but the one time I make an error in judgement, you listen to me! If only you had got Khuda married to that nice Ibn Battuta!' The Sultan didn't think it wise to reply.

Within a fortnight, Saifuddin's boorish conduct landed him in trouble when he physically assaulted the Sultan's own *parda-dar*, the doorkeeper, a crime that was punishable by death. The Sultan declared that the Kazi would make a ruling in the case, and Saifuddin Ghada was imprisoned.

Khuda barely batted an eyelid and did not bother to visit him in prison or even send him bedding or food to make sure he was comfortable.

'He is not without his merits,' she confided in Saira, 'but it wouldn't hurt him to remember that I am the Sultan's sister first and foremost, and my status as his wife will always take second place.'

'At least he had the forbearance not to have him executed,' Saira remarked.

'Give him time!' Khuda laughed at her own joke. But it was tinged with disappointment. Why couldn't more men be like her brother? He was strong, kind and generous and he knew how to treat the woman he loved. As far as she was concerned, the Saifuddins of the world were not worth the Sultan's toenails!

10

Muhammad refused to be discouraged by the disaster that was his proposed Khorasan expedition and give up on his plans for world dominion. Everybody felt it was a fool's dream, but hadn't they said the same about Alexander the Great? Rebellions aside—which had been crushed mercilessly—he was pleased that his empire was stable and flawlessly administered.

He had secured the west by establishing peace in Multan. In the east, Bengal was under his control, and to the south, thanks to his efforts, Daulatabad was a sprawling metropolis that now rivalled Dilli. All that remained was to secure the northern frontier in the Qarachil region, where the Rajput rebels had retreated into the hills and still held sway. From there, they struck out at his military garrisons, interrupted his postal relays, and carried away the treasure chests that were supposed to make up the arrears in pay for his troops.

Muhammad felt confident about taking and holding Qarachil, especially after his recent success at Nagarkot, where he had personally led a force against the Hindu chieftains and subjugated them to his authority. It had felt good to be on the march with his troops, astride his magnificent stallion.

On horseback, he could pretend he was still the wild and carefree youth he had once been. These campaigns made him feel closer to his men and they in turn were delighted when their Sultan dined with them, asked them questions about their families and listened to the ribald humour and folk songs, which was their preferred form of entertainment since wine and women were strictly forbidden to them.

'He seems so regular and he is so easy to talk to,' they commented. 'It is hard to believe what they say about his combustible temper.'

'It is probably jealousy. How can you not envy a man who has everything? People tend to hate those who are this favoured by God and destiny . . .'

'Did you ask him if he is in love with his stepmother?'

'Why don't you ask him? Then we can ascertain for ourselves whether he truly has those who displease him flayed and impaled on stakes!'

'You can say what you want about him, but he is clever and knows his way around a battlefield.'

Muhammad decided he liked the rough company of his simple soldiers much better than that of his courtiers. It was a successful conquest and for once he had an easy time of it. Perhaps his luck was changing. Even his detractors had conceded that he had inherited his father's military genius. Like Nagarkot, he would have liked to undertake the Qarachil expedition personally, but Ahmad had argued strongly against it.

So it had been decided to send young Khusrao Malik, who was a distant cousin's son and an ambitious and bright young man who was anxious to prove himself. He was sent at the head of a large army with a portion of the troops who had been recruited for the ill-fated Khorasan expedition.

Muhammad planned it all down to the last detail, and he did it himself, as was his wont. He had little patience with the fools in his council who did little more than argue endlessly. These people seemed to exist for the sole purpose of taking up space, observing those who actually laboured, commenting on their deeds, proffering worthless advice, criticizing endlessly or conspiring to throw impediments in their path. They were the bane of every empire: the clerks, moneylenders, priests, astrologers, scribes and wastrels.

The Sultan sent surveyors who studied the route across the terrain and charted a course for the army to follow. Their cavalry forces were unstoppable on the plains but up in the steep mountain paths they would be at a distinct disadvantage. Having scrutinized their reports, Muhammad ordered the construction of military posts that were to be stocked with arms, food and other provisions, all of which were to be placed under heavy guard, so his men would have these garrisons to fall back on should they be forced to retreat.

It was the closest thing to a foolproof plan, and Khusrao Malik's troops met with success, managing to take the citadel at Jidya, which gave him a foothold in the surrounding countryside at the foothills of the Himalayas. Muhammad sent instructions to Khusrao to hold fast, consolidate his position and await further instructions.

If only the young fool had listened! His initial triumph had swelled his head and he ignored the royal command. Khusrao led the entire bulk of his army into the formidable barrier that was the Himalayas, eager to take the victory that was within his reach. His timing couldn't have been worse since was it was at the peak of the monsoon season and the slopes were slick and treacherous. Unwary men plunged to their deaths and the Rajput rebels hounded them every step of the way.

The mountains were their enemies' home, and they knew it like the back of their hands. They fought guerrilla style, never forcing open confrontation but nipping at the flanks and harrying them from behind, avoiding pursuit by melting back into the cover offered by the dense forest and the rocky slopes. They triggered landslides and started forest fires. The soldiers fled, convinced that it was the very hand of God that reached down to wipe them out.

Thousands of men were destroyed in moments, buried under chunks of the mountain which came apart before their very eyes, the wall of rock hurtling towards them faster than they could flee. Entire regiments disappeared beneath giant boulders, uprooted trees and swathes of turf, wiped out as if they had never been.

The lucky ones were those who had been killed outright. Worse off were the ones who were grievously injured and doomed to die in excruciating pain or those buried alive in shifting tombs, with no hope of rescue till the elements claimed them in a suffocating embrace.

Even so, they were more fortunate than the ones who were claimed by the fires. The troops ran pell-mell when they spotted the raging fire that roared towards them, seeking frantically for an escape, only to discover that they were trapped in a valley of death with the flames pursuing them every which way, screaming in agony till they were burnt to cinders.

All of a sudden, the hunters had become the hunted as panic gripped the army. Khusrao Malik died in an avalanche, and his men were in disarray, too distraught to make an orderly retreat to the military outposts. It was an unmitigated disaster as their enemy slaughtered them till nothing remained of the mighty force the emperor had put together. When news of the carnage reached the garrisons, they fled in terror, abandoning their posts.

It was the worst defeat inflicted on the Sultan. His war council insisted that they strike back hard and fast. 'The defenders think they can hold out against us forever but if we are persistent then it is only a matter of time before we prevail. And we must give them a fitting reply for the temerity they have displayed in daring to defy the Sultan.'

Muhammad shook his head firmly, heartily sick of the vainglorious claims. 'I intend to put an end to this farcical nonsense. It is futile to expend more of my men on a lost cause. By keeping up the war effort, there will be nothing but dead bodies on both sides, and the land itself will be ravaged and hardly worth taking. It is time to retreat and recoup.'

There was a time to fight and a time to retreat. Sometimes it was prudence that was needed to carry the day. Not false valour and bravado.

He had heard some of the members of his war council remark that 'there is no greater satisfaction than to take the life of your enemies and defile their women even before the blood of the fallen has dried on your armour, watching their faces contorted with pain, fear and molten hatred.' And they called him cruel and a tyrant. None of them seemed to care about the practical considerations that went into waging wars, and he would be damned if he allowed their bloodlust to dictate policy.

Muhammad's decision was met with outrage. Even Ahmad was convinced he was making a grave error, and displayed his new-fangled penchant for expressing his thoughts. 'We cannot ignore a defeat of this magnitude and escape unscathed, your majesty! How can you even suggest it! They have proved that the mighty imperial army is not only fallible but utterly incompetent as well. If the Sultan's aura of invincibility is shattered, then he can expect a spate of rebellions, challenging his authority from every province in the realm. We simply cannot afford to let it happen.'

Muhammad was sick of these prophets of doom. Sick of being questioned all the time. Sick of the burden of expectations that weighed him down. Sick of the incompetent nincompoops who surrounded him and let him down every single time. Sick of their disappointment and distaste. Sick of all the things that went wrong because his subjects refused to make it right.

He spoke through gritted teeth, 'Who dares question the authority of the Sultan? I will teach them all a lesson they will never forget! Since the imperial army has proved itself to be utterly and irrevocably incompetent, the soldiers will pay for their gross uselessness. I want every troop who abandoned his post at the garrison to be brought before me in chains. Every soldier with a black mark on his record—be it for sleeping on duty or farting during a parade—is to be hauled up. The sentence for the lot of them is death! Najib, I want you to behead every single one of them and display the heads around the fortress on sharpened stakes. Let everybody know that such is the fate of those who don't tremble before their Sultan and treat his every word as a sacred command!'

Even Najib seemed taken aback. A deathly silence met the imperial decree. No one dared to even breathe, let alone protest. *Good*, Muhammad mused to himself, *another word and I would have executed the stinking lot of them.*

PART THREE

THE MAD MONARCH

'My kingdom is diseased, and no treatment cures it.
The physician cures the headache, but fever follows;
he strives to allay the fever, and something
else supervenes.'

Muhammad bin Tughlaq

1

Muhammad wished the soldiers weren't dead. He really did. But it couldn't be helped. Was it Bahram who had once told him that regret was useless in life and death? He couldn't ask him now since he had banished the ghosts in his head ever since the lamentable passing of Shaikh Imamuddin.

Still, it was hard not to be filled with regret when confronted with the ghastly spectacle of hundreds of decapitated heads staring accusingly at him from various vantage points across his citadel. Dead though they indubitably were, he could feel their hatred. It was the hatred he felt for himself and which his subjects no doubt felt for him as well. On bad days, he couldn't help wishing that his would-be assassins would just get the job done.

How could he expect his people to understand what it took to wield absolute power? They lived in dread of his sweeping reforms, oftentimes harsh proclamations and terrible punishments, but how was he different from every other conqueror or supreme ruler this world had seen? Did they think Alexander the Great, Genghis Khan or Kubilai Khan had managed their impossible achievements by being embodiments of reason and compassion? Of course they wouldn't understand. Even so, he wouldn't ever stop trying to implement the innovations that he was convinced would elevate this land to the very pinnacle of glory.

Then perhaps history would judge him more kindly. But he doubted it, not if the likes of Barani had anything to do with it. Besides, how would any of it matter once he was gone?

Only the present mattered to him, with the multitudes within and without who abhorred him. Even Saira had set aside her customary reserve to lambast him. 'I have done my best to understand your position and have constantly looked for ways to help lighten the burden of rule . . .'

Really? And did she think her callous indifference to his love would help ease the burden of rule, as she called it? '. . . but I cannot hold my tongue any longer, unlike the others who surround you and daren't speak because they fear for their lives and their precious fortunes!'

She took a few deep breaths to calm herself, and her magnificent bosom heaved with the exertion, reminding him that her body was a masterpiece of exquisite softness and lush curves, which still stirred him like nothing else could. When she spoke again, her voice was softer. More appealing. Feminine wile was a truly beautiful thing to behold.

'Please don't do this to yourself any more,' she begged. 'You have been blessed with a towering intellect and a good heart but ill-luck and misfortune have dogged your steps ever since you ascended to the throne. This has filled you with anger and hate, making you lash out at the innocent with a severity that is simply not acceptable.'

Her eyes were wet with tears. 'I know in my heart that the flood of anger against you will vanish if only you were to set aside your own rage and stop yourself from hurting your people. They look upon you as a father! If only they are allowed to feel warmed by your benevolence, the mutual lack of trust will be replaced with goodwill. Once they know that they need not fear you, they will be more than happy to assist you in every single one of your endeavours. The empire will once again be blessed with peace and prosperity. Future generations will look upon you with love and admiration, and will no doubt be inspired to build upon the solid foundation you have provided to make their own dreams for this land come true.'

By God! Suppressed anger and passion enhanced her natural beauty a hundredfold, and he could not have resisted her even if he had been inclined to try. He reached out and drew her closer to him. She stiffened in silent protest but lay unresisting beneath him while he tried unsuccessfully to merge fully with her. As always, the enforced closeness of their bodies only served to accentuate the vast distance between them. At times like this, he despised himself for settling for whatever little she was willing to give him. Worse, he returned again and again, hoping to breach her unassailable defences.

It was a while before he rose to his feet. Saira lay still and silent as a corpse. He filled the gaping chasm between them with his own bleak thoughts. In the end, she was no different from the others. A hypocrite who would do whatever it took to hang on to her life and fortune. Yet she saw fit to advise him! But she had meant well. And so, he would forgive her. This one time.

Muhammad was feeling far from rested. Saira had been right about the problems erupting everywhere. The way things were going, one would be forgiven for thinking he did actually kill his father and bring down a curse upon his reign. His latest misstep had so angered his detractors, they had put aside their fear of royal retribution and were crying themselves hoarse blaming him.

It had all started with his reverence for the great Mongol emperor Kubilai Khan, who had managed to amass an empire that was thrice as big as Alexander's had been. Muhammad had taken an interest in the system of token currency the Mongols had perfected, though it was the Hans who had been using it as early as the ninth century. Muhammad had quizzed Tarmashirin on the subject, and later, his son-in-law, Amir Nauroz, who had managed to procure samples for him to scrutinize.

Under the great Khan, it was called flying money. The thing was made with paper indicating its value, which could be several

tankas of silver or more, affixed with the signature and seal of the
sovereign. 'The lettering is done using a process called gathered
writing,' Amir Nauroz had told him, 'whereby the words and
characters are arranged on a form which is then locked in place.
The form is then repeatedly inked and inscribed on the paper.'

'Using this technique of gathered writing,' he continued,
'the Han inscribed all the characters of the alphabet on terracotta
moulds, and these could be used to compose whole pages of writing,
which could be made into many identical books. If they had the
alphabets for other languages, the book could be available in other
tongues! This way, they need not deal with the hassle of scrolls.'

It was a brilliant concept and Muhammad was consumed by
it. There was endless potential to make a lasting difference here. He
was convinced that in future, financial transactions made with gold
mohurs and silver tankas would be obsolete. Instead, even large
transactions could be conducted easily and conveniently without
having to carry heavy treasure chests. The sheaves of paper would
be easier to carry, store or hide away for a rainy day.

Since they would be available in all denominations, depending
on a man's need, he could go to a market stall and buy a meal for
himself and flowers for his wife or the entire stall and its owner as
well. And, of course, the paper could be exchanged for the exact
value in gold or silver as well.

While mulling over how best to implement it, he realized
there were a few problematic areas to be addressed. For one, the
Persians under Kaikhatu Khan had tried to mimic this system with
disastrous results. The Khan wound up with his treasury emptied
and his people reduced to penury. Secondly, in order to ink the
alphabet moulds, the Han used brushes made with bristles of the
pig. If word got out that as the Muslim sovereign of his empire,
he had given his blessing to such an unholy enterprise, his scheme
would be sunk before he had a chance to set it afloat, and the Ulama
would ensure that rivers of blood were shed for the express purpose
of toppling him from the throne.

Having pondered over it at length, Muhammad decided to make innovations of his own to help launch the scheme in a manner that would not create too many ripples among the masses. Instead of paper, which his foolish citizenry would never accept as real money, perhaps they could issue thinly beaten copper coins.

Unlike silver, copper was plentiful, and once everybody got acclimatized to it, he could introduce the flying money with a suitable substitute, which did not involve either pig's bristles or anything from a cow in order not to incense his Muslim and Hindu subjects. He was sure horse hair would do just as well, and though the Jains would be sad about his mistreatment of voiceless animals, at least they did not favour violence to express their antipathy.

Muhammad would send a group of emissaries to China, laden with rich presents for their king, with orders to learn the art of gathered writing and making fiery flowers and patterns in the sky. Then, once his people had mastered it, they would make flying money, books, and even perfect the art of using burning powder as a weapon.

If this scheme succeeded, his legacy as a great ruler with vision and enterprise would be cemented for all of eternity, and there was no reason it shouldn't work. After all the effort he had put into its planning and implementation, what could possibly go wrong?

Everything, as it turned out. The entire thing was an unmitigated disaster—from the very start. By the time the naysayers and prophets of doom were done decrying the fact that copper would have the same value as gold and silver, there was widespread panic.

'Gold and silver will no longer have any value if not exchanged for copper! This is madness, we will all be ruined!'

'The Sultan is bankrupt after the disasters of the Khorasan and Qarachil expeditions so he seeks to defraud us and take our hard-earned gold and silver. Our children will starve because of our heartless ruler.'

'His father would never have blundered like this, but the madman killed him too!'

'The ferenghis become rich enough to buy their own kingdoms because the emperor is foolishly profligate. They take his money and laugh at him. We have to pay the price for his foolish adoration of the ferenghis!'

'Ghiasuddin Tughlaq left him a treasury that was filled to overflowing and his son has squandered it all away . . . What will become of us? That father-killer has cursed us all! The mullahs are right. The end is near!'

'Heaven save us all!'

Muhammad had expected some amount of resistance to his revolutionary scheme but even he was not prepared for the sheer scale of the mass hysteria that gripped his realm. His empire nearly came to a standstill in the throes of the anxiety that had gripped the populace. And then the situation steadily worsened.

After all the trouble he had taken to put the freshly minted coins into circulation, every petty thief and swindler in the empire crawled out of the woodwork to set up forges and issue fakes with very little effort. Now the market was flooded with counterfeit coins with no way to tell them apart from the originals.

Merchants and traders were crying fraud and accusing the Sultan of trying to impoverish them out of spite, insisting that the entire thing was a dastardly plot to keep them grovelling under his thumb. The treasury officials flooded him with complaints, insisting that the state exchequer was under enormous strain now that people were converting even their utensils into copper coins and making purchases or paying taxes with worthless currency.

His financial advisers had been at pains to inform him where exactly he had gone wrong.

'The idea itself is sound, your highness,' the prim voice of his finance minister murmured with infuriating condescension. 'However, had you consulted us first, we would have informed you that precautionary measures to prevent forgery have to be taken.

These include making the mint a monopoly of the state and designing special machinery with unique markers perfected by highly skilled specialists that the average artisan would be unable to replicate.'

'Every counterfeiter and worthless infidel thief in the realm has profited from this enterprise.' Another useless wastrel chimed in smugly, 'The corrupt among the landowning classes have shamelessly been hoarding coins of gold and silver, while setting up forges to issue copper coins and spending lavishly.'

'The ferenghi merchants and traders are happy to make purchases with copper coins, which have little intrinsic value of their own, but they refuse to accept the same for the sale of their own goods.'

'There is widespread confusion and chaos everywhere. If we don't do anything to address people's concerns and restore order, the fallout will be more than we can handle.'

'Unfortunately, it is the royal exchequer that has suffered the most. Drastic action must be taken at once, or it is only a matter of time before the treasury is emptied and the realm beggared.'

Muhammad hardly heard the pestilential voices of his accursed financial advisers. As always, the imbeciles were generous with their criticism when it came to his policies but far less forthcoming when it came to finding feasible solutions to an impending crisis. 'Get out!' he barked. 'I want you all gone from my sight immediately, or I'll have every single worthless coin in my realm melted and poured down your worthless throats!'

They fled in terror. All that had remained was the buzzing in his ears. It was the deafening sound of his enemies, laughing and pointing their fingers at him, glorying in his downfall.

2

The Sultan gazed forlornly out of the window at the mountains of copper coins that lay uselessly like trash, seeming to mock him. People walking past murmured that it was a fitting monument to the stupidity of their Sultan. 'Well, if it makes you feel any better, this is not the first time you have made an utter fool of yourself, and I daresay it won't be the last!' Abu cackled away. The raucous sound made his temples throb.

He started slightly when his mother appeared by his shoulder. Muhammad knew that Haniya couldn't see the mounds in his garden, but that wouldn't stop her from knowing all about them. He was steeling himself for what was coming when Haniya gently took his hand in hers.

Muhammad had to stop himself from plucking it away from sheer shock. He had almost forgotten how soft his mother's hands were. They felt frail, but there could be no doubting the strength of their owner. 'What could you possibly hope to gain by blaming yourself for what is done?' She squeezed his hand in a comforting gesture.

'Even if I could go back in time, I would still do it all over again . . .' he told her, his voice sounding childish and petulant even to him. 'In the distant future, when flying money is the only thing in use, they will laud my vision! Then they will be forced to accept that I was right all along.'

'No doubt! But will it be worth making the present and immediate future so miserable, I wonder?' She was in no mood to let him off the hook. 'There are still people waiting with copper coins by the cartload, demanding that they be exchanged for gold and silver. Will you allow yourself to be taken advantage of like that? You have announced that the copper coins will be removed from circulation. That ought to be enough.'

'Will it, though?' He extricated his hand in a sudden fit of pique. 'I don't mind being called a sadist or tyrant but I will not be accused of stealing from my own subjects. My people need to know that I can admit to mistakes and will recompense them accordingly.'

'But you already proved that when you presented yourself to the Kazi and paid the price when a guilty verdict was given against you. If memory serves, weren't you even willing to submit yourself for a beating, though, as it turned out, that was a mistake? My point is that these token gestures are entirely pointless when it comes to making amends. Wouldn't it be more profitable if you were to learn from your mistakes instead?'

Muhammad didn't reply. She tried again. 'Why would you reward those scoundrels who deliberately cheated their Sultan and successfully derailed a perfectly sound enterprise? Sometimes, I simply cannot comprehend your actions. You took harsh action against your soldiers after the failure of the Qarachil expedition, but these counterfeiters are far more deserving of such a fate, in my opinion.'

His mother sighed again. Muhammad looked at her worriedly. Haniya seemed tired, but how lovely she still was! Her blind old eyes brightened when her son broke his customary silence. 'I daresay you are right, but a soldier has a job to do and he is aware that death is what he can expect if he makes careless mistakes. They knew what was at stake and they deserved death for their cowardice. My latest measure, however, may have been sabotaged by a few rotten apples, but a portion of the blame lies with me. Too many innocent people who were only obeying my orders suffered losses they need not have. Therefore, it is my duty to pay them back.'

It all made perfect sense to him. Why couldn't they all see it?

'They are saying that there will be nothing but copper coins remaining in your treasury if you keep up this ill-advised policy of appeasement.'

'Don't you worry, mother.' He smiled sardonically. 'You did not raise a simpleton. Some among my loyal subjects are more unscrupulous than most and have tried to get ahead by failing to pay the taxes owed the state or coming up with the most ingenious schemes to swindle their Sultan.

'Did you know that these charlatans ran a scam to exploit my so-called love for the ferenghi? They would persuade lowborn foreigners just arrived on our shores to pass themselves off as ambassadors representing their kings. The frauds even went to the extent of supplying them with exorbitant gifts to be presented to me, knowing that I would reward them many times over. Then they would appropriate it all, never knowing that their activities are constantly monitored.

'In light of the present crisis, such scum have been arrested and been sent to meet their maker. Of course, their ill-gotten gains obtained from my treasury as well as their extensive properties have all been confiscated by the state and used to set right a wrong.'

Haniya allowed herself a small smile. Of course she knew all about it. 'You have done well! As I knew you would. However, you are as reckless as ever, and I urge you to be cautious. It has come to my attention that many among the nobles were behind these schemes, and your actions have not gone down well with them or their companions.

'But I didn't come here to lecture or berate you. People have always been trying to tell you the many things they think you need to know. But you hate when they do that. You prefer to figure out things for yourself. And that is not the worst thing. I just wanted you to know there is much that is bad in you but even more that is good. Sometimes you just need to remember that.'

Makhduma Jahan reached up to grab his ears, and, pulling him down, she kissed him softly on his forehead. Then she placed her hand on his head in silent blessing and walked away without a word. Muhammad felt the tears stir in his eyes.

'The Queen Mother was actually nice to you!' Abu's voice piped up in his ear. 'Now if that isn't cause for alarm, I don't know what is.'

'Something terrible is going to happen,' Bahram chimed in ominously. 'Or perhaps something terrible has already happened and you just don't know about it. Yet.'

Muhammad didn't bother to reply. He sat down instead, nursing his throbbing head, waiting for the voices in his head to subside and leave him alone.

3

Muhammad expected them to do their utmost to kill him. And as one who did not believe in being a sitting duck, he took a few precautions. Like his father before him, Muhammad recognized the importance of gathering intelligence from every corner of the empire, and had taken pains to establish a labyrinthine network of informers from all walks of life.

With the aid of the information gathered, a certain shadowy state apparatus consisting of personnel handpicked by the emperor made free use of his permission to deploy violence when and where it was needed to dissuade both individuals and groups from plotting to take their sovereign's life or engaging in any activity that wasn't in his best interests. Their efforts were a remarkable success. Those under the faintest suspicion of entertaining murderous thoughts against the monarch were detained and executed without trial.

Muhammad heard the reports with macabre fascination. It surprised him that the people who wished to see him dead were an eclectic mix of tradesmen, artisans, lowly soldiers, high-ranking officials from his court, hired hands sent by his enemies, dancers and musicians, some among his closest associates and even a group of women who had sworn to kill him or die trying.

The only thing they all had in common was abject failure, for none made it to within a mile of him. Every thwarted assassination attempt filled him with delight, almost as if he had been given a fresh lease of life. There was also the unshakeable belief that their failure was indicative of God's will that he was intended to survive and achieve great things.

Which was why he was taken entirely by surprise by the thing that came closest to killing him. He assumed his spies had been too terrified to report what they knew because of the Sultan's relationship with the person in question, but fortunately, they also knew better than to leave the matter unreported.

Even so, it came to the Sultan's attention only when Kazi Kamal paid him a visit. Muhammad had listened without expression. To his credit, the Kazi did not falter beneath his piercing gaze, which barely veiled his rage, and managed to say his piece.

'If I find out that you are lying . . .'

The Kazi's forehead was slick with beads of perspiration. 'I have risked my life by bringing this matter to your notice, your highness. And I only did it because it pertains directly to the Sultan. The law dictates exactly what I ought to do, and I am bound by it as well as my own sense of duty, since the evidence presented is irrefutable. However, I could not proceed without consulting you.'

The Sultan was stone-faced. 'The law shall take its course as it must. I ask only that you stay your hand for a brief period.'

The Kazi bowed low in assent and sidled away. For the longest time, Muhammad sat in silent contemplation. Even the voices in his head dared not speak up. Not this time. Finally, he roused himself long enough to ascertain whether it was true, though he knew in his heart that it was.

There were many who had betrayed him, but none on such a scale. Not even Abu's passing or his father's untimely demise had left him so prostrate with grief.

Muhammad was careful not to let his true feelings show all day. His mother had said his biggest failing was his rashness and undue harshness, so he took his time and waited till the unrelenting waves of pain were replaced with anger. Only then did he send for her.

She came before him, and as always, her beauty took his breath away. If she was feeling nervous, Saira did not show it.

'The Kazi was here to see me,' he said without preamble. 'You stand accused of adultery.[11] The evidence against you is irrefutable, and your guilt is plain as day. How do you plead? But I suppose that is a stupid question.' Muhammad heard the anger in his voice and it made him angrier still.

Outwardly, she was composed. Haughty even. But he saw the faint ripples of stark terror beneath the surface because he had been looking for evidence of her guilt.

Looking at her then, he knew that everything he had heard was the unassailable truth. He ought to have known all along, but perhaps he had been too blind to see it, although his blind mother had warned him about her from the start. Even so, a part of him wanted her to refute the claim. To assure him that despite everything, she loved him and wanted nothing more than to remain by his side forever.

Instead, she looked him straight in the eye. 'I have always tried to be a good wife, your highness, despite the painful position our union put me in. When a woman loses her respectability even through no fault of her own, she spends the rest of her life under attack. It is true that I resented you for that, but nevertheless I knew that your love was true and valued it accordingly. That is all that matters.'

He would have struck her then, if only to watch her quintessential arrogance and defiance shrivel up and die, but he didn't want her to have the satisfaction of knowing what she had done to him with her infidelity. Or how close her affair had come to destroying him. Especially not when she stood before him obstinate and utterly unrepentant, despite being caught in flagrant violation of the laws of Islam.

'It makes no matter if you are inclined to play coy with me.' Muhammad leaned closer, the better to breathe in the fear that wafted off her determinedly unruffled exterior, and stroked her hair gently. 'Najib will have the truth out of you in no time.'

'There is no need for that.' Saira drew away from him, unable to mask her revulsion or sudden terror. 'Your dog is a monster who revels in the suffering of others, and it is he who deserves the punishment and suffering he inflicts. He shall not have the pleasure of defiling my person. I will confess my crime before the Kazi and accept his punishment. Death does not frighten me.' She had raised her voice, but the faint quaver gave her away.

'I have always admired your bravery. Even now, you are bold as brass and hold your head high, despite sinning against God and man. You are an adulteress who has compounded her crime by lying in sin with one who belongs to her own gender. And a lowly maid at that! Despite knowing the Quran has explicitly forbidden sinful relationships in acts of *zina* involving *liwat* and *sihaq*, ever since the people of Lot provoked the wrath of God with their sinful and perverted acts.'

'The holy book has also explicitly forbidden sinful and perverted acts such as murder, tyranny and parricide!'

Muhammad was taken aback by the pent-up fury that exploded out of her.

'*Bismillah al-Rahman, al-Rahim*, Allah of the boundless compassion would never confuse the human need for genuine affection and intimacy with evil acts of degeneracy and debauchery. My conscience is clear and I will meet my maker with my head held high. I wonder if you can do the same when your time is up, having murdered your father, butchered your subjects on callous whims, and reduced them to poverty with your foolish pride and the infinite stupidity of your schemes!'

Muhammad clenched his fists, appalled by her audacity. 'How dare you address your Sultan and husband thus? You will regret having taken advantage of my kindness.'

'Your kindness?' She laughed out loud. 'I wept on the day my husband was killed. And not a day has passed since, when I haven't wished that it was you who had died instead! You have never bothered to secure my consent—I, who am your father's wife and your stepmother. You have degraded me and forced dishonour upon me. It is you who has sinned against God and man, and it is the reason your reign is cursed. It is why failure follows you doggedly, no matter where you go. It is why everything you touch turns to dust. It is why a river of blood flows through your empire. It is why you will go to your death drowning in the blood of the innocent!'

'I am not afraid of death.' He repeated Saira's words, but unlike her, he actually meant them. 'And mine will be an honourable one. I will not be stoned to death for being an adulterous whore. And you clearly had no trouble setting your lofty principles aside to enjoy the many privileges of wedding and bedding two Sultans in a row.'

She quailed on hearing the nature of her punishment, though she knew fully well what she had risked. But now her courage began to fail, and the tears flowed freely down her cheeks. Even so, she was defiant. 'What is it you say after every one of your colossal blunders? Even if I could go back in time, I would do it all over again . . . Well, so would I.'

'I wouldn't throw caution to the winds just yet if I were you, Saira. Perhaps you have forgotten that some among the living still have need of you. I have no doubt poor Masud would appreciate it if his mother doesn't say things that might cause him immense pain . . .'

'Monster! Tyrant! You wouldn't dare . . .' she shrieked and threw herself at him, but his personal guard materialized at once and hauled her back, forcing Saira to her knees as they awaited his command. Muhammad looked at her. She was no longer magnificent, with tears and snot dripping down her chin. Her eyes were those of a cornered animal, and the stink of her shame and fear made his gorge rise. It was hard to believe that this was the woman who had made him lose his head and heart so completely.

'There is no need to make such a scene, dearly beloved,' he said as she stopped struggling against the iron grip of his guards, wracked by an intense bout of weeping. 'Despite my reputation for cruelty, I certainly wouldn't harm your innocent son. And it saddens me that even now you don't know that I could never bring myself to hurt you, even if my own life depended on it. Not even when you put the cuckold's horns upon my head and humiliate me in front of my subjects. All I have ever wanted is for you to be happy.'

Saira lowered her head and wouldn't look at him, wary and uncertain about her fate.

'Besides, if I had really wanted to be cruel, I would have made you watch as Najib and his helpers devoted their entire attention to making your precious maid well and truly sorry for leading you astray.' Muhammad watched as she wrenched her arms free with sudden vehemence, only to bury her face in her hands and blubber incoherently. 'She won't be doing anything wicked any more, I am afraid. On my instructions, Najib had his Hindu attendants scrape what remained of her and feed it all to the vile pigs that roam the streets. Now that the swine have ingested her stinking soul, the gates of paradise will be forever barred to her. I'll admit that the final touch was a tad cruel but there are consequences to stealing what belongs to the Sultan.'

Saira was swaying now, moaning and whimpering. Next to nothing remained of the fiery, feisty woman who had given him the sharp edge of her tongue mere moments ago. 'I had to punish her for putting the Sultan's beloved in the lamentable position of having a Kazi accuse her of adultery and other unnatural acts. You see that, don't you? I think you will agree that the bitch got what she deserved.'

She nodded mutely and wiped her tears away. Muhammad waited patiently for her to spit out the words he needed to hear. 'The b . . . bitch got what she deserved.' She choked on the words but got them out.

'I am so glad that you are finally being sensible. Do you know my greatest desire?' he asked her and she sniffled in response. 'I want nothing more than for things to go back to the way they were. When you pretended you loved me and I was blissfully ignorant of your true feelings, living only to make you smile. Would I also be incorrect in assuming that it is something you would desire too?'

Saira nodded again, unable to articulate a coherent response. She was still wary but there was faint hope on her face as she contemplated the royal pardon dangling in front of her. Deep down she knew that it was too much to hope for but she desperately needed to believe she would be spared. If only for poor Masud's sake. In his veins ran the blood of Tughlaq and Khalji. He would always be a threat to the one who sat on the throne, and without her to protect him . . .

Muhammad watched in silence as myriad expressions flooded her features. She was thinking of Masud, he knew. Her love for life and the unwillingness to let go, despite the foolish claim that she was not afraid to die, was pathetically obvious. Muhammad wondered why she had not thought about all these things when she fell into bed with the scum who cleaned out the chamber pots. He felt his temper flare as images of her making passionate love to another assaulted his senses.

Saira, meanwhile, had managed to get a hold of herself, and she spoke up hesitantly. 'I did not mean to hurt you or say all those dreadful things . . .' She gulped. 'It was wrong of me and I beg your forgiveness.'

She could not go on. Her pride would not allow her to grovel at his feet. Muhammad helped her to her feet and drew her close to his chest. He breathed in her scent deeply and felt the hope burgeon in her chest. They remained that way for a long moment. He waited for her to relax in his arms before he hurled her away from him, allowing the adulterous whore to feel the full extent of his wrath. She hit the floor with a thud, surprise and pain writ large on her face.

'Drag her to the Kazi in chains,' he ordered the guards. 'He will read out the sordid crimes she has confessed to and pass the sentence. Tell Najib that her punishment must be carried out by sundown. Let her be dragged to the town square so everyone can watch as she is stoned to death. The pigs shall feast on her remains. That way, she will be reunited with her lover in the fires of hell.

Never let it be said of Sultan Muhammad bin Tughlaq that he was cruel enough to come between two lovers.'

'Please! Not that!' she shrieked, the last of her pride and strength gone along with the dregs of hope. 'For the love—' He did not bother to hear her out but signalled to his guards and they dragged her out of his sight.

4

It felt good to be astride a horse again. Muhammad's mount was a magnificent war charger, massive, spirited and intelligent, obedient to his every command. A contingent of his crack troops rode behind him, and he dug his heels into the flanks as he led the charge across the dusty plains of the disaster zone that was the Doab. Muhammad had never been afraid to take the lead, and his troops were heartened because they never had to take risks he hadn't braved first. You could say what you wished about Sultan Muhammad bin Tughlaq, but he was no coward. And he had no qualms about doing his own dirty work.

The air was filled with sounds of the hunt, punctuated with the roaring of the troops, the screaming of their victims, and the song of ringing steel as the rebels were cut down mercilessly. There was the distinctive, metallic tang of blood in the air, and Muhammad could sense the excitement of his men. It always amazed him how the scent or sight of blood filled even the gentlest of souls with predatory bloodlust.

Muhammad remembered the first time he had seen a man die before his eyes. It was during Mubarak Shah's reign. They tied him spread-eagled between four horses facing in different directions and a large crowd had gathered to watch the proceedings.

'God have mercy! Spare him!' somebody sobbed.

'Kill the bastard!'

'Rip him apart!' other voices screamed in unison, and the mood had swung just like that. Dozens roared for blood, drowning out the sounds of sobbing and keening. When the command was given, the riders charged and the man was literally torn to pieces. At first, there had been no blood, and then all of a sudden blood spurted explosively through severed and twitching limbs.

Muhammad remembered how the detached leg had kicked spasmodically and how the man's eyes had been open in his head while portions of his body lay separately. There had been unspeakable agony in those eyes which swivelled wildly before they closed forever. His gorge had risen at the sight and he had been revolted. Yet a part of him had been filled with savage glee. Muhammad was reminded of the incident sometimes when they brought in people who faced execution in fetters. He looked back on it now, feeling the familiar, welcome surge of bloodlust.

The Sultan's orders had been clear. 'You shall show no mercy to the treacherous swine who dared to defy their emperor! A quick death is a lot more than they deserve.'

Unfortunately for the rebels, they had very little to offer by way of resistance, especially when confronted with the vengeful wrath of the Sultan. Their ringleaders, who at least had some military experience from their training for the Khorasan expedition, had organized them into a semblance of fighting units. When they were rounded up, the emperor punished what he viewed as their betrayal with customary severity. They had been skinned alive, while their weapons were melted down and poured over their open wounds. They went to their deaths screaming. But the Sultan wasn't quite finished and many more would pay.

Defenceless as most of the rebels were, Muhammad was in no mood to spare them. Not after what they had done. He had given the province of the Doab much leeway and lavished his benevolence and generosity upon the citizens. They had repaid his kindness with treachery and would pay for it with their blood.

Swords rose high in the air and fell with merry abandon as more and more marked for death were trod under the flying hoofs and ground into the dust. Muhammad ignored the arms raised in supplication, cutting them all down without discrimination. Some hefted their axes futilely. It did them no good.

His sword ripped open a human thigh and the bearded man gazed at it with comical horror. Muhammad knew that he would bleed to death in seconds. As for him, he hadn't felt this invigorated in a long time. It was just as the yogis had told him during their sessions together.

'Bhumi Devi, the Earth mother, periodically demands the blood of her children when their numbers and sinful activities become too much for her to bear. The champions enlisted in her cause use the powers at their disposal to bring about death and destruction to clear some much-needed space for themselves as well as others who have been chosen by a higher power to carry on living.'

'That is an interesting way to look at it,' Muhammad had replied, 'though I am not sure that I can agree. My will is my own and I am not a puppet whose strings are pulled by my God or yours. I stand by my actions, and when the time comes to answer for them, I will do so secure in my moral integrity.'

The yogis had smiled at him, their expressions tinged with pity.

'Control is an illusion, and it is only by letting go that you can become the master of your destiny.' Such mumbo-jumbo amused him but he did agree that for his empire to thrive the wretched and worthless deserved to be culled from it. As the emperor, it was a duty which he tried to fulfil without bringing unnecessary emotions or personal prejudice into it.

Death was meted out only to those among his subjects who had well and truly deserved it. It was an exhilarating moment of elucidation. Arrows whistled through the air, burying themselves into the scurrying rodents, felling dozens at one time. Muhammad sliced off a man's head with a powerful double-handed stroke, the impact of which left his shoulders throbbing and shaking.

Those who were still alive had retreated deep into the woods. They were on foot and it wasn't difficult to chase them down.

But some of the vermin had gotten away and Muhammad was determined not to let them escape their misdeeds.

'Smoke them out!' he bellowed. 'Not a single rebel must be allowed to get away!'

His men hastened to do his bidding. Gathering piles of wood, they doused them with oil and set them alight. Muhammad watched as the flames rose higher and higher, the thick pall of smoke bellowing outwards with the deadly intent of avenging angels, stinging their eyes and driving them back. The searing heat and suffocating fumes flushed the runaway rebels from their hiding holes and straight into the arms of the soldiers who awaited them.

Some were on fire and performed a macabre shrieking dance. As they burned, the smell of roasted flesh assailed their nostrils. The ones who were unscathed but sputtering and crawling on their knees were quickly executed by the soldiers.

The rebellion of the Doab ended just as the flames died down. Muhammad was pleased it was all over. He had given orders that the women, children, old and infirm were to be spared and taken to Dilli to one of those homes run by his mother. After all, he was not a coldblooded killer who killed for the pleasure of it. As the emperor, it was merely his prerogative to decide who lived and who died, depending on the merits or demerits of their actions.

Before storming the Doab region, Muhammad would have liked a respite from his duties to mourn the loss of Saira and come to terms with his anger. How could she have allowed herself to risk the scandal, humiliation and death, all for an illicit union? Why did she have to get caught and cause him so much pain? Why hadn't she understood that all he had wanted was for her to not judge him as harshly as he judged himself? That with her by his side he had felt less lonely even though he had always been aware that all he ever would have was his own self, and he wanted no part of himself? Why had she loathed his touch without caring that she was the only one who could arouse desire in him? And more importantly, how could he still love and miss her so much? But he did not have the time or luxury to mourn.

He had been busy ever since he had received reports of what was happening on the Doab, leading expeditions to and crushing insurrections at Baran, Dalmau and Kanauj. Now that he had stamped out the resistance, he looked forward to returning to Dilli and Daulatabad. Hopefully, he could look forward to a period of golden peace. God knew he had earned it.

They were camped near the Ganga, some 80 kilometres from Dilli, where he had erected a residence for himself that he called Swarga Dhar, verily the gateway to heaven. Muhammad had a bit of a soft spot for the river Goddess. He liked cooling off in her waters and divesting himself of the blood, dust and grime that clung to him like a second skin. He envied all those who lived close to her banks, where they were far from the dust and heat, trouble and turmoil of the city. It was not surprising that she was dear not just to the Hindus but to all the people in his realm. Every time he emerged from her depths, he felt like a new man.

The vast tract of land between the rivers Ganga and Sutlej, hemmed in by the Siwalik range in the north and the Rajputana region in the south, extending all the way to Kanauj, had always been a bit of a problem area. It was a fertile region and he had taken special interest, hoping that the Doab would become the food basket of the empire as well as a rich and prosperous domain.

When he had toured the land at the beginning of his reign, he had realized it was going to be an uphill task. For time seemed to have come to a standstill in the villages that dotted these plains. There was little sign of modernity, and nobody had the remotest interest in doing anything but the things that had always been done for hundreds of years. People lived in their little mud- and dried-dung-plastered huts with extended families, though these hovels were unfit for pigs and definitely unsuitable for civilized human beings.

There was no attempt to maintain sanitary conditions, dispose of trash and develop adequate medical facilities or a system for obtaining clean water. People made do with a few wells, though the water was brackish and the carcasses of pigeons or frogs could occasionally be seen floating on the surface.

There were no towering monuments or elaborate structures, but an abundance of humble shrines, consecrated to obscure local deities. Since his Hindu subjects couldn't possibly keep track of the thirty-three crore gods in their pantheon, they wisely picked their favourites and tried not to bother about the rest. The villagers knew little about the world outside and weren't particularly curious. The majority of these people lived and died without ever finding cause to venture away from their homes and farms.

Farming was their main source of livelihood, and they raised crops like wheat, corn, barley and some indigenous vegetable and fruit varieties. However, their system was entirely haphazard, and the illiterate farmers seemed to be merely going through the motions, content to place their faith in their remote gods and hope for the best.

They used ancient equipment and sickly beasts of burden. The sight of the farmers using their rickety wooden ploughs and the puny buffaloes that were used to pull them was a depressing one. The yield per acre was abysmal and absolutely no effort was made to improve it.

The farmers worked their own fields, which were tiny parcels of land. The tenants of rich landowners got marginally better results. These peasants were entirely at the mercy of the elements. They prayed fervently for rain, which was needed for the parched land, but during monsoons and floods their pathetic huts were washed away along with their paltry possessions. If rainfall was scarce, there would be droughts and famines. The crops were also susceptible to attacks by pests and locusts, which could consume the entire yield.

Rather than work on how best to divert water from the rivers and wells to their fields, the morons embraced their superstitious beliefs with foolish fervour. They regularly consulted with astrologers, witch doctors and charlatans who encouraged them to part with what little money they had and advised them to perform elaborate pujas, chant mantras, wear amulets and charms or procure potions made with saliva and chicken blood to sprinkle in a perfect circle around their dwellings.

In difficult times, when money was tight but there were taxes to be paid, many mouths to feed, sick children to be taken to local fraudulent physicians, marriages to be celebrated and funerals to be conducted, the farmers grew desperate and borrowed heavily from moneylenders who charged usurious rates of interest and had no qualms about bleeding the wretches dry.

But despite their plight, the average farmer had a dozen children with more on the way. Muhammad wished there was some way for him to stop them from breeding like rabbits.

Even when all these obstacles were somehow overcome and the farmers managed a bumper harvest, they still suffered from the fluctuating market prices and had to sell the surplus crops at ridiculously low prices or watch them remain unsold till they rotted away. Muhammad had done whatever he could to help this sorry lot, though he couldn't help wishing that his subjects would do more to help themselves rather than look to God or their emperor.

It had been his intention to cultivate vast tracts of land that lay fallow in the Doab region. He had even started a department of agriculture, the Diwan-i-kohi, and stationed experts on growing crops as well as revenue officials to educate and work with the cultivators. The Sultan had invested over 70 lakh tankas in the enterprise. It was too late before he realized that the money might as well have been flushed, along with the contents of his chamber pots, thanks to the ceaseless corruption in his administration.

He had also sought to help them supplement their incomes by encouraging weaving and raising of livestock. He provided funds for them to buy cows, chickens and lambs so they would have a steady income by selling the milk and eggs, and even encouraged them to rear hawks and falcons to be sold to the nobles for their preferred pastimes. But the idiots, flush with newfound wealth, had frittered it all away.

While recruiting troops for the Khorasan expedition, the Sultan had even offered generous incentives for them to join the army, educate themselves and travel around the empire. In addition to all of this, he had recused them from taxes for a while.

Nearly all his efforts had come to nought, and the Doab had become a simmering cauldron of endless conflict leading to open rebellion. Ungrateful wretches! All the money he had sunk into the region had been wasted, stolen by the unscrupulous rascals at the Diwan-i-Kohi, who hadn't bothered to cultivate the land or invest in new equipment to make the lot of the farmers easier.

Muhammad had the corrupt officials arrested and marched naked to Dilli with their wrists pinioned behind their backs and feet in chains. Crowds gathered along the way to watch the miscreants, hurling filth and stones at them. On reaching the fortress, he had them suspended upside down from the battlements with nails hammered into their ears and feet. They were left like that to die as the crows plucked out their eyeballs and tore out strips of their flesh.[12]

'If that doesn't curtail corruption and thievery, I don't know what will, sire!' Ahmad had remarked as they looked up at the gory sight.

The situation in the Doab continued to worsen, though. After the disaster with Qarachil and the token currency, Muhammad needed to replenish his treasury and on the recommendation of the central ministry, the Diwan-i-vizarat, he increased taxation. He thought it was fair since it was less than what Alauddin Khalji had demanded and only slightly more than the percentage fixed by his father.

In the Doab, he reintroduced taxes, and the people were furious at having their former concessions taken away from them. They felt that their Sultan was squeezing them so that he could carry on with his frivolous spending and exorbitant lifestyle. Tax collectors feared his wrath if they failed to hand over the revenue dues, and they used harsh measures to force the peasants to pay.

Things came to a head when many of the disgruntled troops who had been laid off after the Khorasan expedition used their military training to organize themselves into rebel outfits, riled up the farmers, and murdered the collectors and magistrates. Muhammad had sent his centurions to deal with them, but the Amiran-i-sadah were defeated and cut to pieces by the rebel army. Fearing the Sultan's retribution, they set fire to the crops and scurried into hiding in Baran and Dalmau.

In Dalmau, they slew Mubarak Malik, the Sultan's own brother, and nailed his body upside down to the city gate, mimicking the Sultan's actions. When Muhammad and his troops arrived after flushing the rebels out of hiding in Baran, they were confronted with the horrendous sight of Mubarak Malik. Or what remained of him. The blood had rushed to his extremities and left them engorged. His bulging belly rested on his chest. His genitals and his tongue had been lopped off.

Molten rage erupted out of the Sultan when confronted with his brother's mutilated remains. Muhammad and Mubarak had never been particularly close, and yet, the Sultan mourned his loss. Like Bahram, he had done what was asked of him in silence, never asking for anything more than what was offered. More importantly, he hadn't plotted and schemed to take the throne from him that Muhammad knew of.

Muhammad had sworn to avenge his brother's memory and he had. But the massacre of the rebels gave him no satisfaction. All his brothers with the exception of Masud were gone. He wished he had got to know Bahram and Mubarak better. He wished he had not mistrusted them. He wished he could have kept them safe. He wished and he wished before finally giving it all up as yet another exercise in futility.

5

Muhammad wasn't a fool. He knew the people's discontent against him was on the rise and that his hold over the empire was weakening. They were now calling him Kuni Muhammad, the bloody emperor. It didn't help that the very elements seemed to be conspiring against him. The drought, which was the worst in living memory, had begun sometime in the year 1334, and they had no way of knowing that it would persist for nearly seven years with little or no relief, leaving Dilli and almost the entire northern provinces reeling.

When the rains failed, so did the crops. The land became parched, baked into hard clay by the fury of the sun, before it cracked and lay in ruins, utterly unfit for civilization. Soon the soil turned to dust and the hot, dry winds blew it around, making sport with the withered hopes of the farmers. Gaunt and emaciated, they stared listlessly at the destruction that was ahead of them.

The rivers that watered the plains were temperamental creatures who could wash away entire villages and towns but in the scorching climate they had dwindled to a mere trickle. The wells had dried up completely, carrying little more than the bleached scales, bones and withered carcasses of the little creatures that had been their former inhabitants.

Famine followed close on the heels of drought, bringing untold misery in its wake. The Sultan's people came to know the true meaning of starvation, and it was not a fate they would wish on their worst enemies.

Entire flocks and herds died, the flesh having melted away from the bones, making them unfit for consumption, though it didn't stop the people from cracking the bones, chewing and sucking on them in the vain hope of nourishment. Food shortage was reported in all the northern provinces. Thousands were starving. In some places, the situation was so bad people were reduced to eating grass and leaves. Beggars prowled the streets begging for a handful of rice. Emaciated mothers clutching their infants flung themselves on the ground, beseeching passers-by for a bite to eat.

Only the vultures were growing fat. Jackals and dogs roamed boldly among the nearly dead and had been known to attack skeletal children. As the corpses started to pile up, the burning ghats by the sides of the rivers found themselves unequal to the task, and bodies were just dumped into the shrinking water reservoirs. More bodies were simply abandoned. Disease and infection were rampant, compounding their misery.

The wealthy obtained grain from the unaffected parts of the empire and hoarded it illegally, contributing to the grotesquely inflated prices of rice and other foodstuffs. Within their comfortable cocoons, they mourned the privations they were made to endure and were content to sit back and condemn the inaction of the Sultan.

'The sheer folly of the Sultan and his failure to have foreseen and forestalled this natural disaster defies belief!'

'These bloody beggars who gather at the entrance of our homes are a wretched nuisance!'

'I agree! They are filthy and carry disease. The Sultan should send his troops to cleanse the land of them!'

'This entire business is such an inconvenience. I have had to double the guards around my orchards and groves. Soon I will have to hire guards to keep an eye on the guards if this continues.'

Mercifully, Muhammad had little time for their nonsense as he sprang into action, pouring all the effort and resources he could muster to provide relief for his people. Grains were brought in from the south through Daulatabad and Oudh, whose governor, Ain-ul-Mulk, responded to the Sultan's order immediately. Muhammad's relay teams rose to the occasion magnificently, working tirelessly to transport lifesaving provisions with speed and efficiency to the distant reaches of the realm. Muhammad fuelled their enthusiasm with added incentives, bonuses and gifts of land.

Exhaustive measures were implemented in Dilli, the Doab, Malwa and the other drought-afflicted regions. Imperial officials were tasked with compiling registers with the names of his subjects from the affected areas, who were then allotted food, funds and other essentials that were to last them six months. The Sultan suspended the collection of land taxes and people breathed a sigh of relief, calling down the blessings of God on their sovereign. His subjects were also given loans to encourage them to obtain seeds, bullocks and all they would need to return to farming.

Many public kitchens were set up. The indefatigable Makhduma Jahan, despite her advanced years and failing health, worked harder than the lowliest slave to keep the droves who descended on her charitable institutions well-fed on soups, stews, rotis and vegetable and meat dishes from the royal kitchens. Khuda was happy to help as well, though she had her hands full with little Dawar Malik. 'Feeding beggars and hearing them sing my praises is a lot more entertaining than coping with a screaming brat who does little besides eat, sleep and poop. Nobody warned me that motherhood would be so noxious or that future Sultans could be so disgusting.'

Dear Khuda! How she made him laugh! Perhaps he would release that odious husband of hers from prison in a year or two. 'He can remain there for all I care,' Khuda had been dismissive. 'Husbands are even more annoying than babies. And unlike the latter, you can't fob him off to the hired help.'

His mother was too busy for such frivolous talk. Instead, she helped herself to funds he could ill-afford to spare from the imperial treasury to buy buildings at exorbitant prices. She equipped these to provide lodging and medical facilities for the wretched peasants who had thronged to Dilli.

'I have to make amends for the sins of my son,' she informed him snidely, though he had not said a word to protest her extravagances. Haniya had never liked Saira, and yet she seemed angered by her death. Fortunately, she did not give him the rough edge of her tongue.

Muhammad and Ahmad closely monitored the operations to prevent the supplies from being rerouted to undeserving pockets. Justice was delivered swiftly and mercilessly to those tempted to take advantage of the crisis to enrich themselves. Profiteers and petty thieves who preyed on the populace were trod underfoot by his war elephants and their belongings confiscated to be used in relief efforts.

Nobles were nudged towards philanthropic activities after some were caught feasting and holding banquets, and were publicly subjected to a thousand lashes of the whip as well as made to pay crippling penalties.

All of a sudden, the Sultan found himself in the warm sunshine of his subjects' approval. They cheered him on the streets and prayed for his health. Every time he rode out to check the supply trains with the imperial guard in tow, people gathered to bless him, prostrate themselves before him and call out words of lavish praise for his munificence.

Some even kissed the hems of his robe when he wandered into one of his mother's charity houses. Muhammad was not averse to the goodwill, but it bothered him when his subjects pooled their resources in extremely difficult times to build a monument in his name, even hiring a scribe to inscribe the following words:

'Muhammad Shah is the magnificent and magnanimous king of the whole world; in comparison to the waves of his heart the river found itself reduced to a drop.'

He had to admit it had a nice ring to it and was a welcome change from 'tyrant' and 'mad monarch'. Yet, he wished his people would be pragmatists like himself and practice a little moderation, without swinging between the extreme emotions of hate and love, which made them do foolish things like clamour for his death or build him monuments they couldn't really afford.

The Khwaja Ahmad was a pragmatist, too, and had this alone to say of his newfound popularity. 'The enmity of the nobility which you insist on provoking far outweighs the fickle approval of the commoners. Besides, the mood of the mob usually melts away, while the malice of the mighty has the backing of money to make it grow like a malignant tumour . . .

'And the nobility dare not forget they enjoy the privileges of birth only thanks to the munificence of their Sultan. If they do, it would be most unwise of them.'

Muhammad forgave Ahmad his curmudgeonly demeanour. After all, he had lost his good right hand on account of the Sultan. Najib, better known as the Sag-al-Sultan, though he had always been the grand Vizier's man and his loyal lieutenant, had come to the end of a brilliant career and life somewhat abruptly. It had been a bloody business, but had a certain poetic justice to it. Even his mother had approved.

'I had a good mind to have that vile creature poisoned myself,' Haniya muttered with uncharacteristic vehemence, 'for his role in Saira's death. It is good you had the sense to put down that rabid dog.'

'Najib carried his dark secrets with him to the grave.' Muhammad tugged at his beard restlessly. 'He never did reveal why he put together the evidence against her and handed it over to the Kazi. Nor did he confess the full extent of his misdeeds or the names of others who most certainly were involved.'

Muhammad had visited him shortly before the end. He still remembered the stench as he entered the inner apartment of Najib's own torture chambers. The walls were spattered with blood and gore. His own assistant had torn out the hair on his head and beard by the roots and removed most of his scalp. Only stumps remained where his thighs and hands ought to have been.

He was still alive, though, and greeted the Sultan respectfully, almost as if they were merely discussing affairs of state on an average day. 'Why did you do it? And on whose orders were you acting?' Muhammad asked him coldly.

'I have taken many confessions in this room and discovered that there is little to tell the truth from the lie, and it doesn't matter in the least.' Despite his reduced circumstances, he still had much of the swagger and morally ambiguous attitude that had characterized him in life.

'That is not an answer. If you were to tell me what I need to know, I might be persuaded to give you a quick death.'

'If my profession has taught me anything, it is that death hurts less than the infliction of pain or the wounding of others. It had been my duty to mete out all three to others. Now that it is my turn, I see no reason to flinch or be afraid.'

It was hard to ascertain if the sadistic brute was a fool, a brave man or a raving lunatic. Either way, it was hard to pity or respect him. And if ever a man deserved punishment, it was this one. He would die slowly, allowed to sustain himself on bits and pieces of his own flesh and drink his own blood till his beastly heart stopped beating. Muhammad walked away from him without a backward glance.

Haniya was looking at him with a mixture of pity and irritation. 'Isn't it obvious? Those in close proximity to the Sultan run the dual risk of gaining or losing everything. Some feel that a Sultan's most important duty is to bear an heir, and they see nothing wrong with removing all impediments to this most sacred task. Which is why you were urged to marry, father a son or at least adopt one.

'Saira, of course, was blamed for your lapse, and if that weren't enough to make people plot her ruin, she was stupid enough to provide them with an excuse. Not that I blame her in the least. You need not have played into their hands and sacrificed that which you held so dear, making yourself even more miserable.'

Muhammad had nothing to say to that. Haniya softened. 'It is done, and you will do well not to drive yourself to distraction by dwelling on it obsessively, the way you have in the past. The only thing I am curious about is why you saw fit to spare the Khwaja Jahan, when you took such a harsh stand against his toady . . .'

He seldom bothered with explanations. As a Sultan, he was under no obligation to explain his actions to his underlings. But this was his mother. Besides, this whole business was weighing on him, simply because unlike the others he had lost to death, Saira steadfastly refused to speak to him, adamantly cold and unyielding, just as she had been while alive. As his mother pointed out, though, who could blame her?

'I daresay between Ahmad and Najib they have woven a fine tapestry of deceit, extortion, bribery and corruption . . .' he began thoughtfully, 'through shadowy dealings that are a little too convoluted for even me to fully unravel. They have amassed a fortune that in all likelihood surpasses mine, taken possession of enormous tracts of prime land and buried ownership beneath an avalanche of deeds and obscure legalese.

'Ahmad is the holder of a thousand dark secrets and guilty of shadowy deeds. He did well to distance himself from the unsavoury elements of his worst enterprises, which was why Najib took the fall for gathering the evidence of Saira's guilt and handing it over to the Kazi. But unlike the others who provided me with less than exemplary service while striving to rob me blind, Ahmad has always obeyed my instructions and fulfilled his duties and obligations. He may have helped himself, but he has helped his emperor and empire as well. And as Najib told me, there are worse things for the living than death. I suppose I spared him so that we can see things through to the bitter end.'

'I am not sure I understand.' Haniya looked bemused. 'But I am glad that you didn't act with your customary haste and recklessness.

By ridding yourself of the hound, you have muzzled the master. He will be careful to repay you with stellar service.'

She took a quavering breath. 'There, that's enough of that. You did well to put your heart and soul into helping your subjects during a time of dire need. Deeds of genuine kindness outweigh the worst acts of evil, and it is the only true reason for living.'

'She means she is proud of you, though more often than not you have disgraced your father's memory,' Abu whispered helpfully into his ear.

Haniya coughed and reached out for his hand. 'I have always been proud of you. My Jauna is a good boy and nothing you have done or are going to do is ever going to change that.'

Muhammad squeezed her hand in response. Eloquent though he always had been, he couldn't possibly find the words to tell her what her words meant to him. For once, even Abu was speechless.

6

Muhammad was on the march with his troops again. He wished he could have remained in Swarga Dhar and the cool embrace of the Ganga as they went on with relief efforts, hoping the interminable drought would end. However, insurrection had reared its ugly head yet again in the form of traitors and had been dealt with swiftly, but the situation in the far south had worsened and warranted his personal attention.

The traitor Sayyid Ahsan had declared the independence of the districts of Madurai, Tirunelveli, Ramanathapuram, Pudukottai and Tiruchirapalli from his empire and had styled himself as the shah of the south. Most of his generals could not even pronounce the names and simply referred to the southernmost province as the Ma'bar. Muhammad's response had been instantaneous. He sent a detachment of his troops trained for the Khorasan expedition to deal with Ahsan, but the ingrates had been persuaded to throw in their lot with the usurper by the thrice-cursed Orthodox Sunnis in pursuance of their own spiteful vendetta against him. Meanwhile, Ahsan's brother Ibrahim Sayyid had raised the standard of rebellion in Hansi.

The Sultan waited for the surge of anger that usually blinded him to reason. But this time, he saw all too clearly. His empire had taken one blow too many and it was bleeding. Sensing weakness and the whiff of opportunities, his enemies were circling. As they rode to battle, Muhammad saw the depredations of drought and detritus of rebellions fought and suppressed. Despair, his worst enemy, drew close, but the Sultan drove it back with all the determination he could muster.

At this critical juncture, maintaining his hold on Madurai would be difficult, but he owed it to himself to try. He would fight Ahsan Shah and Ahmad would march against Ibrahim. If God was kind, the brothers would be hauled up for an audience with him, minus their heads and grasping hands.

Ahsan Shah had made quite the speech, he was told, while proclaiming his independence. 'The Sultan cares little for those of us who live in the south. He believes himself superior to us, and his northern subjects follow his callous example. They are driven by greed and seek to bleed us of our natural and financial resources. They seek to stamp out the proud culture and heritage of the glorious south. We will no longer stand for this treatment, we will throw off the yoke of tyranny and march forward into a glorious future of our own making!'

Of course, it was a lot of political claptrap and merely an excuse, for Ahsan spoke not a word of the Tamil language and knew even less than Muhammad about the people in the deep south or their customs. Having seen an opportunity, he had simply seized it. Muhammad wished he had followed through on his plan to visit Madurai and stay there for a brief spell after his stint at Daulatabad.

He had wanted to familiarize himself with southerners, their culture, temples, festivals and language, of which he had learned they were most proud. He had wanted to sample their cuisine, which he was told wasn't as spicy as Telangana's but quite tasty. They were seafarers and had travelled to distant lands to trade in salt, silks and spices. He had even conversed with one of the dark-skinned Tamils with the help of an interpreter who had made him a gift of the commodities he traded, in addition to a beautiful casket of precious stones and an exquisitely sculpted idol of a Goddess with bountiful breasts.

Muhammad had asked about the demand for common salt and the trader had been eager to explain. 'This is sea salt and it is very much in demand wherever we Tamils travel. You will find that food seasoned with it can prevent as well as cure goitre.' Muhammad had been suitably impressed.

The man had told him that Madurai was famous for its jasmine flowers, a river named something he couldn't quite pronounce, and steamed rice cakes. And he definitely remembered a Goddess who was the guardian of the city. The Tamilian had felt it would interest the Sultan to know that she had three breasts and that the third one fell off at the end of his convoluted story. Muhammad had made a note then to travel south and make the people feel less removed from the rest of his empire, but there simply hadn't been time. Now he had no choice but to handle this unpleasant business.

Perhaps once Ahsan Shan had been crushed, he would make it a point to try those rice cakes with lentil gravy or even the deep fried minced-meat balls the region was famed for.

Of course, there was more to this rebellion than met the eye, but he would deal with it in good time. In the meantime, they marched, their discomfort growing by the minute. The heat was unbearable, leaving them in a torment of thirst till their lips cracked. Muhammad let his men rest during the hottest parts of the day, and they resumed the march in the evenings and through a good part of the night.

None of them were in peak physical condition following the ravages of drought and famine that had beset the land, but Muhammad was determined to do what he could to build up the strength and morale of his men. He ordered that they be given double rations, and organized archery competitions, running races, sword fights, wrestling and horse-racing, distributing valuable presents to the winners. His men were veterans inured to discomfort and punishing conditions, and Muhammad had every confidence that they would prevail.

And they would have prevailed if it hadn't been for the deadly epidemic that swept through their ranks like a fire, leaving destruction in its wake. The disease afflicted them with the dreaded purging of bleeding bowels that left them too weak to get up, let alone march across a great distance and wage war.

Initially, Muhammad had hoped it was simply an outbreak of diarrhoea, but he was quickly disabused of the notion when his men succumbed quickly and in alarming numbers. Sanitary conditions worsened once the men found it impossible to walk the distance to the latrine pits, soiling themselves where they lay, too weak to clean themselves or fend off the fat flies that had materialized out of nowhere and landed on every exposed inch of skin. Their incessant buzzing was a torment that was as bad as the thirst.

The sickest among them lay doubled up in pain, turning their heads sideways to vomit or hugging their knees to their chests as their bladders and bowels were voided noisily and painfully. Wracked with fever, cramps and insatiable thirst, they burned and shivered, in mortal torment as their eyes turned dull, watery and unseeing. Eventually, they sank into unconsciousness and never woke up.

Dying men dug graves to bury the dead before dying themselves. Muhammad commanded his physicians to do what they could, but their efforts were futile, and most succumbed to the epidemic themselves. 'It is the heat and lack of hygiene that breeds this disease,' said Wasim, the royal physician who alone looked cool and unruffled. 'Once it has taken hold, the epidemic spreads easily enough. Think about it, sire, a travelling army has little access to fresh, clean water, and food is prepared with dirty, unwashed hands by an oaf who has just relieved himself. I can't be sure, but even the flies who flit from one body to the next spread the taint.'

'Can your medicines help?' Muhammad had enquired impatiently. 'And what is to be done to tackle the situation? If this disease is not checked immediately, every man in my army will be dead and drowned in his own shit. Not even Ahsan Shah and the dreadful natural calamities that have besieged us have caused damage on this scale. Something needs to done, and it needs to be done sooner rather than later.'

'If the disease is left unchecked, it will destroy not only your majesty's army but will spread from here to Ma'bar and destroy it, besides the rest of your empire and this land as well. In fact, it could theoretically destroy the entire world.'

Ignoring the Sultan's glare, Wasim examined his own fingernails. Every time the Ulama accused him of believing he was God, Muhammad wondered if they had ever met a typical physician with the aggrandized airs and graces they gave themselves.

'Cleanliness is key, sire,' Wasim lectured him as if he were explaining the obvious to a child. 'The bodies will have to be burned and not left where they are. Only the funerary smoke will deter the flies. Water must be boiled before it is drunk. Food must be prepared only using utensils that have been cleaned and placed in boiling water.'

'Is there hope or is everyone going to die?' Muhammad asked him.

'Some always survive these things, sire, the very young, the old and infirm, the extremely useless, sometimes a few good men,' he was told matter-of-factly. 'I will survive and so will you, since I will be taking care of you. Now, sire, if the condition of your stools are any indication, and they are, the disease has taken a hold of you. It is because you ignored my recommendation and insisted on overseeing your men yourself. You must confine yourself immediately and place yourself entirely in my care.'

'I have never felt better in my entire life!' Muhammad insisted, hoping that if he ignored the ominous symptoms they would go away. His physician sniffed disapprovingly. Soon enough, Muhammad was taken seriously ill at Bidar in the Telangana region and he lay thrashing in a delirium while Wasim attended to him. They were rubbing his abdomen and limbs with heated castor oil, forcing soups and fluids down his throat and making him swallow a pill that was crushed and mixed with honey every two hours. But the Sultan was sinking.

Muhammad lay empty and depleted, feeling his strength and very life force ebb and flow. Voices seemed to address him from a great distance and he strained to hear the words that throbbed with urgency over the clamouring in his own head and the pounding of his heart. Shapes and incoherent forms emerged from the darkness around him as he fought the dizziness and fatigue while his flesh burned.

He struggled to drown out the cacophony of the sounds of a raging battle, the blaring horns, pounding drums, clashing swords and whizzing arrows. He was in the very thick of the madness, using every one of the skills he had taught himself, to kill before he was killed. Every time he struck with his almighty blade of bronze, his victim's head flew off his shoulders. Blood fountained high above his head, and he was bathed in the scalding crimson tide as more and more decapitated heads thudded to the dusty ground.

Others rushed him with their swords, screaming abuse at him, their voices hoarse with hate, but he wouldn't retreat before their onslaught. Rather, he charged them in a ferocious rush, inflicting wounds, pain and death. Bronze rang against bronze as he fended off the attack, keeping his enemies at sword's length with ferocity. Again and again. His blade moved swift as thought and he marvelled at his own skill and boundless energy as the blows of his enemies proved entirely ineffectual.

Yet, they refused to give up. No matter how many of them he killed, replacements sprang up to fight him. He gritted his teeth. He wouldn't give up either. But soaked in perspiration, he felt himself tiring. There was a ringing in his head and every part of his body ached fiercely. The swordplay cost him a world of effort and it took everything he had to hold his blade aloft.

Sensing his weakness, they attacked in a relentless wave, knocking him off his feet, howling like wild animals that had brought down their prey ready for the feast. Relief washed over him and his grip loosened on his blade. It would feel good to let go and close his eyes.

Muhammad held on to the sword. Just a little longer. He wished they would end it, so the decision would be taken out of his hands. The exhaustion had seeped into his very soul and he barely had the will to go on. He was so weary; all he wanted was for it to end so that he could allow himself to sink to the depths of the ocean of blood. It was too hard to stay afloat! He couldn't do it any more. And yet he had to. For as long as he could. There was no one else.

So many mistakes. Too many mistakes to atone for. And yet he had to go on. He felt compelled to try. At the very least. For the sake of everyone, he had failed. For his own sake, before the despair proved too much. So he tried. To fend off the attacks, to get back on his feet and keep on fighting till it was all over. Only then could he lie down, shut his eyes and get some rest. Until then, he would fight.

When he came to, it wasn't to the beauteous countenance of a houri but the grim visage of Wasim, who had pulled back his eyelid to stare into his pupil. 'I told them it would work,' he told him with a grimace of self-satisfaction. 'Asafoetida, opium and black pepper when taken in the right proportions and administered using my method can bring a man back even from the brink of death.' He went on muttering, 'But if only you had listened to me, when I spoke about an ounce of prevention being worth more than a dozen cures, you wouldn't have come so dangerously close to shitting your life away.'

Muhammad thanked him, though he was tempted to have him throttled.

The Sultan recuperated in Daulatabad. They said it was divine will that he had survived, much to Wasim's outrage. The bulk of his army had been decimated. His generals and thousands of soldiers were dead. Meanwhile, as he lay incapacitated and the surviving soldiers huddled together in miserable groups, Ahsan Shah had struck coins and established what he called the Madurai Sultanate.

It was a bitter potion to swallow and Muhammad gagged on the taste. But there was no point wallowing in misery when the Sultan's work awaited. There was trouble afoot in Lahore and Bengal and he could not dally in Daulatabad. Muhammad sent for Qutlugh Khan, the governor. 'You will have to hold down the fort here. Once news of my illness spreads, there will be rumours of my impending death, and every opportunist will make his bid for power. It will also be your responsibility to bring Ahsan to his knees or make as much trouble for him as you possibly can!'

'I won't let you down, your majesty!' he replied fervently. Muhammad wished he could believe him. If he had a silver tanka for every time somebody said those words before letting him down, he would be able to remount his Khorasan expedition and leave for parts unknown. Alas! But it wasn't to be.

He promised himself that he would win his southernmost province back after rebuilding his army and sending for reinforcements to aid Qutlugh Khan, but something told him it was a lost cause.

Muhammad had received heartening news from Ahmad. The blackguard had somehow steered clear of epidemics and covered himself in the glory of a stupendous victory. Ibrahim had been defeated and killed, and the Khwaja Jahan sent his sovereign the pickled head of his late adversary to cheer him up.

Then he received dire news from Swarga Dhar. His mother was dying and it had been her desire to be taken to Tughlaqabad. Muhammad did not tarry a moment, though Wasim insisted that he was in no condition to make the journey back. Despite his weakened state, he rode like the wind to be by his mother's side.

Haniya was far gone. She did not even recognize her son, though she clutched his hand and held it close to her. 'Is there anything you can do for her?' Muhammad pleaded with the hakim. 'You did brag that you could bring a man back from the dead.' But Wasim could only shake his head in chagrined helplessness.

'She doesn't have long, sire. All I can do is make her comfortable and give her a drought to ease the passage to the other side.'

Muhammad cradled her head in his arms, refusing to leave her side. He hoped she knew that he was close in her weakened state, frail and weightless as a little bird. Khuda sat by his side and sang to their mother. He felt the last breath she drew as she left him for good. Slowly, and with infinite care, he placed his forehead on her lips. 'Goodbye, mother!' he breathed. Khuda sobbed gently by his side.

He knew that she had tarried as long as she could only for the sake of her hopeless firstborn. He was more grateful than he could say. Now she was by his father's side, which was where she had always wanted to be. Muhammad could not begrudge her that. So he buried Haniya in his father's mausoleum, and left her to rest in peace.

7

Muhammad asked them to bring the Moroccan traveller before him. Despite his fondness for Ibn Battuta, the Sultan had found it necessary to place him under armed guard at the luxurious house that had been turned over for his use. Muhammad looked forward to seeing him. Ibn Battuta was always amusing, even when he was disapproving. He could use the laughs after what felt like a lifetime of putting out political fires.

Even as he mourned the passing of his mother, Muhammad received word that Hulagu, one of the Mongol chieftains, had overthrown Malik Tatar, the governor of Lahore. The Khwaja Jahan had fought the rebel on the banks of the Ravi and slain him.

Truth be told, Muhammad's sympathies lay with the Mongol and others like him, or the new Muslims, as they were called. The orthodox sects hated them even more than the other infidels, if that were possible, having never forgiven Genghis Khan and his descendants the violent raids they had carried out in Hindustan.

Consequently, the Mongol converts were treated like dirt and Muhammad was convinced it was going to blow up in *his* face. They usually made up the front ranks in battle but were paid less than others in the same position and begrudged their paltry share of the war booty. Despite Muhammad's best efforts to treat them more fairly and his elevation of the deserving among them to higher posts, he had known it was only a matter of time before the Mongols retaliated.

'It is on the petty spite and foolishness of imbeciles that the fate of an empire depends,' he had remarked somewhat obliquely to Ahmad, who took inordinate pride in presenting him with the decapitated head of a slain enemy. 'Hulagu was a good man, Malik Tatar would have done well to make use of his talents, instead of alienating him.'

'Hulagu was a rash and reckless man who made his bid for power and lost. I do not share your sympathy for men like that, your highness!' Ahmad had replied.

Dwelling on it depressed him and Muhammad let his thoughts return to the man bitten by wanderlust. Battuta had left home at the age of twenty and had been travelling the world ever since: North Africa, Egypt, Arabia, Jerusalem, Damascus, Mecca, Medina, Khorasan, Anatolia and the lands of the Golden Horde.

The Moroccan was made welcome by his fellow kazis wherever he went and clearly had a taste for the good life. He had an easy manner about him and told the most exciting stories about his journeys through dangerous terrain, surviving shipwrecks and bandits, bragging about bedding and wedding the most beautiful and exotic women, sampling the finest vintage of wines, and his acquaintance with the most powerful kings in the known world.

Muhammad was fascinated by his inability to stay in one place too long and leave behind his accumulated wealth, wives and offspring behind without a backward glance, wild and free as a feather picked up by the wind, content to simply glide through life. Battuta did not speak Persian, so Muhammad practised his rudimentary Arabic on him, hoping to become more fluent in the prophet's tongue. The man was refreshingly honest and the Sultan had learned more from their occasional conversations than the reports of a hundred spies.

He remembered the first time they had met, Muhammad had been effusive in his greeting and Battuta had responded in kind as they exchanged gifts. He knew people would accuse him of fawning over yet another ferenghi but he did so like listening to their perspectives. He enjoyed living vicariously through their experiences of a larger world outside the confines of his suffocating empire.

'Everything I heard about your generosity is true, sire,' Battuta had said.

'I don't think that is all you heard about me . . .' Muhammad had prompted him.

'Well, your highness, the kind folks on the border who helped me to assemble the gifts to be presented to you, especially since I arrived with little more than the clothes on my back, assured me that you would reward me with valuables that far exceed their value. They were wrong only in that they undervalued the bounty I could be expected to receive.'

The Sultan threw back his head and laughed. If the unscrupulous rogues on the border had apprised him of this much, then they would have certainly told him about his so-called partiality to the ferenghis and penchant for assigning the scholars, scribes, administrators and judges among them key positions in his court. He certainly hoped to make a fortune here. He was a sly one, this Battuta, with an eye for gold. Still, it was valuable information, and Muhammad made a note to monitor the situation. It would most certainly come in useful later.

Since Battuta came from a family of judges, Muhammad offered him an honorary position as the Kazi of Dilli, with two assistants to help him. It all seemed to suit Battuta most admirably.

He cleared his throat. 'I am told you encourage the citizenry to speak openly with you, sire . . .'

'I certainly do. It is hard not to appreciate a man who says what is on his mind without prevarication. The process of divining the true meaning of the words most use to obfuscate their thoughts tries me sorely.'

'I feel the same way, your highness,' Battuta said. 'While on the way here, I passed Sehwan, and to my shock, men of the true faith—Muslim chieftains, members of the Ulama, the khatibs, preachers of the word of God, and devoted Sunnis—had been nailed to crosses across the ramparts of the city. It chilled my blood that such a travesty had come to pass in the empire of a Sultan known for his faith and devotion.'

'It is quite a common sight in the realm of a Sultan not quite known for his faith and devotion but who is nonetheless a true believer, since it is a capital offence to use the name of God for the foul purposes of hate-mongering, sedition and treason. Those who are guilty wind up nailed to crosses to deter others inclined to do the same.'

'May I enquire about the especial nature of their crimes, your highness?'

'Barani here will tell you.' Muhammad had smiled knowingly. 'He has strong opinions on these matters but can seldom be convinced to speak out. I think he is saving it all for the histories he intends to write one day.'

Barani flushed with embarrassment and a touch of resentment at having his intentions exposed so cavalierly before a ferenghi, just arrived in court. Even so, he spoke up. 'The Sultan in his infinite wisdom named a kafir, Ratan Singh, as the governor of Sehwan. It is wrong to speak ill of the dead, but at the time many among us expressed our doubts about giving such a high post to one who hadn't even converted to Islam and denounced the Hindu adoration of idolatry. It was predicted that such an unconventional decision could only lead to trouble but the Sultan dismissed our concerns.'

'Barani also disapproves of bright and ambitious Hindus who convert for furthering their career prospects and to avoid paying the *jizya*. He thinks of them as abominations. Ratan Singh—may Allah and his gods have mercy on him—was not one for pretence and it was only one among his many virtues.' Muhammad examined the rings on his fingers for a moment. 'The old guard among the nobles composed entirely of Persians, Turks and Muslims are keen to preserve their incestuous little circle and refuse to make place for representatives from other races. On the other hand, when foreigners are brought in to fill the empty places in my administration, I am accused of partiality.'

Muhammad nodded for Barani to continue, enjoying the sight of him squirming in discomfiture. 'In Sehwan, two Muslim chieftains, Wunar and Rumi, angered with Ratan Singh's aggressive measures to encourage the Hindus to rise up against the Muslims, deposed him . . .'

'That is an interesting choice of words, Barani, but I think you mean Wunar and Rumi were bitterly resentful that a man of merit was promoted over them and killed Ratan in a manner that can only be described as treacherous, after fabricating claims that would bring his integrity under question,' Muhammad corrected him. 'And their actions had been precipitated by the Ulama and the zealous preachers. On my instructions, Malik Sartez marched from Multan to punish them, and our distinguished visitor subsequently bore witness to the plight of sinners and traitors in my empire.'

Battuta shook his head. 'I am not sure it is the right message to send, sire, especially in a land where far too many practise idolatry openly, with blatant disregard for the true path of Allah.'

'It was their land before it became mine,' Muhammad retorted. 'And I am mindful of that. As long as my subjects maintain the peace, I couldn't care less if they worship idols, Buddha or the saviour. I am told that the Christians are determined to wipe out Islam and drive us away from the holy lands. Which is why I thought you might be a little more sympathetic to the plight of the Hindus in these parts, Battuta.'

He remembered the pained looks on both their faces and the words Battuta had left unsaid. *How dare he make light of the holy wars and use it to shore up his hollow argument?*

Muhammad smiled bitterly at the memory. He was heartily sick of God's followers and often found himself praying earnestly for the Almighty to strike them down. They had robbed the land of precious peace and thrown one wrench too many in his administrative wheel. Alauddin Khalji wouldn't have believed it, but the present Sultan had discovered that the biggest threat to his rule was not the Hindus but the Muslims: an amorphous body of holy men with their vested agendas, who were determined to sabotage every aspect of his rule.

Despite his brutal reprisals, they had grown in strength by pretending to be martyrs while establishing themselves as formidable foes. Infuriated with his refusal to kowtow to their religious dogma or seek their approval and endorsement, they denounced him as a blasphemer, harped about his alleged crimes of parricide and incest, calling all the while for his abdication.[13]

Things had taken a dangerous turn now that the holy hyenas had gone one step further, urging every true Muslim to rebel against him and issuing a fatwa declaring that the Sharia decreed that he be killed for his crimes against the faith and the faithful. It was a massive blow and an insidious one, for the poison had spread to every part of the empire.

Clearly, it was the reason he had lost Madurai to Ahsan Shah. Qutlugh Khan had been unequal to the task of winning it back. Warangal, Bidar, Kampila and Dwarasamudra had fallen as well, but to the Hindus who had seen a resurgence of power. Ironically, by undermining his efforts at every turn, it was the Ulama who had paved the way for the rise of the Hindu kings, and what they were calling the Vijayanagar kingdom in Telangana.

The only silver lining in this cloud was that the Hindus had sworn to take Madurai back from the false Sultan and carve an independent southern realm for the Hindus. Harihara, the upstart founder of this kingdom, and his brother, Bukka, had been survivors of his own Warangal expedition during his father's reign.

They had converted to Islam but soon renounced it, appalled at how those in power were using religious sentiments for their own gain. Muhammad had to admit that his own impetuosity and reckless rage hadn't exactly smoothed things over between the warring factions in his empire. But that was hardly reason to abdicate his throne, as some were suggesting.

His informers had also found Battuta consorting with a charlatan Shaikh. On the Sultan's command, they had forced human excrement down his throat, plucked out the hair on his head and beard, placed hot coals on his newly bare scalp and finally beheaded him in full view of the public. Battuta had been placed under house arrest ever since and had spent the time fasting and praying.

They brought Battuta before him then. Anxiety had taken its toll on the Moroccan. He looked thinner but strangely serene in the face of the grave accusations levelled against him.

'I see that confinement has done you a world of good, Battuta,' Muhammad remarked genially. 'You seem to radiate peace and calm, just like the holy men whose company you like to seek out. Those despicable creatures who endorse violence.'

But Battuta's boldness had not deserted him. 'The Sultan may disapprove of the company I keep, but allow me to clarify that it is the higher mysteries of Sufism and spirituality which I sought rather than the thankless politics and conniving I am accused of. For what it is worth, his majesty has my assurance that I have never acted against his interests.'

'Not even when the interests of your religion decreed otherwise?' Muhammad's voice was soft. He didn't really expect a reply, though. 'If I weren't so religious, I would have been fully convinced that religion is the only true evil in the world that kills even more people than faith heals. But moving on, I believe congratulations are in order! Your father-in-law is now the proud founder of the Madurai Sultanate.'

'Your highness, you couldn't possibly think that I had anything at all to do with his rebellion?' Battuta pleaded. 'As you know, my wife does not approve of my wandering ways, and preferred to move to Ma'bar with her father when you appointed him as governor.'

'It makes no matter,' Muhammad said airily. 'Especially since I was going to offer my condolences to your poor wife, who has been deprived of her usurper of a father.' Battuta blanched and his face froze with disbelief and fear. He was no coward, but he did have a care for the safety of his own person.

'I have just received the sad tidings,' he continued, 'that the brief but glorious reign of Ahsan Shah ended with his murder at the hands of one Alauddin Uddauji. May Allah have mercy on his soul, though he is guilty of base treachery.'

Battuta lowered himself on to his trembling knees. 'I beg the Sultan's permission to renounce this world and leave on a pilgrimage. It is all I seek.'

Muhammad helped the distraught Battuta to his feet. 'Get a hold of yourself, Battuta! Otherwise people will have difficulty believing you are the intrepid traveller they have heard so much about. I have one task for you, which you are certain to enjoy. You shall go as my ambassador to China to discuss trade and other matters, bearing rich gifts for the emperor. I want to know what happened to the delegation I had sent earlier, as well as learn more about flying money and flaming powder. It may delight you to ascertain for yourself if what they say of the Ming women being exquisitely beautiful and skilled in the art of love is true.'

Battuta stared at him with a mixture of wariness and relief, before bowing repeatedly, kissing the rings on his proffered fingers a dozen times, and taking his leave.

'There was enough evidence to condemn him!' Ahmad pointed out drily. He had been watching the proceedings in silence. 'Your majesty's actions are going to do little to refute the claim that he is soft on ferenghis.'

'On the contrary, my dear Ahmad, the evidence clearly established his innocence. Battuta may be a little too pious and steeped in the sterile dogma of the Muslim clergy for his own good, but as a hardened wanderer, he'd rather observe than get involved.'

'Be that as it may, sire, the fact remains that he was well and truly present when the Shaikh spouted his seditious sermons against you and failed to report the matter or take action, as his office dictates.'

'He was a Kazi merely in name,' Muhammad pointed out. 'Besides, despite the aversion most Muslims claim to feel towards yogis, have you noticed that the very same are drawn to the Sufi mystics who have appropriated many aspects of the yogic way of life?'

'I don't quite see what you mean, sire . . .' Ahmad glanced at Barani, who looked affronted.

'Isn't it obvious? The pirs as well as the yogis preach against an obsession with worldly goods and power struggles, while endorsing direct communion with God. They sing with abandon, dance wildly in the case of the former and contort their bodies into impossible positions in the case of the latter, and have a shared belief in magic and mysticism. Both have been known to use drugs to intensify their communion with God . . .'

Understanding had finally dawned on his slow-witted audience, Muhammad noted with satisfaction. 'Battuta has a restless disposition, which explains why his bursts of energized activity are interspersed with bouts of depression. Which is why he sought out the company of those Shaikhs and ended up with a certain vile habit that left him bouncing endlessly between the highs of pleasure and the lows of distress.

'The guards told me that during the period of his confinement, they were alarmed to hear the strangest sounds emanating from his chambers, as he lay tossing and turning, moaning and groaning in a delirium. Giggling and wild laughter would give way to sobbing and lamenting. And the gibberish he spoke! Levitating yogis and floating sandals that attacked him, men with the mouths of dogs, tigers in human form and humans inhabiting the bodies of tigers, enchantresses who could extricate the heart of a man through his orifices, and monkeys that lay with maidens . . .'

Ahmad found it most amusing but Barani's expression was one of distaste. 'He may not have been in any condition to betray the Sultan but men like him are nevertheless dangerous to themselves and others because of the reckless abandon with which they conduct their lives.'

'That is a little harsh, don't you think?' he replied to Barani. 'What stories he will have to say about his time with us! The best stories are the ones stitched with the needle of truth threaded with the finest lies a deluded imagination can conjure up, wouldn't you say?'

'As a serious historian, I'd rather not answer that, sire!'

'As you wish, Barani. But I still think we will all get along better if we learn to enjoy the stories without taking them too seriously.'

8

Muhammad was seething. His legion of detractors, on the other hand, were wild with mirth over the losses the Sultan had sustained. Sonargaon, Lakhnauti and almost the entire Bengal Province was lost to him. It was the latest in a series of crushing blows that had shaken the very foundations of his power and prestige, leaving the empire crumbling. The triumphant conquest of Bengal had been the crowning glory of his father's myriad achievements, and it was hard to believe that he had lost it. Possibly for good.

He wept when he heard the news, glad that his mother had not lived to see him brought so low. It had happened in the blink of an eye. After Bahram's death, Malik Tatar had been named the governor of Sonargaon, while Khader Khan took charge of Lakhnauti. The lowborn Fakhruddin, the *silahdar*, a mere armour-bearer of Malik Tatar Khan, had assassinated both the governors in a fell swoop and taken power for himself, declaring Bengal's independence.

He had sent forces under his amirs—Malik Hisamuddin and Azam—to deal with Fakhruddin while he himself had been busy with the rebellions that flared up in Sunam and Samana. He had crushed the rebels and beheaded them in the thousands, leaving their heads spiked on spears and planted all around the town. Thousands more were taken captive and led in chains ahead of them on the route they would take on the way back. As night fell, they were tied to wooden crosses in neat rows, doused in oil and set on fire to light their path.

Muhammad would have liked to turn his attention to Bengal then but Ain-ul-Mulk chose to betray him at this precise and crucial juncture. The governor of Oudh, he had been a dear friend of Muhammad's. He had provided him with invaluable assistance during the famine at the Doab and helped him crush the rebellion at Kara. Thanks to a steady influx of the Ulama to Oudh, who had fled to escape the Sultan's 'persecution and tyranny', events had come to this dire pass.

Muhammad heard the muezzin then, calling the faithful to prayer.

Allahu Akbar! Allahu Akbar!
Allahu Akbar! Allahu Akbar!
God is great!
Ashhadu an la ilaha illa Allah
Ashhadu an la ilaha illa Allah
I bear witness there is no God except the One God
Ashadu anna Muhammadan Rasool Allah
Ashadu anna Muhammadan Rasool Allah
I bear witness that Muhammad is the messenger of God
Hayya 'ala-s-salah
Hurry to the prayer
Hayya 'ala-l-falah
Hurry to success
Allahu Akbar! Allahu Akbar!
God is great!
La ilaha illa Allah
There is no God except the one God.

The blood throbbed in his temples as his nobles—having washed their hands, feet, heads and faces from jars of water—knelt on their prayer mats facing the west, waiting for the Sultan, who always led them in prayer. But today he was standing, his sword belted firmly by his side, glowering at them from the throne.

'Enough!' his voice boomed across the hall, with all the strength of his angst. 'What has prayer ever done for any of us? It is merely the opiate offered to the sheep-brained so that their faith may be better manipulated towards destruction by the evil-minded.

'To kill or endorse killing in the name of God, the merciful and compassionate, is the greatest sin. The crimes against humanity in the name of religion have gone on long enough, and I for one am sick unto death of it! Not a day goes by when my empire is free of violent deeds motivated by religious fanaticism. The Hindus bewail the killing of their sacred cows for meat, the destruction of their temples, the burning of their homes and people. They are roused to throw off the yoke of Muslim tyranny and they respond in kind. On and on it goes . . . For shame!

'Can't you see that this land will never flourish if the present is blighted with the malaise of communal hatred? Religious persecution and barbarism must end. Compassion is supposed to be the cornerstone of religion but terrorism has taken its place!

'From this moment, none shall utter a prayer aloud in my empire or mount a podium to blather on about religious doctrine. They are welcome to do all their praying in silence in the privacy of their homes, as long as their toxic faith does not extend to public spaces. From now on, my subjects no longer need concern themselves with being good Hindus, Muslims, Buddhists, Jains or tree worshippers, but rather on being good human beings. This is the decree of Sultan Muhammad bin Tughlaq. Those who flout this decree are guilty of a capital offence and will be punished accordingly. Pay heed to my will or face my wrath!'

Muhammad could feel the gaze of Ahmad and Barani, who were standing apart, secure in their mutual disdain for each other. Both were watching their Sultan as he shared a meal with Ain-ul-Mulk, laughing and talking as if they hadn't been bent on each other's destruction mere days ago.

'I can't tell you how happy it makes me that this misunderstanding has been cleared up, old friend!' the rebel governor of Oudh who had been roundly defeated in battle and taken captive remarked happily.

'It just serves as a reminder that even the soundest of friendships cannot be taken for granted,' Muhammad replied. 'It is fortunate that I remembered the many times you came through for me when all others let me down.'

'Your magnanimity is unmatched and the mercy . . .'

'Enough of that now. Let us talk of other things.' Muhammad's tone was affectionate. He had practically forgotten what it was like to have a laugh with a dear friend. He had remembered that his mother would never have forgiven him if he had executed Ain-ul-Mulk, of whom she had been exceedingly fond. He was the only one among his childhood companions who would always help himself liberally to the platters of rich food she liked to feed them.

'We shall talk of other things then,' the rotund Ain-ul-Mulk agreed, belching softly 'but it will not be to your liking.'

'That should be interesting,' Muhammad lied.

'You know better than to intrude in matters of a person's faith,' Ain-ul-Mulk said, emboldened now that he had escaped the executioner. 'It is even worse than attempting to legislate the sexual activities of your subjects.'

Muhammad glanced at Ahmad, who looked worried that Ain-ul-Mulk was putting wrong-headed notions in the Sultan's head. But wouldn't it be funny if he tried to frame laws pertaining to sexual congress?

'We used to talk about it even back in the day,' Ain-ul-Mulk was saying. 'Don't you remember? As I recall, you insisted that faith is a private interaction between man and God. In your own words, things took a turn for the worse when third parties interfered. You have cause to be angered with the clergy, who have been dogged in their disapproval and criticism, but I must point out that in this particular situation, you are the third party who has put himself between man and God. It behoves you to step aside immediately.'

Muhammad sighed. 'I may have overstepped even the supreme temporal powers of a Sultan,' he admitted grudgingly, 'and I have already been working on reversing the effects of my latest decree.'

Barani and Ahmad were straining to listen, so he lowered his voice. 'I have decided to approach the Abbasid Caliphate in Egypt and secure a confirmation decree recognizing my sovereignty. Once the investiture from Caliph Al-Hakim II is received, every Muslim shall pray five times a day as per the dictates of the Quran, and celebrate Eid and Ramzan as before.'

'That is wonderful news!' Ain-ul-Mulk paused, looking at him with a hint of suspicion. 'But these things take time, years even, which you can ill afford to spare if you truly seek to appease your subjects.'

'As you know, patience is not one of my many virtues,' Muhammad said with a wink. 'I am expecting Hajji S'aid Sarsari, the envoy of Caliph Al-Hakim II, this very Friday. He will bring with him the confirmation decree and a truly magnificent robe of honour, sent by the Caliph himself. It is going to be a grand spectacle, you will see! I shall abase myself while welcoming the Kalifa's representative and prove that I am little more than a servant of Allah, who shall dedicate what remains of his life towards upholding the word of the Prophet. Coins—not copper ones, mind you—have already been struck in the name of the Caliph and his faithful friend, Muhammad bin Tughlaq. Then the muezzin shall sound the call for prayer, and it will be the most beautiful, poignant and powerful moment in the entire history of my reign.'

Ain-ul-Mulk seemed torn between laughter and frustration. 'You are overdoing it just a bit, as usual. I am merely going to impress upon you the importance of the only rule we swore as children never to break.'

'Thou shalt not get caught!' they said together, and burst out laughing, embracing each other in the manner of rambunctious boys.

Ahmad had raised his eyes heavenward, almost as if he were beseeching God to grant better sense to the emperor. As for Barani, his relief had given way to barely concealed irritation. *How very like him! If the fraudulent envoy is exposed, the Sultan would be subject to more ridicule and hatred, and he would have only himself to blame. Serve him right too!*

Muhammad ignored the perennial scepticism of Ahmad and Barani, confident that his latest scheme would succeed. But that was hardly unusual for him.

9

'I request your permission to return to Baran, your highness. It is something I have been meaning to ask you for a while now.'

'Baran is your native place, Barani? After my treatment of the rebels thereabouts, I am going to assume there is a scarcity of goodwill for me in those parts . . .'

Barani lowered his eyes to the floor in his customary manner.

'The recent changes made among the administration officials are not entirely to your liking, I suppose.'

'It is not my place to question the Sultan's decisions, sire,' he hurried on when Muhammad made an impatient noise. Everybody knew that all the Sultan's decisions were questioned every step of the way. 'But it is hard to comprehend why you would dismiss the old officials of impeccable lineage and rub salt in their wounds by installing lowborn drunkards, barbers, cooks, gardeners, weavers and rogues in their place. Whatever do you propose to do next, your highness? Hand over the reins of rule to women perhaps? To nautch girls and courtesans even . . .'

His anger clearly knew no bounds since he had the temerity to address his Sultan in those strident tones, but Muhammad forgave him his lapse in decorum.

'Why ever not, Barani?' the Sultan looked at him with fond indulgence. 'I am sure the ladies will not make a hash of things, unlike us men, who have reduced this bountiful land to a battlefield. The trouble with you is that you are a snob and a hardened reactionary, who will resist progress to preserve the old way, even though it has repeatedly proved to be ineffective.'

'But what is wrong with that, sire? The wisdom of the ages has been handed over to us for a reason.' It was fascinating to watch Barani finally cast aside his caution. 'What will become of this land if the mean-spirited and squalid take the places of mighty men? What will become of order in a structured society if the master is replaced by a slave, as if there was no difference between the two and both are equally qualified for the role allotted them by birth? Does a common whore have a right to believe herself entitled to the respect a virtuous wife or mother is accorded?

'Do the young have a right to cast aside the elders who have the benefit of hard-earned experience and have won the right to hold exalted positions, having devoted their entire lives to serve the emperor? How could you find it in your heart to remove those who have served the throne for generations in favour of lowborn wastrels? Why do you deliberately insist on doing these awful things?'

Muhammad felt the familiar surge of anger for his subjects, who refused to let him or themselves rise from their base level and regressive mode of thinking.

He controlled his temper with an effort. 'My people need me to provide them with protection and a reasonably good life. In order to do that, I must allow the affairs of state to be handled by capable, courageous and clever men, irrespective of their origins. Rogues and fools are present not just among the peasantry but are equally distributed among the nobility as well. Yet you would have me make no attempt to help my people free themselves from the limitations of class and caste.'

Barani refused to back down. 'The poor and downtrodden are no doubt grateful for the compassion and opportunities you have shown them, but even you will admit it is a wasted effort. Wouldn't it be far more practical to extend the same courtesy to those who share your faith and noble antecedents? At the very least, you could refrain from punishing them so severely . . .'

'If you are suggesting that I deal with my enemies who plot and scheme behind my back with love and affection as opposed to the lash of the whip and the executioner's block, then you are the one who needs to be practical. We live in troubled times, and he who has qualms about killing is the one who gets killed instead.'

Barani could think of no response and merely looked dejected.

'Do you think me quite mad, Barani?' Muhammad enquired.

'Sire?'

'You are free to depart for Baran and you shall be compensated for your many years of loyal service. I have enjoyed our conversations on all things related to history and other matters besides. It saddens me that you seek to leave my side when the end is so close but I shall not stop you. But first you must answer my question honestly.'

'I know for a fact that you are not mad, your highness.' Barani looked him in the eye for the first time since the regrettable events leading to the death of Shaikh Imamuddin. 'But you are always in the midst of madness, and a lot of it is of your own making. Your generosity is boundless, as is your genuine concern for the welfare of your subjects. There can be no denying your intelligence, competence and innate goodness, but for reasons known only to God, none of it has worked in your favour or that of your subjects. If you will forgive my boldness, I will suggest that you set aside your doubts about the benevolence of God and surrender to his will completely. Therein lies your sole hope for success as well as salvation.'

'What a memorable occasion this is turning out to be!' Muhammad clapped his hands in glee. 'Why, Barani, this is the first time your words and thoughts haven't been at odds with each other, and I appreciate your honesty. Your suggestion is sound but one that I cannot follow, for surrender has never been an option for me. I have carved out my destiny with my own hands, and I always will. It may have filled me with hubris but it is also what helped me survive. You may go now, Barani, may God keep you safe and ever guide your writing hand.'

Barani bowed. There were tears in his eyes. Despite everything, he could never find it in his heart to despise the Sultan.

'Why would you want to leave?' Ahmad asked him, somewhat uncharacteristically, as their paths crossed briefly. 'You will drive yourself mad by isolating yourself in Baran, which is little more than a boil on the bottom of the empire. Have a care that you don't squander away all your savings and become a broken, bitter old man with nothing but bile to pour on to his pages.'

Without waiting for Barani's reply, he approached the Sultan, who reproached him. 'Why do you insist on teasing him, Ahmad? You know he is sensitive. But I suppose you have come to me with unpleasant tidings as per usual.'

'Your majesty's wisdom exceeds even his generosity!' Ahmad took less and less effort to mask his sarcasm nowadays. With all the heads that had rolled in vain, everybody seemed to have become acclimatized to the bloodshed.

'Unfortunately, trouble has broken out on multiple fronts,' the Khwaja Jahan went on in clipped tones. 'The Amiran-i-sadah have rebelled and their members stationed in various parts of the empire have joined hands to throw off the yoke of imperial authority.'

He was waiting for instructions on how best to deploy the imperial troops to deal with the series of rebellions, but Muhammad dismissed him and leaned back, eyes closed and brows furrowed. His joints ached and he was fatigued. This one was going to be even worse than all the others put together. He could feel it in his bones, which were creaking in protest.

The Amiran-i-sadah—his centurions, cobbled together from amongst the Mongol and Afghan nobles—had always been loose cannons. He had given them a free rein and had enlisted their aid in keeping his subjects in line, but they had proved themselves to be no less susceptible to the seductive pull of corruption and disaffection than the others. Now they had turned on him like the rabid dogs they were, stealing from the Sultan as well as his subjects. He had been riddled with the thankless task of hunting them down.

This lot had the sympathy of the sainthood, and he had heard that they had pooled their considerable resources to depose of him and put someone they approved of on the throne. It was why he had sent for Malik Firoz before making plans to mop up this ungodly mess.

'You wished to see me, your highness?' his cousin knelt before him in that formal and stiff manner of his.

'My dear cousin! You are just the person whose counsel I need in this disastrous time.' Muhammad grasped his hand warmly.

'Is this about the rebellion of the centurions, sire?' Firoz asked worriedly. 'It was most imprudent of Aziz Khumman, the recently appointed governor of Malwa, to summon the centurions for official purposes and then have them slaughtered en masse. He claims he was acting on your orders.' Firoz hesitated during that last part. Muhammad saw no reason to elucidate further. He was tired of giving explanations.

'What do you think, cousin? It sounds like something a tyrant known for his devious stratagems would do.'

'It is not impossible that you would have done such a thing,' he said in his careful manner, 'but it is highly improbable, given that the mass killings have led to a wave of fury among the Amiran-i-sadah and near-frenzied levels of agitation in an already prevalent mood of fear, unrest and disaffection. It has all resulted directly in civil war, which certainly does not work in your favour.'

Not for the first time, Muhammad admired his cousin's ability to always say the right thing, though he seldom said much.

Malik Firoz had never chased fame or fortune. Unlike Muhammad himself, he had a pacifist attitude that somehow pleased the hardliners as well as everybody else. In the eyes of his enemies, he also had the added virtue of being a most orthodox Muslim who had taken pains to give the impression that he deferred to the Ulama while maintaining a healthy distance from them. It was why the rebels had chosen him as the one to replace the tyrant Sultan.

Muhammad stroked his beard and looked at him closely. 'It has come to my notice that the Ulama have chosen you as my successor.'

His cousin shook his head with distaste. 'I am aware of that, sire, and I told them the same thing I told you at cousin Khuda's wedding years ago, when you had the kindness to inform me that I was your chosen successor. The throne demands skills which I neither have nor am inclined to acquire. May Allah in his infinite wisdom confer the sceptre of rule on the one who is equal to the impossible task of bringing peace and prosperity to this troubled and divided realm. For my part, I am content to serve the Sultan.'

Muhammad allowed himself a smile. Only Firoz could refuse the Ulama and win their admiration and unstinting support in place of the scorn and contempt they were ever ready to heap on all else. 'You will find, cousin, that power is more likely to fall into the hands of those who run away from it rather than those who run towards it. But that aside, not reporting treason counts as treason, and, as you know, that is a capital offence.'

'Your majesty doesn't need me to inform him when his vast network of spies are there to do the needful.' Firoz spoke firmly. 'And I refuse to have the blood of fellow Muslims on my hands. Besides, as he most certainly knows, even before the passing of Sultan Ghiasuddin Tughlaq, malcontents have been trying to pin their ambitions on me and my response has always been the same. However, if you feel the need to put the question to me under torture, I am not a coward, but a confession is very likely to be wrung out of me.'

'If you are referring to the tragic circumstances that led to charges of conspiracy and treason levelled against Masud Khan, it was his confession that led to his public execution. Despite my dubious reputation, in all matters related to the judiciary, it is my policy not to interfere, unless of course there are exceptional factors involved.'

'It was a most distressing affair, your highness! Your half-brother was just a boy and there were too many who tried to manipulate his grief over the demise of Saira Begum against you. Ultimately, though, he was innocent, and it pained me to bear witness to his passing.'

Muhammad frowned at the memory. The fools with their love for all things theatrical had carried out Masud's execution in the very spot where Saira had breathed her last, just to generate a grand spectacle and create an almighty uproar. He had always avoided the boy and had wanted nothing at all to do with the charges levelled against him, incidentally by the same Kazi who had caused the downfall of his mother.

Saira had tormented him for days and nights afterwards, flooding his dreams with her hate and fury. How magnificent she was when her anger was roused!

'You always resented the fact that my son is the only member of the opposite sex I truly loved. It was bad enough that you treated me like property you owned, on which nobody was allowed to trespass. The least you could have done after my passing was to spare my innocent child your malice! May Allah make you pay for every one of your evil deeds over the course of eternity!

'I never loved you! Your father was always the better man and you are not worth his toenails! Even your mother is ashamed to have borne a wretch like you!'

He had to admit that her words were hurtful. Even so, it had been nice to see her and hear her voice, and definitely worth doing nothing to save the boy.

Firoz was looking at him expectantly, and Muhammad cleared his throat. 'I have decided to deal with the rebels personally. It is going to be a bloody business but I don't trust anybody else to handle it. You are hereby named the regent and will take command here in Dilli during my absence. If it is Allah's will that I don't come back alive, you will take your place as the rightful Sultan of the Tughlaq dynasty.'

'I thank you for your faith, sire and will pray to the Almighty to grant you a mighty triumph over your enemies and a safe return.' Firoz accepted the onerous chore placed on him with dutiful resignation, though nine out of ten men would have literally killed to be in the same position.

'You mean every word, don't you?' What a strange creature his cousin was! Muhammad remembered the naked ambition of his own youth.

'I have always admired you, sire!' he said simply. 'Your talent is matched only by your kindness. And you have never been afraid to do what you think is right, even in the face of universal and vehement opposition. Which is why this land needed you to be its ruler. And yet, you always deserved better . . .'

Muhammad was strangely moved on hearing the same words he had uttered to his father so long ago. 'This land needs you too! And you certainly deserve better. But you should stop worrying about Khuda's disapproval, Ahmad's ruthless ambition, and all who would seek to strike you down. There is a quiet strength to your personality which the empire will find to be a refreshing change.'

'I thank you again for your trust and I will strive not to let you down,' Firoz promised him. 'As for cousin Khuda, in her eyes you can do no wrong and she is never going to forgive me for presuming to take something that she feels is the rightful due of her son. But perhaps none of it will come to pass. I wish you Godspeed and every success, sire.'

'Thank you, cousin! God knows I need it!'

Something told him he wouldn't be coming back. And truth be told, he didn't mind a bit.

10

Muhammad went to see Khuda before he left. She flung her arms over his shoulders and burst into tears. 'I hate those nasty centurions and wish they were all dead. Why can't you send your Khwaja Jahan to deal with them? Dawar needs you to be close to him and teach him how to be a good Sultan. I need you too! And whatever possessed you to release my husband from prison? I have a good mind to leave him behind and march by your side.'

'When did you become so sentimental, Khuda?' he teased her. 'Cousin Firoz will take good care of you while I am gone. He has far more patience than I ever did for your little eccentricities. I still don't understand why you refused to marry him. He is a good man, you know.'

Khuda made a face. 'Firoz is a bore and a poor man's Muhammad. He is better than my husband, but that is not saying much. I don't want to be around the two of them. Why won't you let me accompany you?'

'You son needs you,' he reminded her. 'Besides I don't think you will enjoy the rough life of a soldier, the stench of latrine pits and the bloodcurdling sight of rude buttocks exposed and in the throes of diarrhoea. As I recall, you refused to go anywhere near your own son till he was properly toilet trained.'

She sniffed in distaste. 'If only mother could hear you now! But if I can't come with you then you must make haste to come back to me. Don't spare the blasted Amiran-i-sadah and kill every last one of them. You have always been too kind and people take advantage of your large-heartedness. Only you could have found it in your heart to spare Ain-ul-Mulk after he dared to betray you. Don't make that mistake again. Make them pay for daring to rebel against the greatest Sultan this land has seen.'

Muhammad embraced her and held her close to his chest. 'Only you could say that.'

'That is because everybody else is too stupid. Promise me you will come back!' she murmured. 'If you don't, I will never ever forgive you!'

The days, months and years passed by in a strange blur of frenzied activity as the rebels led him on a merry dance. They dared not meet the imperial forces out in the open where the latter's superior numbers and training would have made short work of the rebellion. Instead, they preferred to strike in a series of attacks like gnats worrying a lion, dancing just out of the reach of the royal troops.

He journeyed across Gujarat, pursuing them into Dabhoi and Baroda, where the rebels were forced to fight. It was a long and bitter battle. It always was for him. Muhammad watched men on both sides disappear into the depths of a river of blood. Chunks of bloodied, mutilated flesh and severed arms littered the battlefield. Battle formations were cleaved and shattered over and over again. But they retreated, fled, reassembled and came back for more. The process went on and on. It felt like he had been running all his life, only to discover that he hadn't moved an inch.

Muhammad rode to battle on his horse or elephant. But he always led the charge, lopping off heads and limbs, wielding swords and releasing showers of arrows and spears that tore through flesh.

So much fighting and bloodshed in his lifetime. Was peace an impossible dream? Would this land never be free of the ravages of war? Perhaps he should have named Khuda as his regent and successor. A woman's touch would be just the thing, though Khuda was at heart twice the savage he himself was.

His enemies fled before his advance towards the Muslim clergy and the Hindu muqqaddams, who helped them with weapons and supplies. While he fought them in the north, they took Daulatabad. Muhammad would have been shattered, but he didn't have the time. All he could do was vent his feelings on the banks of the Narbada when he overtook the rebels yet again and exacted bloody vengeance. Another day, another massacre.

Barani was right. He was always in the midst of madness, while all around his men were swept by the tides of battle, helpless as driftwood, on the waves of their Sultan's will. He didn't know whether to laugh or cry at the endless saga of butchery that had come to define him. His mother would have told him that it didn't have to be that way. But it *had* been that way for him. And it was too late to do anything about it.

Muhammad liked to spend time with the men. They taught him their bawdy battle songs and they would roar the words together in rough, hoarse voices with scant regard for tune or harmony. All of it warmed his heart. He questioned them about their families and wanted to know everything about their lives so that he could somehow make it all better for them. They seemed so grateful that he cared. He wished he could do more. He wished he had done more.

'Being a soldier is not as easy as being a Sultan,' one of the more insolent ones told him. 'Maintaining a wife and mistress is a bloody business on the wages we are paid. It is why I have decided to content myself with the humble camp followers.'

The men around him fell silent and the chap clapped his hands over his mouth. They all knew of the Sultan's famous disdain for sexual excesses, which was why camp followers had been banned, not that this imperial decree had been successfully enforced.

'Am I going to be executed, sire?' he asked in hushed tones.

'Why should I bother?' the emperor replied. 'If you persist in pursuing the prurient, it is only a matter of time before the rot sets into your manly parts, causing them to blacken and fall off, and then you will be screaming for death.' The Sultan left them to it, and not for the first time, his men wondered if he was serious or joking.

The citizens always gathered to see the Sultan, even though they had little fondness for marauding armies. However, the imperial forces were a disciplined lot. Muhammad liked conversing with those among the common folk who weren't scared speechless in his presence. His legendary largesse was in full display as he handed over bags and bags of gold mohurs and silver tankas to the wretched masses who wept and insisted on kissing the ground before him.

He was not very fond of little boys. They were noisy and troublesome, with dried snot plugging one or both their nostrils, which was why he had never grieved over the lack of an heir in his life. But he adored the sweet little girls who showered carefully gathered flowers on his path, and had been known to present them with strings of pearls and sweetmeats. On one memorable occasion, he even entertained a request by a bold young girl who wanted to get atop his elephant. She had thrown her arms around him in a rapture. 'If you come back when I grow big, I'll marry you!' she promised. The Sultan presented her with a magnificent necklace that he had worn around his own throat, much to the chagrin of his officials. They felt even his generosity was coloured with madness.

The Sultan's retinue encamped at Broach, Gujarat and Malwa respectively. There were tax collectors to be appointed, administrative reforms to be made, traitors to be brutally disposed of during the day and raucous singing sessions with the troops at dusk. Nobody knew what to make of him and he didn't either.

Muhammad marched to Daulatabad in pursuit of the rebels who had escaped him in Baroda to join those who had seized control of the fort. He arrived on the battlefield which he knew with the intimacy of a lover. His divisions of cavalry and foot soldiers stretched behind him and they charged at the enemy ahead. The archers fired and he saw the gaps open up in the opposing rank in bright bursts of blood.

The initial charge had been very successful and heartened his men, encouraging them to move in for the kill. Volley after volley was released into the massed ranks, scything through them. Then the mauling began in earnest as the two armies locked horns.

Muhammad circled round the fighting, heaving multitudes gauging the tempo of battle, bellowing instructions, sending in the reserves where they were needed and pulling back the troops when they risked being encircled. He did what was needed with the unerring precision of one whose instincts had been honed over the course of countless battles.

Soon, it was all over. The rebels fled in disarray, their army routed, while his foot soldiers gave chase. The Sultan, standing knee-deep in blood and bodies, knew that it wasn't over. They could not make an end of it. His men deployed to chase down the rebels who had too much of a head start gave up all too soon, eager to begin celebrating their victory. A sizeable number of the rebels got away, headed by Hasan Gangu. It was not over. It never was.

Ensconced within the fortress, Muhammad was still restoring order and sorting out the mess made by the rebels when word reached him about yet another rebellion that had broken out in Gujarat, headed by Taghi. He set out again, heartsick and weary, but filled with a feverish energy born of his fierce will that always made him indefatigable.

This time he would make an end of it, he promised himself. It was his intention to secure peace for good or perish in the attempt. He had sent word to Altun Bahadur, the king of Tansoxiana, who had agreed to help him deal with the rebels once and for all. Fifty thousand Mongols were on the move and would join him soon. In the meantime, Taghi was also on the move, never staying long in one place as he raced from Broach to Asawal and then Patan to evade the wrath of his emperor.

Muhammad met with the Hindu muqqaddams at Naharwala and negotiated a truce with them. They feasted together and the rajas swore their allegiance to the emperor after they kept their word and chased Taghi out of Gujarat. The Sultan appreciated their efforts but would have appreciated it even more if they had presented him with Taghi's head.

The rebels had gathered in Thatta. He was on his way there with the freshly arrived Mongol troops when the rains began, bringing with them his old foe: pestilence.

Muhammad was taken ill and laid low. Again. The fever wracked his body and Wasim attended to him night and day.

'Have my enemies paid you to poison me, Wasim? You can tell me . . . I am too weak to have you executed.'

'I am a merciful man, your majesty. If I wanted you dead, I would have given you a draught that would put you into a deep sleep from which you would never wake, rather than expend my considerable skill to coax you back to good health.'

'My body aches so much. I always wanted to die in battle with a sword in my hand or go off gently while sleeping in my own bed, not in some swamp in the wilderness with mosquitoes buzzing in my ear.'

'I would like to die having taken my pleasure with a beautiful woman nestled between her lush body and silk sheets. But let us talk about how we are going to live instead. You need to get better so that you can execute Taghi and his ilk at the earliest. Before you do that, you need to rest and focus on getting better,' Wasim responded.

He offered him medicines and potions to dull the ache in his body, but Muhammad refused them, determined to live every single moment left to him. Pain was just another enemy to be conquered by the force of his iron will. But this was his last battle. He knew it and he was eager for the end. Finally.

He turned back for one last look. He had been derided as a tyrant and murderer and sinner. They had been wrong about that.

The good he had done may not have wiped out the evil he had wrought but had neutralized it. And, as his mother would have said, that counted for something.

How he had lived! All he would take with him were the memories of the many truths and lies he had experienced. They would keep him company through the darkness of death and the endless corridors of eternity. Along with everyone he had loved and lost. Sultan Muhammad bin Tughlaq was thankful. And grateful.

Muhammad saw them all again as his eyes closed, never to open again. Abu, Mahmud, his father, Bahram and his mother. Even Saira held her hands out to him. They were smiling. His mother had tears in her eyes. They did not look angry or disappointed. All of them looked proud. Of him. It was such a relief. He had never been afraid in life, and after everything he had been through and survived, death held no terrors for him. Muhammad closed his eyes and let go with a gentle sigh. It was time to rest. At last.

Notes

1. Alauddin Khalji's son, Mubarak, by all accounts did not acquit himself with even the barest modicum of competence as a ruler. The Persian historian Ferishta went so far as to call him 'a monster'. Apparently, his excesses were too sordid to even merit a mention, but Mubarak's bizarre practice of 'leading a gang of abominable prostitutes, stark naked, along the terraces of the royal palaces, and obliging them to make water upon the nobles as they entered the court' (Keay, p. 260) has been recorded. It makes one wonder about the rest of those unspeakable sybaritic excesses, though, doesn't it?

    Mubarak Shah's reign lasted four years. According to Ziyauddin Barani, a contemporary of Muhammad bin Tughlaq who served in his court and the author of the *Tarikh-i-Firoz Shahi*, 'the sultan attended to nothing but drinking, listening to music, debauchery and pleasure, scattering gifts, and gratifying his lusts . . . the sultan plunged into sensual indulgences openly and publicly, by night and by day' (Eraly, p. 134). His debaucheries, utter dissipation, complete negligence of his many responsibilities as a ruler, recklessness and disregard for decorum and decency is generally believed to have brought about his ruin.

    Curiously, the beginning of his reign was hopeful and Mubarak Shah was very popular. His downfall could have been brought about partly by his own inability to handle the pressures of rule, and those around him who sought to take advantage of his weaknesses by encouraging his fondness for intoxicants and inebriants to make him more malleable to their own will and in furtherance of vested interests.

2. In the words of Barani, 'He [Mubarak] cast aside all regard for decency, and presented himself decked out in the trinkets and apparel of a female before his assembled company . . . Sometimes he made his appearance in

company stark naked, talking obscenity' (Eraly, pp. 134 –35). Historians have recorded with marked disapproval Mubarak Shah's feelings for Nasiruddin Khusrau Khan. Barani noted that 'his infatuation for this infamous and traitorous Parwari exceeded that of Ala-ud-din for Malik Kafur' (Eraly, p. 136). He was so madly in love with Khusrau and trusted him so blindly he refused to listen to well-wishers who sought to warn him about his paramour's treachery and even punished them severely for speaking against him.

Khusrau Khan, though perfectly happy to bask in the sunshine of Mubarak Shah's favour, seemed not to have reciprocated his overlord's amorous feelings, and it may be surmised that he did not have the same taste as the Sultan with regard to his sexual preferences and peccadilloes and may have been humouring him all along with an eye on the throne.

3. Chroniclers have made much of the prevailing tension between Shaikh Nizamuddin Auliya and Sultan Ghiasuddin Tughlaq. It all started when Ghiasuddin clamped down on those who had profited at the expense of the throne or helped themselves to public funds during the rule of Nasiruddin Khusrau Khan. 'Shaikh Nizam-ud-din Auliya, the famous saint of Delhi, was ordered to refund what he had received as a gift from the usurper. The saint's inability to comply with this order led to strained relations between him and the emperor' (Husain, p. 54).

There are those who attribute the untimely death of Sultan Ghiasuddin Tughlaq to his quarrel with the saint. It certainly did not help that the Shaikh had predicted that Prince Jauna's rise to the throne was imminent during one of his trances. The news spread like wildfire and reached Ghiasuddin's ears. The emperor was not happy and sent messengers with a warning that when he returned to his capital he expected to find Auliya gone since the city was too small to hold them both, to which the saint famously replied, 'Hanuz Dihli dur ast'. That, as they say, is truly the stuff of legend!

4. Then, as now, it seemed to have been par for the course to manipulate religious sentiment for political purposes. Muslim historians of that period believed Khusrau's coup to be a Hindu victory, though he had converted to Islam. Barani says, 'preparations were made for idol worship in the palace . . . The flames of violence and cruelty reached to the skies. Copies of the Holy Book were used as seats, and idols were set up in the pulpits of mosques . . . Hindus rejoiced greatly . . . boasting that Delhi had once more come under Hindu rule' (Eraly, p. 138).

Subsequently, Ghiasuddin tried to win over the nobles to his cause by stating that Islam needed them to unite and make common cause against the tyrant who favoured Hindus and sought to root out the Muslims from Hindustan. In a fiery speech, he said, 'The Hindus have captured the realm of Islam, and have subverted the Alai house. I hereby wish to avenge the wrongs done to that house. Just as you have readily and actively co-operated with me for years in the past, I wish you even at this juncture to help me' (Husain, p. 36).

This ploy was ineffective, though, because many of the Islamic nobles and even those among the Muslim clergy continued to ally themselves with Sultan Nasiruddin, who had won them over with generous gifts of land and gold. This episode notwithstanding, Sultan Ghiasuddin Tughlaq enjoys a well-deserved reputation for fairness and tolerance as he did his best to put out the flames of communal violence, which plagued his reign as well as his son's.

5.   In all matters pertaining to religion, Muhammad bin Tughlaq displayed the same perplexing contradictory manner that was unique to him. As a devout Muslim, he practised the faith in keeping with the rationalism and spirit of inquiry that were a part of his own scholarly attributes, and did not seek to promote or propagate Islam using state-sponsored machinery. He even tried to understand other religions and had lengthy discourses with holy men of other faiths, and this, coupled with his harsh treatment of the Muslim clergy, made them his enemies. It did not help that to prove himself to those who questioned his faith, the Sultan chose to implement a policy compelling people to say the prescribed prayers in the strictest orthodox manner under threat of capital punishment.

Ibn Battuta, the famous Moroccan traveller and author of *Rihla*, was impressed with the Sultan's insistence on the strict observance of ritual prayers, 'making congregational attendance at them obligatory, and punishing any dereliction of them most severely. Indeed, he put to death for neglecting them on one day alone nine persons, of whom one was a singer. He used to send out men, specially charged with this duty, to the bazaars; any person found in them after the commencement of prayers was punished . . . He gave orders also that the people in general should be required to show a knowledge of the obligations of ablution, prayer, and the binding articles of Islam. They used to be questioned on these matters; if anyone failed to give correct answers he was punished' (Batuta, *1971*, p. 693).

6. Bahauddin Gurshasp's rebellion was one of the earliest, and an important one, since it exemplified the savagery Muhammad bin Tughlaq was capable of when he was angered or felt betrayed. He has been roundly criticized for his actions in having his cousin flayed and ordering that his flesh be cooked with spices and rice, and rightly so, but it must be remembered that it was a cruel age and wielders of absolute power felt they had little choice but to deal with traitors and rebels with an iron hand using brutal means of execution for the ostensible purpose of serving as a deterrent for those who felt inclined towards treason and treachery. The Sultan was simply no better and perhaps only slightly worse than those who held similar positions both before and after him. For those interested in the various versions of this grisly episode by noted historians, I suggest you refer to Husain (pp. 142–44).

7. Battuta has given the Sultan's petty grievances against his subjects as the reason for the ill-advised move to transfer the capital from Delhi to Daulatabad, which most modern historians feel is too simplistic and reeking of bias in its assessment of Muhammad bin Tughlaq's true motives in addition to being historically inaccurate. According to Battuta, 'One of the gravest charges against the Sultan is his forcing of the population of Dihli to evacuate the city. The reason for this is that they used to write missives reviling and insulting him, seal them and inscribe them, "By the head of the Master of the World, none but he may read this." Then they would throw them into the audience-hall by night, and when the Sultan broke the seal he found them full of insults and abuse of him. So he decided to lay Dihli in ruins' (Battuta, *1971*, p. 707).

    He then proceeds to give a graphic and exaggerated account of the move to Daulatabad, claiming that the Sultan sent his men to search the city to see if any of the citizens remained, and they returned with a cripple and a blind man. The former, on Muhammad bin Tughlaq's alleged orders, was hurled from a ballista, and the latter dragged to Daulatabad. Over the course of the journey, the poor man was supposedly torn to pieces and only his leg reached the new capital. None of this has been sufficiently corroborated and is taken with a dash of salt by contemporary scholars.

8. Malik Isami, a historian from Muhammad's times who served the Bahmani Sultanate and authored the *Futuh-uh-Salatin*, seemed to have an axe to grind with the Sultan and is scathing in his condemnation of the decision to transfer the capital; he narrates the ordeal suffered by his grandfather, who did not survive the harrowing journey.

'Much is in common between Isami and Ibn Battuta; and the latter's story of the cripple and the blind man, which remains unconfirmed, appears to have been a concoction based on the hardships to which Isami's grandfather, A'izz-ud-din Isami, was supposed to have been subjected. Again, Ibn Battuta's version that Muhammad bin Tughlaq was pleased when, on mounting the roof of his palace, he saw no trace of fire and light in any house, seems to have arisen from Isami's report that the Sultan ordered the city to be set on fire' (Husain, p. 122). The version presented here about the fate of Isami's grandfather is fictional.

9. Ibn Battuta has dwelt at length on the gruesome treatment meted out by the Sultan to those among his subjects he believed were guilty of a host of offences, ranging from the trivial to the grave. The Moroccan seems to have been particularly galled by his treatment of the Muslim clergy, who were humiliated by having their beards plucked out one strand at a time, being force-fed ordure, tortured, having urine poured over their wounds, flayed or executed. While some of it may have been exaggerated, the Sultan did have a proven record of punishing the members of the Ulama, the Sayyids, Mashaikhs and Sufis most cruelly for he believed not without sound reason that they sought to undermine his authority and cause trouble. For a detailed account of 'This Sultan's murders and other reprehensible actions' please refer to Battuta (*1971*, pp. 695–708).

10. Ibid.

11. Ibn Battuta alone describes the execution of the Sultan's half-brother, Masud Khan. He seems to have believed that his rebellion was triggered by his mother's sentence to death by stoning for the crime of adultery.

'He had a [half] brother named Mas'ud Khan, whose mother was the daughter of the Sultan Ala-al-din, and who was one of the most beautiful persons I have seen on earth. The Sultan accused him of rebellion against him and questioned him on the matter. Mas'ud Khan confessed to the fact through fear of torture, and people consider execution a lighter affliction than torture. The Sultan gave orders for his execution, and he was beheaded in the midst of the bazaar and remained exposed there for three days, according to their usage. The mother of the executed prince had been stoned to death in that same place two years before, on her confession of adultery. Her stoning was by [decree of] the qadi Kamal al-din' (Battuta, p. 696).

It is a pity not much is known of this daughter of Alauddin Khalji. My version of her story is entirely fictionalized.

12. Barani's account of the Doab rebellion does not show the Sultan in a favourable light. He has levelled grave charges against the emperor, accusing him of rashly implementing administrative policies that forced the officials to harass the people and force them to pay taxes they simply could not afford, prompting them to rise in rebellion against the administrators which led to the emperor leading 'man-hunting expeditions' and murdering the inhabitants of the Doab.

Husain, however, is of the opinion that the accepted theory of the Doab rebellion, attributed to the Sultan's incompetence and gross hiking of taxes, is not supported by facts. His thorough assessment of the events leading up to the hotbed of conflict in the Doab and the Sultan's handling of it makes for interesting reading (pp. 148–57).

13. 'The discontent was fomented by the Ulama, the Sayyids, Mashaikhs and Sufis, who had personal differences with the emperor on account of (1) his peculiar views with regard to religion and administration, (2) his disregard of the time-honoured sanctity and privileges that the Sayyids and saints enjoyed, and (3) his cold-blooded murder of the Sunnis, Sayyids and Sufis, all supposed to be sacrosanct' (Husain, p. 131). They went one step further, and the kazis are believed to have declared war on the emperor, calling for his execution and actively encouraging rebellion. Muhammad bin Tughlaq retaliated by having them ruthlessly killed. This turned public opinion against him and led to venomous condemnation by Barani, Isami and Battuta.

References

Batuta, Ibn. *The Travels of Ibn Batuta.* The Rev. S. Lee B.D, tr. (London: Oriental Translation Committee, 1829).

Batuta, Ibn. *The Travels of Ibn Batuta: AD. 1325–1354*, Volume 3. H.A.R. Gibb, tr. (Cambridge: Cambridge University Press, 1971).

Chandra, Satish. *Medieval India: From Sultanate to the Mughals*, revised edition (New Delhi: Har Anand Publications, 2006).

Chaurasia, Radhey Shyam. *History of Medieval India: From 1000 A.D. to 1707 A.D.* (New Delhi: Atlantic Publishers and Distributors, 2002).

Husain, Agha Mahdi. *The Rise and Fall of Muhammad Bin Tughlaq* (Bristol: Burleigh Press, 1938), https://archive.org/details/in.ernet.dli.2015.282325

Karnad, Girish. *Tughlaq* (New Delhi: Oxford University Press, 2012).

Kumar, Raj, ed. *Essays on Medieval India* (New Delhi: Discovery Publishing House, 2003).

Eraly, Abraham. *The Age of Wrath: A History of the Delhi Sultanate* (Gurgaon, Haryana: Penguin Books India, 2014).

Farooqui, Salma Ahmed. *A Comprehensive History of Medieval India: Twelfth to the Mid-eighteenth Century* (New Delhi: Dorling Kindersley, 2011).

Jackson, Peter. *The Delhi Sultanate: A Political and Military History* (Cambridge: Cambridge University Press, 2003).

Jayapalan, N. *History of India from 1206 to 1773*, Volume 2. (New Delhi: Atlantic Publishers and Distributors, 2001).

Keay, John. *India: A History* (New Delhi: Harper Collins, 2000).

Mehta, Jaswant Lal. *Advanced Studies in the History of Medieval India, Vol 1: 1000–1526 A.D.* (New Delhi: Sterling, 1986).

Miller, Sam. *A Strange Kind of Paradise: India through Foreign Eyes* (London: Vintage Books, 2015).

Sharma, Sudha. *The Status of Muslim Women in Medieval India.* (New Delhi: Sage, 2016).

A Note on the Author

Anuja Chandramouli is a bestselling Indian author and new-age Indian classicist. Her highly acclaimed debut novel, *Arjuna: Saga of a Pandava Warrior-Prince*, was named by Amazon India as one of the top five books in the Indian writing category for 2013. *Yama's Lieutenant*, its sequel *Yama's Lieutenant and the Stone Witch* and *Prithviraj Chauhan: The Emperor of Hearts* are her other bestsellers. Her articles, short stories and book reviews have appeared in various publications like the *New Indian Express* and *The Hindu*.

An accomplished orator, she regularly conducts storytelling sessions and workshops on creative writing, empowerment and mythology in schools, colleges and various other platforms.

This happily married mother of two little girls lives in Sivakasi, Tamil Nadu. She is a student of classical dance and yoga.